Time Limits

By
Kim Megahee

The Kimmer Group

GAINESVILLE, GA

Copyright © 2019 by **Kimberly M. Megahee**

All rights reserved. No part of this publication may be reproduced, distributed or transmitted in any form or by any means, without prior written permission.

Kim Megahee/The Kimmer Group
Gainesville, GA
www.authorkimmegahee.com

Publisher's Note: This is a work of fiction. Names, characters, places, and incidents are a product of the author's imagination. Locales and public names are sometimes used for atmospheric purposes. Any resemblance to actual people, living or dead, or to businesses, companies, events, institutions, or locales is completely coincidental.

Book Layout © 2017 BookDesignTemplates.com

Time Limits/ Kim Megahee. -- 1st ed.
ISBN 978-1-7340190-0-1

Dedication

To Martha Rice Megahee – You are a force of nature – my own personal hurricane. Your faith in me and the impact of your encouragement is beyond measure. I can't wait to see what's next for us as a team.

Cover Design By
Aleaca / 99Designs
Vesna Tišma

*"Whatever suits you just
tickles me plumb to death."*

—HOWDY LEWIS (HENRY FONDA)
FROM THE 1965 MGM FILM "THE ROUNDERS"

CHAPTER 1

1:02 pm – May 20, 2034 - Fort Benning, GA

Captain Marc McKnight had a new mission assignment.

It was a warm Spring afternoon in Georgia. He traveled here to Fort Benning to recruit his second in command. His current destination was Infantry Hall in the Post Headquarters Building.

The last few days of his life were both unusual and exciting.

First, he had a strange meeting with General Flynn. Flynn told him to drop everything and report to retired General Michael Drake for a long-term assignment. When he asked about the project, the General smiled and handed him an envelope.

Flynn's parting comment was both cryptic and encouraging. He said, "You won't be sorry." The envelope contained Drake's cell phone and address.

McKnight knew General Drake by reputation. Who didn't? Early in his career, Drake distinguished himself in battle against near-impossible odds. While time and retelling magnified the story into a legend, the mission facts were irrefutable. If you mentioned "The Dragon," everyone knew you were referring to General Drake.

As Drake rose through the officer ranks, he showed a knack for leadership, getting the job done, and fairness. His men's respect for him bordered on worship. It would help McKnight's career to work with the Dragon. He called Drake and set up a meeting.

They met at Drake's home in Maryland the next day.

He recognized Drake from appearances on TelExtraVision, but was impressed by the man's physical presence when he saw him in person. Even in retirement, Drake carried himself like a general. Upon meeting him, the first thing McKnight noticed was bushy eyebrows below a prominent forehead. At five-foot-ten, Drake was shorter than McKnight by three inches. He was less handsome than rugged, his gray eyes were steady and clear and his complexion was fair. His cheeks showed the wrinkles McKnight's mother called laugh lines and his once blond hair was thin and mostly gray. The wrinkles and thinning hair were the only clues of his sixty-plus years. He looked much younger and his physique was that of a man who religiously exercised, trained, and fueled his body.

The meeting began with breakfast and lasted until 10:00 pm that night. After outlining the project mission and McKnight's possible role, the men talked about philosophy, leadership, and ethics. Drake reiterated General Flynn's promise that he could pick his own team with few exceptions. McKnight would lead the project, but Drake would set the strategic direction.

By the end of the day, McKnight was sure of two things. He wanted the job and Drake was a man worth following.

A pair of sergeants crossed McKnight's path. Their salute brought him back to the present. He returned it and bounded up the stairs to Infantry Hall. The welcome breeze of air conditioning gave him a slight chill as he entered. Colonel Stewart's assistant advised him his candidate had arrived and was in the colonel's office.

He strode down the hallway and paused outside Stewart's office. The door was open, and he heard voices coming from inside the room.

McKnight recognized the first voice. "I'm being transferred, sir?"

A booming voice responded. "At ease, Mr. Tyler. That's a possibility, provided you pass the interview."

"Permission to speak freely, sir?"

"Granted."

"Colonel Stewart, I've only been here for four months. Did I screw up something?"

Outside the door, McKnight smiled.

"If you had, I wouldn't be sending you somewhere else. I don't transfer my problems, Lieutenant. No, there's a new project, and you were requested by name."

"What's the project, sir? Excuse me... by name, sir?"

McKnight stepped forward where Stewart could see him through the doorway. Tyler was standing at ease in front of Stewart, his back to the door.

"Damned if I know, Lieutenant. You might ask the Captain."

"Do you know where I might find him, sir?"

"Yep," Stewart said. "He's standing right behind you." He beckoned McKnight to enter the room with a flick of his hand as he looked at the request on his desk.

Tyler whirled around, and a grin broke out on his face.

"Captain McKnight, this is the man you requested, Lieutenant Winston Tyler." Looking back and forth between the two men, Stewart added, "Have you two met before?"

"Yes, sir," McKnight said. He turned to Tyler and stepped closer. "What the hell are you grinning at, soldier?"

"Just naturally happy, sir," Tyler replied, still beaming.

"I don't know why, Lieutenant. You have the misfortune of working for me again. Wait for me outside." He waved Tyler toward the door.

"Yes, sir!" Tyler saluted Stewart and left the room.

McKnight turned back to Stewart. "Thank you, Colonel. When can I have him?"

"In a week," Stewart said. "He needs to transition his duties. He hasn't been here long and took on a bunch of shit." In a softer voice, he added, "Damn good soldier."

"I know. Thank you, sir." He snapped to attention, saluted and left.

As McKnight entered the hallway, Tyler fell in step with him. They walked down the lengthy hall in silence for a few seconds.

"Well, how the hell are you, Marc?" Tyler said. "It's been a few months since we've heard from you."

McKnight stopped, grinned and stuck out his hand. "I'm five-by-five, Winnie. How's Sarah?"

Tyler grasped the extended hand and slapped his friend's arm with his free hand. "She's awesome as usual. Still the best thing that ever happened to me. And how is Barbara?"

"She's fine."

"Are you positive? When was the last time you talked to her?"

"A couple of days."

Tyler crossed his arms. "Really? Think back."

McKnight paused. "A week, I guess."

Tyler nodded. He stepped closer to McKnight and lowered his voice. "Marc, we've been friends for a long time, and I'm probably the only guy who can say this to you. Barbara is a wonderful woman and cares about you, but it's only a matter of time before she dumps you."

"Why? I've been busy. It's not like I'm seeing someone else."

"In a way that's worse. It's your business, but I'm your friend and I've done my duty. I warned you. You're screwing up."

McKnight smiled and nodded. "Okay. Thanks for the heads-up. I'll call her."

Tyler raised an eyebrow. "Soon, if you're smart. Hey, let's get outside and enjoy the weather."

They left the building and Tyler stopped in the parking lot.

"Okay," he said. "So, what's this all about?"

"I have a job for you if you want it."

"You're kidding, right? Of course, I want it."

"Better wait for the details. Let's get away from ears and eyes."

"Yes, sir. I know just the place. There's a running path in the woods next to the gym. Follow me."

As they walked, McKnight made a mental note to call Barbara. *He's right, she deserves better.*

Tyler was McKnight's first choice to join the HERO Team. They became friends when they roomed together at West Point.

Few officer candidates were more different than Tyler and McKnight. Tyler was fair-skinned, blond and blue-eyed, McKnight was one-eighth American Indian with dark brown hair and brown eyes. Tyler was almost five-foot-nine to McKnight's solid six-foot-one. Tyler possessed an outgoing personality, McKnight was introspective. Tyler grew up in Atlanta in an affluent neighborhood while McKnight spent his formative years on a farm in rural Oregon. Tyler gravitated toward mission planning and McKnight showed ability in combat leadership.

At the Academy, they worked well together and had fun doing it. After graduation, they teamed up for a string of successful projects. Tyler was the logical choice for McKnight's executive officer.

A few minutes later, they were on a path in a pine forest. A light breeze eased the heat of the Georgia sun and the pines whispered to them as they walked further into the woods.

McKnight glanced back in the direction they had come, then at the trail ahead. There was no one in sight. He pulled a form and a pen from his pocket and handed them to Tyler.

"First, the paperwork, Lieutenant. What I'm about to tell you is top secret and cannot be shared with unauthorized personnel, regardless of whether you accept the assignment. Is that understood?"

"Yes, sir."

"Good. Sign the paper."

Tyler signed and handed it back.

"Very good. Lieutenant, they've asked me to assemble a team to plan and execute missions using a new technology. The size of the team is fewer than ten, including two civilian scientists. I'd like you to be my exec for operations. I need a mission planner with leadership ability, and you're it. The rest of the team's still under construction, except for one scientist. We'll be reporting to General Drake with oversight from Senator Lodge."

"Working for the Dragon would be good. Oversight from Lodge? That's not so good. He's my Senator, but I didn't vote for him. He's a damned crocodile. I don't trust him."

"Lodge is the General's problem. We're the grunts. Our job is to execute."

"So, what'll we be doing?"

"The team is being called the HERO Project."

Tyler rolled his eyes.

"Yeah, I know. Stay with me, Lieutenant. HERO stands for Historical Event Research Organization. In a nutshell, we're going to be researching and validating historical events. Here, let's take a load off."

They sat on a wood bench alongside the running trail. McKnight looked across the path at a dogwood in full bloom and a bank of azaleas in unrestrained spring glory. Bumblebees hummed in and around the flowers.

"If you're trying to sell me on how exciting the project will be, you're failing miserably. Sounds like we'd be spending the next few years in the library and on the net, writing papers. Doesn't sound like fun to me. Is there something I'm missing here?"

A thin smile formed on McKnight's face. "Well, Lieutenant, I daresay we'll be doing paperwork. I didn't mention libraries or the net."

Tyler scrunched up his face. "Then how? No library, no net. Where's that leave us? Interviewing elderly witnesses?"

McKnight shook his head, waiting for Tyler to make the leap. Tyler sat on the bench, his elbows on his knees, his hands clasped together and his head down. After a moment, he looked at McKnight.

"You can't be suggesting what I'm thinking."

He's getting there. "And what is that, Lieutenant?"

"Nope. I'm not going to say it. I must be missing something." He paused. "All right. How do we witness an event in the past? We don't have the technology to.... Wait, you mentioned a new technology, didn't you?"

"I did." McKnight allowed himself a little smile. *One last hint.* "You took physics at the Point, right?"

"What? Of course."

"Um-hmm."

Tyler stared at him. His eyes narrowed and darted around. He resumed the position with his elbows on his knees and his eyes on the ground.

"Who's the scientist?" he said without looking up.

"Robert Astalos. He does research at MIT–"

"I'm familiar with him. I read a white paper he and his family wrote last year about interstellar propulsion. Son and grandson, I believe, all with the same name. Let's see... Einstein related speeds close to the speed of light with time slowing down. Nobody has proved that wrong. And gravity is not a force, but a distortion of time-space. Everitt validated that." Tyler sat up straight and looked McKnight in the eye. "Astalos invented time travel?"

Bingo. "Well, I'll let him share the specifics with you, but that's the bottom line. Interested, Lieutenant?"

"Are you kidding? Who wouldn't be? Anything else you want to tell me? Do we have aliens in Area 51?"

McKnight laughed. "Not that I know of. Want the rest of the details, Lieutenant?"

"Yes, sir. You bet I do."

"I thought you might. Here's the short form. We'll operate out of the DC area. Only a few people know about this. The charter for the HERO Team is strictly research. We're forbidden to do anything that might affect history. There's a mandatory risk/benefit analysis and research period required before traveling to make sure we cover the bases. No options, no exceptions, unless the President issues an Executive Order to bypass the process.

"The other civilian on the team will be another planner, your civilian counterpart. He or she hasn't been picked yet. The General's reserved the right to pick that person. You and I get no say," McKnight said, holding up his hand to cut off any objection. "We need a shitload of testing before we can do any work. We don't know enough about the technology yet. Questions?"

"Ha! Only a few hundred. This is supposed to be secret? Nobody outside the organization knows about it?"

"Well, for as long as that lasts. Congress is involved, right?"

"Yeah. I'm surprised the word isn't out already."

McKnight shrugged. "The day is young. But yes, until we hear otherwise from the General, the project doesn't exist and we're working on special projects for Colonel Stewart."

"Okay. Why do we need the civilian planner?" Tyler asked.

"The official word is to balance the team. I suspect it's because Congress doesn't trust the military. I assume it'll be an egghead guy with serious credentials and no government ties. Drake wants someone with no agenda."

"Got it. Do you have anyone else in mind for the team?"

"I do," McKnight said. He pulled a folded piece of paper from his breast pocket and handed it to Tyler. "What do you think?"

"Lieutenant Mitch Wheeler. From North Georgia College, right? Good pick. Has a degree in physics if I remember correctly."

"Yep. That one was easy. And his buddy Hatcher, too."

"Yes, sir. Should be a good team." Tyler handed the list back.

"Glad you approve." McKnight checked the time on his phone. "I need to go catch a plane, Lieutenant. Transition your work ASAP and report to me in DC Monday week. Questions?"

"Yes, sir, but they can wait until next week."

"Very good. I have two more instructions for you." He stood and Tyler followed.

"What's that, sir?"

McKnight smiled at his new executive officer. "Number one, don't bring any preconceptions about time travel with you. Doctor Astalos says most of what the science fiction writers came up with was wrong."

"And number two?"

"The other two Robert Astalos's? The men that coauthored that paper?"

"Yes?"

"They aren't his son and grandson. They're all him. They call themselves Robert, Rob and Robby, but they're all the same guy."

CHAPTER 2

<u>2:00 am – October 23, 2034 – The Sandia Mountains near Albuquerque, NM</u>

Lieutenants Mitch Wheeler and Karen Hatcher met as freshmen in calculus class at the University of North Georgia and discovered their birthdays were one day apart. It was the first of many commonalities that drew them together.

Both grew up in urban communities in large Midwest cities and completed secondary school in three years. Both excelled in math and physics. The college environment in Dahlonega Georgia was a wilderness paradise for these two city kids.

Despite his name, Wheeler was of Hispanic descent. With an olive complexion, jet-black hair and dark brown eyes, he spent most of his free time in the gym lifting weights. He was five-foot-seven on a tall day and compensated with hours of practice in the martial arts. He had a quick wit and always found the upside of any situation.

Hatcher was taller than Wheeler with a slender, athletic build. She wore her raven hair in a ponytail most of the time. Freckles she never tried to conceal augmented her nose and upper cheeks. But her bright blue eyes were her most striking feature. She was introverted and rarely smiled, but was all business with her job in the military.

She was first in their PT class for hand-to-hand combat. Wheeler took second place, setting up years of competitive friendly matches between the two. Hatcher's fighting ability and direct manner earned the respect of male and female cadets alike.

While Hatcher excelled in combat, Wheeler surpassed everyone in physics and quantum mechanics. He read doctorate dissertations in his free time. His curiosity about the subjects might have been considered obsessive if he wasn't having so much fun learning about it.

Hatcher and Wheeler both had serious romantic interests back home, so their shared academic direction and abilities caused them to gravitate toward each other as friends. After graduation, they still regarded themselves a team and sought assignments where they could work together. This was a factor in McKnight's decision to recruit both for the HERO project.

Tonight, they breathed in cool desert air and basked in starlight atop a secluded hillock in the Sandia Mountains of New Mexico, just east of Albuquerque. At an altitude of 7000 feet, this region of the country was called high desert because of the low humidity and clear skies. They chose this location because of the elevation and the absence of light pollution. There was no moon tonight, and the sky was bright with stars.

"So, Wheeler, we ready yet?" Hatcher said.

Wheeler glanced at the timer on the Engine console. "Another couple of minutes and we can start recall. What time is it, anyway?"

Hatcher checked her phone. "Almost 0200 hours," she said as she typed in the camera's return beacon signature.

"Copy. Which test is this, Hatcher?"

"This is test number thirty-seven. The target time is October 23rd, 1934, one hundred years in the past."

The purpose of the experiments was simple. They needed to learn how to calibrate the time travel engine to send a team to a specific date with accuracy. The tests were all the same. For each experiment, they changed the engine's calibration, sent the camera back to photograph the stars, brought it back and calculated what time the camera landed in from their positions in the pictures. It was a tedious and painstaking process, but it was the easiest way the scientists could think of to collect the data they needed.

"Okay, it's time. Bring it back," Wheeler said.

Hatcher punched the recall button and a globe of light appeared over the stainless steel platform twenty yards away. As its brightness intensified, they could see the camera chariot, a four-wheeled chassis the size of a lawn mower. A stellar camera sat on it with the lens pointed up toward the stars.

As they watched, the light bulged to twice its size and dissipated. The chariot now stood before them on the platform. Following procedure, the two officers re-checked the travel calibration to confirm they recorded them correctly and Wheeler ran to the chariot to retrieve the film disk drive.

As he approached it, he thought he saw debris on top. *Did something fall on it?*

He hurried to the device and realized he was far too close. An angry western diamondback rattlesnake coiled around the camera. Its rattle stood upright and buzzed furiously.

Wheeler threw himself backward as it struck at his leg. He twisted as he fell, trying to avoid the exposed fangs. The snake missed his thigh by an inch, but landed next to him. It coiled again, ready to strike as he rolled away from it.

Before the rattlesnake could strike, Hatcher dove on it from behind, grabbing its head in one palm and a coil of its body with the other. Using the forward momentum of her dive, she regained her feet and stood there, grinning at Wheeler and holding the furiously writhing reptile at arm's length.

"I swear," she said. "Leave you alone for a couple of seconds…"

Wheeler rose and panted as the adrenaline surge subsided. "Damn, Hatcher, you are one crazy woman."

"Stop flirting with me," she said. "You know I have a boyfriend."

"Shit! We brought back a rattler from a hundred years ago. You're holding a hundred-year-old snake!"

Hatcher waved it at him. "I don't mean to break your train of philosophical rambling, but I'm already tired of wrestling this asshole. Could we please focus on the problem at hand?"

"Absolutely." He ran to the camera chassis and pushed it off the platform. "Let's send that bastard back to where he came from. Hang on a second." He raced to the console and reset the Engine.

When finished, he ran toward Hatcher but stopped halfway there. "Wait," he called over his shoulder as he sprinted to the truck and pulled out two shovels.

"Now we're ready," he added, as he dropped one at Hatcher's feet and the other on the other side of the steel platform and ran back to the console.

The snake struggled furiously. With effort, Hatcher kept it under control.

"Okay," he said. "When I start the engine, toss it on the platform. We'll use the shovels to keep it there until it goes. Got it?"

"Yes, dammit, I got it. Start it already."

Wheeler pulled the trigger and returned to the platform as Hatcher threw the angry reptile onto it. It coiled again and struck repeatedly at them as they worked to confine it inside the spinning globe of light.

After being poked hard twice, the snake advanced on Hatcher, forcing her to retreat a step. It slithered to the edge of the light globe, coiled and struck at Hatcher. The sphere bulged and dissipated with a bang.

The serpent's body and the part of the shovel inside the globe disappeared. Still in flight from the strike, its severed head bounced off Hatcher's midsection, the fangs snagging her fatigue blouse and spotting it with venom and blood. It landed on the platform with a thud, its mouth opening and closing reflexively.

They stood motionless for a long second.

Hatcher recovered first. "I hate snakes."

"Damn. Sorry about that. But we learned something important."

"What's that?"

Wheeler grinned. "If you're going to travel through time, you'd better make damn sure you keep your body inside the sphere."

CHAPTER 3

2:55 pm – February 5th, 2035 – Russell Senate Office Building

Two enlisted men saluted the group of men as they passed in the hall. The corporal stopped and turned after the officers went by. "Holy shit. Did you see who that was?"

The private halted and looked. "What? No, it was a bunch of officers."

"No, you dickhead. One of them was a civilian. It was *the Dragon*."

"No way. General Drake?"

"Yeah. A fucking legend just walked past."

The private breathed a low whistle. "Man, I heard he killed fifty Taliban single-handedly, with nothing but a knife."

"Aw, that's bullshit."

"Says who?"

The corporal touched his chest with his thumb. "Me, you asshole. I got the straight shit from Sergeant Saunders over beers last month. He was there."

"Sarge was there?"

"Yup. He told me that's where Drake got the nickname Dragon. His squad got ambushed and four were KIA in the first assault. The enemy got overconfident and tried to overrun them. Total dead was five Rangers and forty-nine Taliban. Sarge said Drake had sixteen confirmed kills, seven in hand-to-hand."

"Jesus H. Christ. He must have been one bad motherfucker back then."

"Back then? Shit, Sarge said Drake showed up for one of their PT sessions right before he retired last year. They did a ten-mile run, and he smoked almost everybody. Then he took over the hand-to-hand training. Man, I wouldn't fuck with that guy."

The private shook his head. "Me, neither. Hey, I wonder what the hell he's doing here?"

****

Senator Lodge's secretary led McKnight, General Drake, his aide Tom Clary, and Tyler into his conference room. After motioning them to have a seat, she said, "Senator Lodge will be with you in a few minutes. He's talking to the President."

"No problem, Kathleen. Thank you," Drake said. The three officers sat at the table while Clary took up station behind Drake against the wall.

"Isn't Doctor Astalos supposed to be joining us, sir?" McKnight asked.

"He should be here already," Drake said, tapping his fingers on the table. Turning in his chair, he addressed his aide. "Tom? Could you please check if—"

The door opened and an old man slipped past the secretary. McKnight saw his Marine escort standing outside the door. After acknowledging the officers with a nod, the old man shuffled toward them.

They stood as he approached. "Hello, Doctor Astalos. How are you?" Drake said.

"Hello, gentlemen," he said as he shook their hands. "General, has our host made an appearance yet?"

"No, sir, but we're expecting him at any moment. Would you like to sit?"

"Thank you, General. I believe I will," Astalos said. He set down his coat and hat and sat next to Drake. "Before we meet with the Senator, can we agree to table any discussion on the recombination issue until we learn more about it? There are people who, given the chance, will try to use it to end the HERO program, correct?"

McKnight noted the nods around the table. *Yep. Nobody objects to that.*

"I have questions about it myself, Doctor," Drake said. "But I agree we need to know more before sharing outside the team." Turning to McKnight and Tyler, he said, "Okay, no mention of recombination unless directly asked. Defer to me. Any objections?"

"No, sir," the two officers responded in unison.

"Thank you," Astalos said. "That takes a load off my mind. On another topic, General, how's your search for the civilian planner coming? Any good prospects?"

"Yes, sir. I have an excellent candidate. We're setting up the final interview."

"Excellent! Who is he and what are his credentials?"

"He's a she, Sir. I–"

The door banged open as the Senator entered. "Sorry for being late." He smiled without warmth.

He sat in the executive chair at the head of the conference table, laying out his calendar in front of him. "I have ten minutes, General Drake. What have you learned and what has my two billion dollars of funding bought me?"

McKnight glanced at Drake, whose face betrayed no hint of his thoughts. His respect for the General had grown over these last nine months on the project. Unlike the Senator, General Drake wasted no energy on power posturing or politics unless it was important to the mission.

"More than ten minutes worth, sir," Drake replied. "But I'll do my best to summarize it. First, we can send a human from the present to a designated time in the past and return them safely, with the help of technology Doctor Astalos came up with—the return beacon, the targeting mechanism and the travel platform. We haven't tried to go forward in time. And there are limitations."

"Like what?" Lodge said.

"For example, sir, we have experimented and proven it's easy to go back twenty-five years, but we can't go back one year. We don't understand why, but we have some ideas–"

"What does that mean?" Lodge said.

"It's simple, sir." Drake shifted in his chair. "A specific amount of power can take you back exactly twenty-five years. That twenty-five-year interval is the key, because if you want to travel twenty-five years and a day, the power required is higher. Twenty-five years and three days requires even more power and the requirements go up exponentially after that. All things considered, the limit of the travel window is two weeks, a week on either side of the anniversary."

"You can only go back twenty-five years?" Lodge said. He sounded disappointed.

"No, sir. Sorry, I should be more precise. We can go further back, but only in increments of twenty-five years. From our experimentation, it takes the same amount of energy to travel fifty, seventy-five, even a hundred or more years as it does to travel twenty-five years. Based on this, we believe time is folded, for lack of a better way to express it. And the fold is at twenty-five years."

Lodge smiled at this information, then continued. "You can't travel back just a few minutes or something like that?"

Drake nodded his head. "Actually, you can, sir. This is one of the components of time travel technology we have chosen not to make public. The zero multiple of twenty-five years also works. A few minutes back is within effective range of the zero multiple of twenty-five years. Almost all our human tests were travels to times close to the zero multiple. To minimize the potential impact to history, all the training missions went back less than two days. Except for two trips made by Doctor Astalos, the furthest trip was thirty-six hours."

It occurred to McKnight that Lodge was up to something. The man had a strange gleam in his eye.

"So how do you know we can travel back further?" Lodge asked.

"Well, we have the first travels by Doctor Astalos. Those two twenty-five-year leaps he made are undeniable, but we have independent verification. There's considerable detail around this, Senator, but in short, we sent back a probe in each test. Wheeler and Hatcher from our team did the bulk of the research under Doctor Astalos's direction. They conducted the travel experiments at night from a plateau in New Mexico. After traveling to a different time, the probe photographed the night sky. Based on the position of the stars, our experts can pinpoint the time. In the subsequent tests, we sent a lizard, then a chimp along for the ride to prove a living being could survive the trip. We executed three trips at fifty years, seventy-five years and one hundred fifty years with no failures. Regardless of the time interval, the power required was basically the same."

"I see," Lodge said, making notes in his calendar. "Another question. Can we boost the power enough to overcome the limitations on travel, so we can travel to any time we want?"

Drake glanced at Astalos. "Doctor, would you care to comment on this?"

"Of course," Astalos said with a steadiness that belied his advanced age. "We performed over fifty tests, collecting data. If we increase the power much more, we'll melt the power cables and the Engine. Until we find a power conductor that can handle the load without melting, I'm afraid we are out of luck. For the immediate future, I expect we must resign ourselves to living with this limitation."

"All right," Lodge said. Turning back to Drake, he said, "Tell me about the return beacon and the platform. What do they do?"

"The return beacon allows us to recall the time traveler or the time traveler to recall himself. Without the beacon, we can only return by waiting out the passage of time, which isn't very practical. The platform removes the need to touch the Engine to travel. You need only stand on the platform. Doctor Astalos developed both tools for us."

"Okay," Lodge said. He wrote in his calendar. "Let's talk about possible missions."

"Yes, sir," Drake responded. "I've asked Captain McKnight to cover this for you. Captain?"

McKnight opened the folder on the desk before him. He cleared his throat and faced at the Senator. "Sir, we've done some preliminary research and identified several events that might be of interest. Unfortunately, our desire to get to events of interest in the short term narrows the choices. We had a much bigger list, but we can't address many of them for years, due to the twenty-five-year limitation."

"Give me the big list," Lodge said. "All the events you considered."

"Yes, sir." McKnight looked at his notes. "1972 - the Watergate break-in, 1945 - Hitler's death in Berlin—"

"Hitler? Does anybody still care about that?"

"Apparently so, sir. It's still showing up in gossip media and historical papers."

"Okay, go ahead."

"Yes, sir. 30 or 33 AD - the Resurrection of Jesus-"

"The Resurrection of Jesus? Are you kidding me? We'd get murdered in the press—"

"Sir, you asked for important events. this event is the basis for several major religions—"

"Hmmpf. Okay, I get it. Please continue."

"Yes, sir. 1587 - The lost colony at Roanoke, 1918 - the disappearance of the USS Cyclops in the Bermuda Triangle, 1937 - the disappearance of Amelia Earhart, around 9000 BC - the existence of the continent of Atlantis, 1888 - the Whitechapel murders in London—"

"What are those murders on the list?" Lodge asked.

"Some of them were the murders attributed to Jack the Ripper, possibly the most famous unsolved murders."

"Okay, I understand why people might be interested in these. But I don't see the benefit. What I'm interested in are events that underscore the need for this project. There are members in Congress who fear we'll use the team to gain political advantage. That's my biggest headache right now, and I need ammunition to fight that battle."

"Understood, sir. The last event I have here may fit your bill. On November 22, 1963, the thirty-fifth President of the United States, John F. Kennedy, was assassinated in Dallas. As you are no doubt aware, the authorities detained and questioned a suspect, but he was murdered before the investigation got off the ground. There are dozens of conspiracy theories related to it."

Lodge shifted in his armchair. "Do people care about this anymore? It's been nearly a hundred years since it happened."

McKnight leaned back in his chair. "Have you ever been to Dallas, sir? Where Kennedy was killed?"

"No," Lodge said. "I've been there, but I didn't have time to go sight-seeing."

"Yes, sir. I visited there as a teen. My dad told me about the day of the assassination. He said every American alive then remembers where they were that day. I noticed something very interesting."

Lodge leaned forward and said, "What? What did you notice?"

"On the street are two large X's that represent where Kennedy's limo was when his body was struck by bullets. Even to this day, the grass by the street is trampled bare from the feet of Americans who visit the site each year. People *do* care about this event, sir, so it might be a candidate for investigation."

"Something to keep in mind, sir..." Drake said. "Sorry for interrupting, Captain."

"Not at all, sir. Please go ahead."

Drake turned to Lodge. "If we investigate this event, we might not like the answer we find. We should think long and hard before going after this one. Once we commit to it, we must go through with it and produce evidence. Otherwise, they'll add us to the long list of conspiracy theories."

"Thank you, Drake. I'll keep that in mind. Captain, how soon could we travel to check out the assassination?"

"Four years from now, sir. There are two women who died under suspicious circumstances, a prominent actress in 1962 and another in 1964. Both have been linked romantically with Kennedy. To get the whole picture, we should check out those deaths, too. We could travel on the first one approximately thirty months from now."

"That's still too far in the future for help with my problems. So keep looking for opportunities we can act on sooner. But let's put that one on the list for planning. I'd like a detailed plan for the event at Event minus six months. Does that work?"

"Yes, sir," McKnight replied, adding a note to the folder.

"Thank you, Captain McKnight. Anything else?"

"No, sir. We'll have more events to discuss at the next briefing."

Lodge grunted and made notations in his calendar, then looked back at Astalos. "Doctor Astalos, are you sure you won't change your mind and take a larger role with the project? I'd like to see you making a larger contribution to it."

Drake started to respond, but Astalos beat him to it.

"No, Senator, I think I've made my position clear. I'd prefer to work with Rob and Robby on the light speed drive. The project team respects that decision and supports it. I invented the targeting mechanism, the beacon, and the platform to make them independent from me, though I am reviewing the test results and providing suggestions. They don't need my help and, to me, the drive research is more important. Besides, we're on the verge of a breakthrough for that project."

"Well, Doctor," Lodge said. "You can't blame me for trying. And your funding for your drive research is secure?"

"Yes, sir, it is."

"So as long as you have your funding, you'll be unavailable to work on this project?" Lodge stared at Astalos.

With an effort, McKnight chose not to speak.

"Senator." Astalos paused, looking Lodge in the eye. "If I lost my federal funding tomorrow, I have three corporations with standing offers to double my existing funding. I'd rather keep it where it is, but if I'm forced to take my light speed drive to the private sector, that's what I'll do. If that happens, I'm sure I won't have time to work on government projects. No, my funding is secure." Astalos stared back at Lodge and didn't blink.

McKnight relaxed. Doctor Astalos had learned the game of power politics.

"Well, that's mighty good to hear, Doctor," Lodge said with a humorless smile. "How are your other... selves doing? Rob and Robby? Everyone in good health? What are they up to?"

They're fine, Senator. Robby is planning to go to Europe for an extended sabbatical and write a book. I'm not sure where Rob got off to. He was really secretive about it. I suspect he is following his interests somewhere close by."

Lodge stared at him for a moment, then nodded. "Good, good. Glad to hear it. Let me know if you change your mind about working on the project."

"I will, sir."

Lodge turned to Drake. Before he could speak, his secretary stuck her head into the room. "Senator, that call you were expecting is on hold now. Shall I take a message?"

"No, Kathleen, I'll be right there. Please ask him to hang on for a second." He turned back to Drake. "Drake, I'm satisfied with the progress you've made and will make a recommendation to extend the HERO project funding. I want another status report in..." He thumbed through his calendar and made a notation. "Six months. Will we be ready to start missions by then?"

"Yes, sir. We're ahead of schedule, thanks to Captain McKnight and Lieutenant Tyler here. Barring any unforeseen problems, we'll be ready by then."

"Okay. One more thing. Have there been any complications from the President's public announcement about the technology?"

Drake shrugged. "Not that I know of, sir, except it's causing inconvenience for Doctor Astalos. Because of the publicity, he needs a security detail to walk down the street. And everyone he talks to becomes a target of the media, hoping to get a tidbit for the evening news."

"I'm sorry that's happening," Lodge said. "Since that journalist broke the story, the President had no choice but to go public with it. Do we know the source of the leak yet?"

"No, sir, but I assure you we will identify the source."

"Good. Thank you, gentlemen, and have a good afternoon," Lodge said, as he hurried out and closed the door.

For a moment, there was silence. "That went well," Astalos said with a laugh.

"We accomplished what we came here to do," Drake said. "Doctor Astalos, is there anything I can do for you?"

"No, sir," said Astalos. "You've helped me immensely, especially your advice on how to deal with politicians and bureaucrats. I am in your debt."

"Well, no problem, sir. Let me know if I can help. Captain? Lieutenant? Let's get back to work." McKnight, Tyler, and Sergeant Clary filed out of the room behind Drake.

****

Astalos and his Marine escort walked through the front door of the Russell building to where his security detail and vehicles were waiting. There were four Marines in the detail, all in dress uniforms.

While the others scanned the area for threats, the escort offered his arm to Astalos and together they walked carefully down the building's stairs to the waiting limousine. Astalos climbed in the back seat while the escort slipped into the driver's seat. The other soldiers got into a lead car.

The driver peered at Astalos through the rear-view mirror. "Where to, Doctor Astalos?"

"Home. Thank you, Sergeant."

The car was soon out on the freeway, headed to Andrews Air Force Base.

Astalos smiled to himself. *Thanks for keeping your mouth shut, Rob.*

The voice in his head laughed. *You're welcome. It was an effort.*

CHAPTER 4

<u>6:55 pm - Friday, July 6th, 2035 - Silver Springs, MD</u>

As was his custom in the evenings, General Drake sat in a favorite armchair to read with a cup of decaf coffee. He had finished reading the first chapter of "The Once and Future King" when the TelExtraVision communicator chimed.

The ringtone told him it was not an ordinary call. One member of the HERO Board or the President was trying to reach him.

He answered the call with the remote. The monitor came to life, displaying the frowning face of Senator Lodge.

"Good evening, Senator. What can I do for you?"

"What's the status on the HERO project tests? Are they completed?"

"Yes, sir, they are. We wrapped up the final set of tests yesterday. There are a few issues to be worked out, but–"

"Good," Lodge interrupted. "I want to discuss something with you, Drake. A new opportunity for your HERO team has come up. Is your team available? How quickly can you mobilize them?"

"They can be ready to go in one week, once the mission is approved, Senator. The approval process takes longer, as you know, sir."

"Bear with me for a minute, General. If I remember correctly, the team must time travel on the fiftieth anniversary of the incident for it to succeed. Is that right?"

"Sir, that's partly correct. I'm presuming when you say *succeed*, you're talking about the travel itself, right? Not the specifics of the mission?"

"Yes, that's what I'm asking."

"Yes, sir. But it's not just the fiftieth year. It's every twenty-five years after the event. When is the event in question, sir?"

"Good," Lodge said. "I need your help, Drake. What would it take to cut through the bullshit and get a mission in progress today? I'm talking next weekend. We need HERO to investigate an event right away."

The conversation was a few seconds old and Drake didn't like its direction. "Excuse me, Senator, but the approval process is not optional. You know that better than anyone. We're required to go through the approval process–"

"No time for that."

"–before we can undertake any mission," Drake continued. "No exceptions. Since this would be our first mission, it's even more important that we stick to procedure. That's part of our safeguard to make sure that nobody gets killed or makes a catastrophic mistake."

"This is a special circumstance, Drake. As the Chairman of the Oversight Board, I'm making a special request for a short, simple mission. Just event observation. Nothing else."

What? "Senator, I'm confused. You're asking me to circumvent the approval process? You designed it yourself to make sure no one abused the technology for personal gain. Why would you–"

"I will not debate this with you, Drake. As the board chairman, I'm directing you to authorize and schedule the mission." His voice rose in volume and pitch. "I own this team and I'm not letting a damned scheduling problem keep me from..." Lodge stopped talking. His face looked ashen. When he spoke again, his voice was soft and steady. "Look, Drake. I recommended you for this project because you get things done. If you can't do it, there are others who'd jump at a chance to try. I need you to step up and make this happen."

Drake straightened and, keeping his voice level, responded. "Senator, I have the utmost respect for you and what you went through, getting this program funded and operational. You've built a good process that puts national security first and–"

"Fuck that. I need—"

"Let me finish, sir. You've built a good process that puts national security first and prohibits missions for personal or political purposes. I admire that, I really do. But as far as this assignment goes, you and the rest of the board can fire me and bring in whoever you want, whenever you want."

"Drake—"

"I'm serious, sir. If you have someone else in mind, bring them in. Since I have more than a year with the team and the technology, bringing in someone new will likely jeopardize the mission. Is that what you want?"

"No, but—"

"Senator, you brought me in to do this job. Until relieved, I'll do it legally and ethically to the best of my ability. Federal law prohibits you and me from circumventing the approval process. Only the President can do that with an executive order."

Lodge grunted. "So, if the President approves the mission, your team can be ready in a week to move?"

"That's correct, Senator. Sir, may I ask what the—"

The image on the monitor changed to black. Drake swore and moved to throw the remote across the room. With effort, he controlled his temper and laid the remote back on the side table. He picked up his book and tried to read.

After he stared at the same page for ten minutes, he closed it and dropped it on the footstool. He took a sip of coffee. "Ugh. Cold," he muttered.

In the kitchen, he poured another cup, took a sip, and leaned back against the counter with his arms and ankles crossed. For a few moments, he stood motionless with his eyes closed, replaying the exchange with the Senator.

Okay. What happened fifty years ago that he's so damned interested in? He walked back to the library and sat at his desk.

Cradling the coffee cup in both hands, he leaned back and studied the ceiling.

Let's see. Maybe newspaper database? No, search for it.

"A-S-E?" he said to the black TelExtraVision monitor.

An image of a young woman appeared on the screen. "Yes, General. What can I find for you?"

"Search for *Lodge, 1985, July*. Associate and correlate."

"Please wait," the automated search engine said. Drake took another sip of coffee as a spinning icon replaced the image.

The woman's image reappeared on the screen. The voice reported, "There are 24,345 hits. Would you like to refine your search?"

"Hmmm... Yes, A-S-E. Please add *Atlanta*. Associate and correlate."

"Please wait." Another image appeared. "There are 254 hits. Would you like to refine your search?"

"No, thank you, A-S-E. Show me the first hit... Okay, next hit, please... Next... Next..."

After ten minutes, an image caught his attention. It was an old newspaper story.

"Open, please," Drake said.

The newspaper article filled the TelExtraVision screen.

When he finished reading the article, he leaned back in his chair and rubbed his eyes with the heels of his hands.

Shit. This could bring down the HERO program. And all of us with it.

CHAPTER 5

10:23 am – Sunday, July 8th, 2035 - Washington, DC

McKnight sipped his coffee and set the cup on the table. He had avoided making this call as long as he dared. Sitting at the breakfast table of his apartment in the Bachelor Officers' Quarters, he picked up the phone and dialed Barbara's number. He wasn't looking forward to this.

It rang eight times before she answered it. Her quiet voice came through the line. "Hello, Marc."

He detected no emotion in her voice. *She's pissed.* "Hi. Good morning. Sorry I didn't make it to the party last night. It was–"

"Work, right?" she suggested.

"Yes, it was. I just couldn't break away. I'm sorry."

"I know. It's happened before."

"I'm very sorry. It was… well…"

"It's classified. I know that. It's always work." A long pause. "I'm really trying hard here."

"Barbara, I know you're disappointed—"

"Disappointed? I was disappointed the first time. The second time you did it, I was hurt. The third time, I got irritated. Now, I'm… just…"

"Pissed? And you should be. I have no excuse. It can't be easy to date a guy with a classified job and crazy hours. I wish…"

"What? What do you wish? Tell me."

He didn't know what he wanted to say. He had strong feelings for Barbara, but the pull of his work was stronger.

She filled in the silence. "You don't know what you want, do you? You have no damned clue."

He had that sinking feeling he'd been here before, and more than once.

"You could have called," she said, her voice quivering. "It wouldn't have taken more than a minute. You could have…"

McKnight couldn't think of anything to say. Barbara was a remarkable woman and didn't deserve to be treated this way. There was no acceptable reason he shouldn't be in love with her, but he wasn't. She cared for him and they had a lot in common. He was the source of her misery and his heart filled with empathy for her. He felt hollow and guilty inside.

"Say something," she said.

"I don't know what to say." He stumbled over the words. "You know I care about you. You're right, I should have called you. But when duty calls, I have to answer." He paused. "I can't tell you how sorry I am."

"Tired. That's it. Tired."

"What?"

"I'm tired. I'm not mad or hurt or irritated anymore. I'm just tired. Tired of waiting for you to call. Tired of wishing and hoping. Tired of being alone most evenings. Tired of—"

"Barbara, I—"

"Sarah and Winnie told me and I should have listened to them. I didn't because I thought maybe I was… maybe I could be the one who could break through to your heart. But I was wrong. I shouldn't have started a relationship with a married man."

"Married?" he asked. "No, I'm not m…"

"Yes?"

"You mean married to my job."

"I do. That you catch my meaning without explanation speaks volumes."

"I... I don't know how to react to that," he whispered, struggling to keep the emotion from his voice.

"Say goodbye, Marc."

"I don't want to."

"Marc, listen to me." Her tone softened. "You're not ready for me. I know you better than you think I do, and maybe better than you know yourself. I don't know what you do in your day job, but for now, it is all consuming. You don't have time for anything or anyone else right now, so I'll spare myself a lot of grief and you a lot of embarrassing moments like this one."

McKnight felt a sharp sense of loss mingled with a slight wave of relief. He said the sole thing he could think of.

"Can we still be friends?"

"Friends? Of course, but not for a while. I need space to pull myself back together. Seeing you around would only make it tougher. When I'm myself again, I'll call you. Maybe someday you'll be the guy for me, but right now, I need someone who is front and center. Someone who needs me as much as I need him."

He heard her voice becoming stronger. In that moment, he knew he hadn't done critical damage to her. She would recover.

"Barbara, I wish I could be that guy for you."

"You think I don't realize that? Of course, you do. I know you, Marc. You didn't mean to hurt me. You have so much spirit and you're the type of man I want, but you're not there yet."

McKnight smiled a little, despite his feelings. "You may be right. I feel pretty one-dimensional sometimes."

"Of course, I am. You can't help it. You're a kind person and I adore you. But I'm not waiting for you any longer. I can't afford it. Know what else? You know in your heart I'm right."

He sighed. "I can't argue with you about this. It's too close to home."

She laughed. "It's been fun, Marc. Maybe if the timing was different or whatever. Anyway, it's time to call it a day. I'll always remember you and I hope you'll do the same, my friend."

"I will."

"Say goodbye, Marc."

"Goodbye, Barbara."

"Bye."

She hung up. He set his phone on the table and stared at it.

His mind raced. His emotions flooded with sensations of guilt, loss, and… relief.

After a few minutes, he became conscious of the world again. He glanced out the window. The sun was still shining, and he was still alive. He could hear the grounds keeper's lawnmower and a PT class running by, singing as they passed.

His eyes settled on Winnie Tyler, stretched out on his couch. Tyler crashed on his sofa after their work session last night.

McKnight smiled. "Okay. I know you're awake. You heard?"

Tyler opened his eyes. "Is it morning? Oh, yes it is. What's going on?"

"Shut up."

"What? What'd I do?"

"You heard?"

Tyler grunted. "Just your part. Enough, I guess. I'm sorry, Marc."

"Me, too. I suppose it was predictable. I'm not exactly good boyfriend material."

"Ha! Sarah disagrees. I don't understand why. She fixes you up with her friends, but then she warns them about you. Go figure."

"I'm not sure she's that great a judge of boyfriends," McKnight said. "After all, she chose you, God knows why."

"Just lucky, I guess," Tyler replied. He rose from the sofa and walked across the apartment to the kitchenette and poured himself a mug of coffee. "Need a warm up?"

"Yes, please."

Tyler filled McKnight's cup to the rim, replaced the carafe in the coffeemaker and sat at the table. "Besides, I have a new idea for you."

"Uh-oh."

"Now hear me out. What you require is a nice, hot Southern lady. From Atlanta, for example."

"Don't you think it's a little too soon? Barbara and I just broke up."

"Perfect timing if you ask me. You haven't found anybody else yet, right?"

"What?"

"Just as I expected. So, a nice, hot Atlanta girl. Sweet and beautiful. Oh and did I mention she was hot?"

McKnight laughed. "And why the hell would I choose to go out with anyone you think is hot?" He grinned at Tyler across the table.

"Are you kidding me? You've met my fiancée. You know I can pick 'em."

McKnight saw his opportunity and pounced on it. "Winnie, Sarah is a brilliant and lovely woman, but she had a brief lapse of judgment. She got engaged to you before she realized what a dick you are. She's such a sweetheart, she'll marry you anyhow, rather than let you down."

"Ah, stick it. You have no taste. You'd have no social life except for the ladies I set you up with. When was the last time you had an actual date, huh? Two months? Three months?"

"Last week, thank you very much. I don't need help."

"Bullshit. You need all you can get. I'm right, and you know it."

A faint melody interrupted their banter. Tyler pulled out his phone and smiled at the display. He lifted it to his ear and spoke. "Hi, Mom."

McKnight leaned backward and savored his coffee.

Tyler listened for a few moments. "I haven't forgotten... Sure, I can make it, barring an emergency at work. I can't speak for Sarah, though. Let me call her and find out if she's available... What?" he said, shifting sideways and lowering his voice. "That stick-in-the-mud? Well, I don't know. He's such a social midget I... Ma'am?... Yes, he's here with me... Okay, if you really want me to, I'll ask him.... Right... Yes, ma'am, I'll see you then, regardless... Yes... Love you, too."

Tyler turned back to him with a wide grin. "We're flying to Atlanta on Wednesday."

"What amazing event am I *not* attending this time?" McKnight asked, futilely struggling to maintain a straight face.

"My Grandmother's birthday. They always have a big picnic in her backyard to celebrate. You haven't met her yet, have you?"

"Don't think so. Was she at our graduation?"

"Nope. Gramma and Granddad were in Europe, some kind of business-slash-pleasure trip. They do that sometimes. Anyway, it's a big celebration. Mom thinks it'd be a good opportunity to introduce Sarah to the rest of the family. And it wouldn't hurt you to be there. Mom has someone she wants you to meet."

"Oh, great. No offense to your mom, but I don't think–"

"Hey, I know the girl. You'd like her."

"Yeah?" McKnight said, raising an eyebrow. "Why do you say that?"

"Because she's got a great personality," Tyler said, grinning and shooting him with his finger.

"Bite me," McKnight said with a scowl. He balled up a napkin and threw it at Tyler, who laughed. Despite himself, he laughed with him. "Now I know I'm not going," he said.

"I'm kidding, I'm kidding," Tyler said, regaining his composure. "At least partly. I know her and she does have a great personality. She's my cousin and she also happens to be hot."

"You're calling your cousin hot? What is this? I hear some people in Georgia have family trees that don't branch."

"Not this again," Tyler said, rolling his eyes. "I can appreciate good looks without incest being a factor. And I reiterate, she is hot. I guarantee it."

"Oh, here we go again, with the hot guarantee." McKnight paused. "Okay, so why don't you call Sarah? She might actually be interested in going to this thing."

"Good idea," Tyler said. To the phone, he said, "Call Sarah."

McKnight leaned back in his chair and thought of Barbara again. What was the real reason their relationship failed? Like Tyler, he did see it coming. But he didn't try to stop it.

Why not?

She was everything he wanted in a woman, and yet he couldn't make himself take the next step. It was all there, but he stopped at the edge of letting her in. *Why can't I just surrender to it? What's wrong with me?*

Something was missing and what it was escaped him. Was he waiting for a giant revelation, a two-by-four between the eyes from the universe that said, "This is the one, Marc?" *That only happens in fairy tales and the movies.*

Another part of him breathed a sigh of sad relief. *It's over, but I'm alone again.*

The sounds of Tyler happily chatting with Sarah filtered into his thoughts. He experienced a tiny twinge of jealousy at his friend's happiness. He pushed the emotion away.

Although the project was challenging, it was also stressful. *Maybe I just need a change. Some R and R.*

He resolved to join Tyler on the flight to Atlanta on Wednesday.

CHAPTER 6

9:37 am - Tuesday, July 10th, 2035 - Atlanta Police Department

Detective Trevor George drummed his fingers on his desk. His current case was now history. He breathed a sigh of satisfaction, seeing a serial killer would soon experience justice.

George loved working cold cases and he was good at it. He had an aptitude for spotting and acting on the odd detail that contributed to solving the crime. He devoted weeks to each case, reading extensive files in a single sitting and wearing headphones to channel in familiar music.

But today, he was on the verge of being bored. It was time to select a new case. He opened his file drawer and drew out his backlog.

He was assessing the third folder when a tap on his shoulder brought him back to the present. The duty officer stood next to his desk.

"Chief wants to see you, George."

Chief Wilson was his boss's boss and seldom asked to talk to him. "What about?"

The duty officer grinned at him. "Well, let me see… She usually tells me everything she thinks, but this time…" He tapped his temple, shook his head, and gestured at the ceiling. "Man, this time she didn't. I guess she forgot."

"Okay, okay," George said. "I'll drop by her office later." He looked back at his pile of cases.

"She said, now."

"Right now?"

"Yes, right now. Hope you didn't screw up too bad," the duty officer said. "See you later."

Chief Wilson was a no-nonsense leader who didn't hesitate to tell you if she wasn't happy with your work. He couldn't imagine what he had done to make her unhappy.

Well, better get it over with.

He walked down the hallway to the Chief's office. A curt order to enter followed his knock on her door. She was on the phone. She acknowledged George with a nod as he entered and pointed at a side chair. He sat while she wrapped up her call.

"Yes sir," she said. "I'll put my best man on it... No sir, we won't let you down... Yes, thank you, sir." She hung up the phone.

She stared at George for a moment. "How's your case load? You got any bandwidth?"

Relieved he wasn't in trouble, George said, "I concluded the serial murder case. I was searching through my files for the next case to focus on. What's up?"

She pointed at her phone. "That was Senator Lodge. Looks like the Feds are here to work on a homicide."

"A murder case. Not a cold case? Who's here? The FBI? NSA?"

"Oh, it is a cold case. One of yours. And it's not the FBI or the NSA. It's the Army."

"The Army? That's weird. Which case?"

The Chief leaned forward and put her elbows on her desk. "The James Lodge case. Are you familiar with it?"

"Sure. Cold case about fifty years old. Someone murdered a senior executive at NewT Communications on the top floor of their headquarters. No one captured DNA evidence back then, and they never solved it. I have my theories about it. Have they uncovered new information?"

Chief Wilson shrugged. "If so, they're not saying. The Governor called last night and told me to expect a call from Senator Lodge. What's on your plate tomorrow?"

"Nothing else as of now. What's going on?"

"There's a meeting at NewT Center tomorrow afternoon at five." She gave him a sticky note, then pointed at it. "That's the number for Walt Matthews. He's a friend of mine and he manages the security team there. Call him and he'll give you the details. Until further instruction, this is your only case."

"All right. I'll review the file tonight and call Mr. Matthews. Think he'll mind if I come earlier in the day? I'd like to look around before the meeting, and we have evidence we can share with them, too."

"Ask Walt about coming down early. Make me proud, Detective George."

"I will. Will you be there, Chief?"

"No, they didn't invite me. You'll be our only representative there."

"Really? That's even weirder. Why don't they want you there?"

"He didn't say. But he did say it was to be kept in the closest confidence and they would only allow the case officer in the meeting. That's you. Maybe they have new evidence that's super-sensitive or something. Who knows? Just don't screw it up."

"No, ma'am, I won't."

"Good. You're dismissed."

George rose and walked to the door. He gripped the doorknob and turned back toward her. "Chief?"

"Yes?"

"You're aware the murdered man was Senator Lodge's father, right?"

The expression on her face told him she wasn't.

"No," she said after a long pause. "I noted the name was the same, but didn't connect the dots. You appreciate what that means?"

"Yes, ma'am, I do. It explains why the Feds are concerned, and it's all the more reason not to screw up."

CHAPTER 7

Wednesday, July 11th, 2035 - 1:30 pm - Atlanta, GA

Tyler and McKnight arrived in Atlanta on the 10:00 am flight from Washington. With their bags on their shoulders, they engaged a news limo for the ride. Tyler gave the address to the operator who switched on the media feed to the passenger compartment and steered the bullet-shaped vehicle to the interstate's ultrahigh-speed acceleration lane. As the limo reached entry velocity, the Maglev high-speed lane captured it and propelled them toward downtown Atlanta. "We're only a few minutes away from Gramma's," Tyler said.

McKnight turned off the media transmission. "So, what were you saying about your grandparents?"

"Oh, yeah, I love this story. It's a slender thread of coincidence that they met and got together. He saw her at the Varsity restaurant and thought she was cute. Two days later, he ran into her where she worked and struck up a conversation. If that hadn't happened, yours truly wouldn't be here."

"Really?" McKnight said.

"Yeah. She was a security guard and he walked by her station on the way home from a concert at the Fox Theatre. He recognized her, said hello, and the rest is history. If he hadn't gone to that concert, or if she hadn't been working the security counter that night, chances are they wouldn't have met. Oh, and it was her birthday. So they have a double celebration every year in honor of her birthday and the day they met. Thin threads, eh?"

"Cool," McKnight said, as he watched the skyscrapers of Atlanta hurtle past. "I've never been to Buckhead. How far is it from here?"

"Not far at all. We'll be there in no time."

The cabbie commanded the limo to leave the Maglev lane and exited the freeway, turning east on West Paces Ferry Road. After a brief ride through a business community, the view outside his window turned residential. McKnight relaxed and admired the meticulously landscaped properties as they passed.

This part of Atlanta was akin to time travel. Many of the homes were a hundred years old or more. They passed one large white mansion after another, with expansive green lawns, filled with oak and dogwood trees. This was a different world from his home, a three-bedroom ranch on twenty acres near Pendleton, Oregon.

The limo turned off West Paces Ferry Road onto a quiet lane. After two blocks, it swung into a short driveway. McKnight and Tyler collected their bags, and Tyler paid the operator.

They climbed the front steps of the first antebellum mansion McKnight had ever seen up close. It was the family home of Tyler's grandparents, Churchie and Meredith Tyler. At the top of the steps, McKnight turned and watched the news limo pull from the driveway.

Oh, boy. This is way out of my league. This was a world he could hardly imagine. Yet to Tyler, it was home.

Through the fog of his thoughts, he realized Tyler was talking to him.

"Come on, Marc. I want to see my folks."

McKnight took a deep breath, exhaled and followed Tyler inside. The foyer was as impressive as he expected. It was two stories high. A huge crystal chandelier sparkled overhead and illuminated a pair of circular staircases with a hallway between them that led to the back of the mansion.

"Everybody's probably out back," Tyler said. He motioned for McKnight to follow him. As they approached the back door, they passed a group coming inside. To McKnight's amazement, Tyler greeted each one by name.

As he stepped through the door, McKnight took in the sight. The property the mansion stood on was bigger than he guessed when they arrived. A dozen children dashed around the yard, enjoying a game of tag. By McKnight's estimate, there were two hundred people standing and chatting in small groups.

The back yard covered over two acres. The lawn flowed downhill from the home to a small brook that crisscrossed it, then more steeply uphill to a stand of mature oak trees and tall pines. Small clusters of dogwoods decorated the slope. Small white bridges crossed the stream in three places. A blue and white gazebo between the stream and the trees completed the picture. To his right, a refreshment table with hors d'oeuvres and drinks stood in the shade of a large oak.

McKnight followed Tyler to one group, where he recognized Tyler's parents, Charles and Bonnie. He didn't know the other couples. Bonnie greeted them and introduced McKnight to the rest of the group.

"Hi, Honey," Bonnie said to Tyler, touching his arm. She glanced over his shoulder. "Where's Sarah?"

"She had a meeting at the hospital she couldn't avoid, Mom. She's taking a later flight." Tyler checked the time. "I'm picking her up at the airport in two hours. Where's Gramma?"

"She's around here someplace," Bonnie answered, craning her neck, looking over shoulders. "I don't see her, though. She's probably button-holed somebody, making them tell their life story."

"She was here a moment ago," another woman said, leaning left and right to peer around the others.

"I want Marc to meet her. C'mon, Marc." He turned toward the snack tables.

"Come back later, dear," Bonnie called after him. "I want to know what you've been up to. And bring Sarah around as soon as you can." Tyler waved assent over his shoulder. He let McKnight catch up to him, and they continued on to the nearest refreshments.

"Needed to get you away from that group," he said. "Get Mom started and we'll be all afternoon, recounting what we've been doing since I was here last. Want a beer?"

"Best idea you've had today," McKnight said.

"Two Blue Moons," Tyler said to the barman, and turned back to McKnight. "I see ten people I haven't seen in a while and I need to catch up with them. I still haven't seen Gramma though." He took the beers from the barman and handed one to McKnight. "Salud," he said and clinked the neck of his bottle with McKnight's. "I haven't seen Megan, either."

"Megan? Who's that?"

"My cousin I mentioned. She's supposed to be here now."

"Oh, I forgot. The *hot* cousin." McKnight rolled his eyes. "I can't wait."

"Bite me. Hey, there's one of my high school buddies. Let's check out what's going on in town tonight."

"Go ahead. I'd like to have a sandwich, finish this beer and relax. You don't have to entertain me. I'll come find you if I get bored."

"Are you sure? Mom will kick my ass if you don't meet all the eligible women."

"No problem, Winnie. I'll be fine. I'm not much for the social crowd and I wouldn't mind kicking back and relaxing a bit. There's plenty of time later to appease your mom."

"Okay," Tyler said. "I suggest the gazebo if you prefer to remain outside. It's hot today. Otherwise, I recommend the rec room. There're drinks at the bar, plus TelExtraVision, pool table and video games set up for the kids. If that appeals to you, go back inside, turn right, and take the stairs to the basement."

"Thanks. I think I'll stick around out here. If you can't find me, ping me."

"Will do."

McKnight made his way to the sandwich table and picked up a turkey on wheat and a napkin. Armed with his Blue Moon and sandwich, he crossed a bridge and trudged up the hill to the trees, looking for shade. Like most summer afternoons in Georgia, it was hot and humid.

Under the largest tree, a small group of men were discussing the upcoming college football season. McKnight didn't want to join the discussion, so he kept his distance. He finished his sandwich and strolled down the hill toward the gazebo. *This looks like a great place to sit and watch people. Or grab a quick nap.* He climbed the steps and slipped inside.

It wasn't empty. An elderly woman sat in a white Adirondack chair, hidden by the latticework. She was fanning herself and reading an old, battered book.

"Oh, excuse me," McKnight said. "Sorry, I didn't mean to intrude. I didn't see you sitting there."

Closing the book, the woman turned toward him and smiled. "Oh, you're not intruding. I was escaping for a minute." She paused and searched his face. "Have we met before?"

"No, ma'am," he replied. "At least, I don't think so. I've never been here before. I'm Marc McKnight." He bowed in her direction. "Winston Tyler invited me. I guess you know him since you're here at his grandparents' place."

The woman smiled. "Yes, I do. I'm Merrie Tyler, his grandmother. And you are his friend and commanding officer. I'm very pleased to meet you. Please sit down."

McKnight hopped forward and took her offered hand in his. Her grip was firm, but feminine. "Yes, ma'am. It's my honor. Winnie's told me so much about you, I feel I already know you."

He sat in the other chair and scooted it around to face Mrs. Tyler. She was a striking woman, trim and attractive in a stylish, royal blue summer dress. Her hair was silver, but with a slight hint of blonde, and pulled back into a ponytail. There were few lines on her face, and her eyes matched her dress and sparkled with humor and intelligence. She didn't look old enough to be Tyler's grandmother.

She must have been something else when she was young. Attractive women always made him nervous. "Have you lived here long?" he asked.

"Thirty years in this house, but I've lived in Atlanta my entire life," she said. "Is this your first trip here, Captain?"

"No, ma'am. I've been through Atlanta a few times, but this is my first time to visit anyone who lives here. And please call me Marc."

"I will, but only if you promise to call me Merrie. Winnie will insist you call me Gramma, but I try not to let handsome young men call me that." She laughed, and her eyes danced.

"I promise, Merrie. Thanks."

"Oh, your beer is nearly empty, Marc. Can I get you another?" She moved to rise from her chair.

McKnight jumped to his feet. "Oh, no, ma'am. I'll run over and get one. And can I get you anything? A glass of wine or something?"

Relaxing back into her chair, she said, "You're drinking my favorite now. If you don't mind, get yourself another Blue Moon and bring me one as well."

"I'd be happy to. Whatever suits you, tickles me plumb to death, Merrie."

As he turned to fetch the beers, her eyes widened, and she asked, "I'm sorry. What did you say?"

He paused on the step. "I said I'd be happy to."

"No, after that. Something about being tickled?"

"Oh. I said, 'Whatever suits you, tickles me plumb to death.' It's just a line I picked up as a kid. I liked it and got in the habit of saying it." He stepped off the gazebo.

"And you're sure we haven't met before?" she called after him.

He turned around to face her. "Yes, ma'am, I'm sure. I'd have remembered you." He waved at her and walked to the refreshment table.

When he returned with the beers, Merrie was staring across the lawn. At his approach, she perked up and smiled at him. He handed one to her and sat beside her. As he did so, he got a whiff of her perfume. She didn't smell like his own grandmother.

"What are you reading, Merrie?"

"Oh, it's my favorite. The Lord of the Rings. I've read it many times. I never get tired of it. Have you read it?"

"Wow."

"What? Is something wrong?"

He pointed at her book. "No, not at all. It's my favorite, too. I've read it ten times, though I read it on my phone, not from an old hardback."

"Most people do. I got this copy many years ago, and it has sentimental value. So who's your favorite character?"

"I'm a Ranger," he said with a grin. "It would have to be Aragorn."

"Of course, it would." With a gleam in her eye, she said, "'All that is gold does not glitter.'"

McKnight responded with the poem's next line. "'Not all those who wander are lost.'"

"Ha! You *are* a fan. I'm glad to have a new friend to talk with about Middle Earth." She gestured toward the crowd in the yard. "The rest of my family, they don't get it. Folks either love the story or they find it boring."

"Well, it isn't for everyone. I tell people to read the first two chapters and, if they aren't excited about it, stop reading. It's a waste of time."

"You're exactly right," Merrie said, the passion rising in her voice. "I gave up trying to excite folks about it long ago. They either are, or they aren't. Now it's just my private pleasure. Except, now I have you to talk with."

"Yes, ma'am, you sure do. And who's your favorite character?"

"I have many, but if I must pick one, it would be Eowyn. She's delicate, but strong. And she has love for Aragorn that can never be returned. Courageous, with a huge capacity for love." She glanced at McKnight with glistening eyes, then looked away. "How beautifully tragic."

"Yes, it is. But she finds her knight in shining armor in the end."

"Yes, she does. And she's happy."

McKnight nodded. Her voice trembled as though her emotions had overflowed and he was uncomfortable.

He changed the subject. "You have a beautiful place here. Regardless of the heat, it's very relaxing."

Warmth radiated from her smile. "Hang around until this evening. Late in the afternoon, just before the sun sets. At twilight. It's our little piece of Heaven. I often come out here to relax after Churchie and I play tennis. It's nice at that time of day."

He followed her gaze to a line of trees at the edge of the lawn where he guessed the sun would set.

"Funny you should say that," McKnight said. "I love that time of day, too. Right before dusk. Everything gets peaceful. The shadows get long and the world cools off. I used to sit out on my deck and do my best thinking then."

Merrie turned back toward him. "Yes, that's precisely how I feel." She paused. "You know, you should meet my granddaughter. She feels that way, too. She often comes by to enjoy the twilight and sunset with me. We have wine and solve the problems of the world. Of course, later, we can't remember any of the solutions."

The sound of her laughter was a balm to McKnight's tired and cluttered mind. He was more at ease in that moment than he had been in a long time. He sensed he was wound up. Tight as a drum. *When was the last time I was this relaxed?* He sighed.

"What?" Merrie said. She was watching his eyes, with interest and perhaps concern. *Nothing gets past this lady. She's sharp. And direct.*

"Oh," he said. "I was thinking how pleasant your home is. And you have a talent for making people welcome. I appreciate that. Thank you."

Her concerned look softened and turned into a smile. "I'm glad you feel that way. Are you and Winnie taking a few days off? Why don't you both stay here with Churchie and me? Churchie would be delighted to have Winnie here and you could relax." She paused for a second, searching his face. "I do believe you could use the rest."

"Well, we planned to come for the weekend, but I have leave coming–"

McKnight's phone chirped. He reached for his hip.

The clear device had turned opaque and the incoming banner read "Drake, Michael." A call from the General could mean only one thing. HERO business. He excused himself, stepped out of the structure and answered his phone.

"Captain, this is Mike Drake. I understand you and Lieutenant Tyler are in Atlanta. How soon can you be available?"

"I'm at an event at the Tyler family home, sir, but I'm available." McKnight glanced around to see if he could locate Tyler. He found him thirty yards away in a group of people. Tyler was staring at him. McKnight motioned for him to come over.

"Do we need to go back to DC, sir?"

"No, I'm on my way to Atlanta in five minutes. Meet me at the Pulse bar in the Marriott Marquis Hotel this evening at 1800 hours. Kathy Wu's with me and we'll brief you there."

Kathy Wu, the civilian planner. "Yes, sir. I presume you want Lieutenant Tyler to join us?"

"Negative. Just you." Tyler was now front and center. The question on his face was obvious. McKnight mouthed the word "Drake" and Tyler nodded.

For Tyler's benefit, McKnight said, "Understood, sir. Just me. I'll be there at 1800." At his words, Tyler's face fell.

"Very well, Captain. Get some rest beforehand if possible. It will be a long night. See you at 1800." Drake ended the call and McKnight holstered his phone.

"Just you?" Tyler said. "He's here?"

"On his way, Lieutenant." *If Drake will be here at 1800, he's coming by private jet. Something important is going down.*

"Very good, sir," Tyler said, taking the hint. "How can I help?"

"No idea, Winnie. I don't know anything myself yet."

Merrie approached and touched McKnight's arm. Both men pasted smiles on their faces. She glanced at Tyler, then back at McKnight.

"Bad news?" she asked. Tyler stood still and said nothing.

"My apologies, Merrie," McKnight said. "That was our boss. I'm afraid I have to leave earlier than I expected. But I'd love to talk with you more about our favorite book. May I have a rain check on our conversation?"

"Certainly, Marc. When must you report? Will you still be able to stay with us?"

"Six o'clock. I don't know how long I'll be, so I'd better take my gear with me."

Merrie checked her watch. "It's three o'clock now. You've had a long trip. Why not grab a hot shower and a short nap? Then you'll be fresh and ready to go. Winnie can show you where everything is."

Tyler nodded. "I sure can. Sounds like a good idea, Marc. C'mon, I'll give you the grand tour. Thanks, Gramma."

Tyler stepped off the gazebo and headed for the house.

McKnight took Merrie's hand in both of his. "Thank you for your hospitality, Merrie. Meeting you has been my honor. I hope I can visit again soon to continue our discussion and to meet your husband. He must be quite a guy to win a woman like you." He turned on his heel and followed Tyler down the hill to the house.

Tyler looked back at McKnight and frowned. "Jeez, Marc? Are you hitting on my grandmother?"

McKnight laughed and dismissed the comment with a wave.

"If she was fifty years younger, you might have something to worry about."

He was apprehensive, but excited. General Drake was coming to Atlanta. Their first time travel mission must be imminent.

CHAPTER 8

5:50 pm - Wednesday, July 11th, 2035 - Marriott Marquis Hotel, Atlanta, GA

McKnight paid the taxi driver and walked to the hotel entrance, his travel bag slung over his shoulder. The bellman from the motor lobby trotted over. "Checking in, sir?"

"I don't know yet. Where can I find the Pulse Bar?"

"Straight in, sir. Bear to the right. Look for the big green sail and you'll find it, no problem." McKnight fished a tip from his pocket and thanked him.

He entered the hotel through the revolving door and crossed the lobby. Fifty stories above, a skylight formed the roof. When looking up, one had the sense of being inside an enormous beast whose ribs were showing.

McKnight spotted the green sail and headed in that direction. He saw a large TelExtraVision monitor in the base of the sail and the neon word "Pulse" above a mahogany bar. Brown leather armchairs and couches defined several conversation areas on a red and blue carpet. He didn't see Drake in the immediate area.

A sultry voice behind him said, "Come here often, trooper?"

McKnight smiled and turned around. Doctor Kathy Wu stood there, giggling into her hands. She snapped to mock attention, saluted with an exaggerated gesture, then offered her hand.

He hadn't known Wu long, but her intellect and her professionalism impressed him. He liked her irreverent sense of humor and her penchant for quoting old movie dialog to underscore a point. An excellent judge of character with an eidetic memory, she had a flair for reading and understanding human motivation. She wore black slacks and a shirt with her raven hair pulled back into a ponytail.

"Hi, Kathy," McKnight said. "Where's General Drake?"

"Upstairs. He's talking to people about the mission. And Captain?"

Captain? So this isn't a social conversation. "Yes?"

"Senator Lodge is here, too," Wu said.

McKnight frowned. "Why? A kickoff meeting for the first mission? I could do without that."

Wu glanced around the bar. "Let's sit for a minute." McKnight followed her to the armchairs and sat. He verified no one was near enough to overhear the discussion, then focused his entire attention on her.

Something's bothering her. "What's on your mind, Doctor?"

"Well, don't sugarcoat it, Sundance. Ask her what she really thinks," she blurted out.

"What's up? What's bugging you?"

"I wanted to talk to you before the mission briefing. I have concerns."

"Are there specific details that bother you? Whoa. Aren't we getting ahead of ourselves?" He looked around. "Before voicing concerns, shouldn't we wait for the General to give the briefing?"

"Actually, I'm giving the briefing. General Drake brought me on board Sunday and I have most of the plan in place."

"Okay. Let's get to it then."

"Not yet." She paused, meeting his gaze. "Here's the bottom line. This won't be a standard project and we won't execute it according to our defined protocol. We've known about it for less than a week and you go tonight. I'm telling you this in advance so you don't waste time in the briefing."

"Excuse me?"

"I know. Tell me, Captain," Wu said, studying her fingernails. "Would you argue against the mission because it has insufficient lead time, it doesn't conform to protocol, and a half dozen other reasons?"

"Yes, I would." McKnight paused before he spoke again. "You're saying that'd be a waste of time."

"Yes, I am. I doubt you'll come up with any risk the General hasn't pointed out. I rode on the plane with him and got the story behind the story."

"But what about the approval process? Drake's a stickler for procedure. It requires a month to approve a mission and that can't be circumvented, unless..." He was beginning to understand. "Unless..."

"Yes?"

"Unless the President issued an Executive Order to go forward with the mission."

Wu nodded. "Correct. The President called the General Sunday morning. She gave him a direct order to carry it out as soon as possible."

McKnight rested his elbows on his knees and studied the floor. "He kept me out of the loop. Why?"

"I understand where you're coming from, Captain, I honestly do. Don't forget, General Drake has known about this for four days. And he's been lobbying her to reconsider. Once he was certain he couldn't stop the project, he activated you. He had no doubt you'd get up to speed in time."

He looked up at her again. "So we go tonight, prepared or not, no matter what?"

"Yes, Captain. That's what I am saying."

It's a done deal. If I don't do it, they'll send someone else. Maybe someone less capable. I'm the leader. It's my job. He sat up straight and slapped both thighs with his hands.

Wu smiled. "Just so we understand each other, Captain. I think you've decided to get the project done, no matter what. Am I right?"

"Yes, ma'am. I won't waste time in the briefing talking about approval and protocol circumvention. Thanks for the heads-up, Doctor. So what's the mission?"

She stood. "Okay, now we can have that briefing. Let's check what's going on upstairs." She pulled out her phone and touched a speed dial. After a moment, she said, "We're ready when you are, sir."

She snapped her head around toward the elevator. McKnight looked in the same direction.

Drake walked out with a frown on his face. "Good evening, Captain. Doctor Wu bring you up to date?"

"Yes, sir. At least on the matters of planning and protocol. We haven't discussed the details."

"Okay," he said. "Let's discuss it on the way upstairs."

They boarded the elevator that brought Drake to the first floor. No one spoke until the doors closed and it started to move.

"Okay, Captain. Here it is, in a nutshell," Drake said. "Ordinarily, I wouldn't share this with the unit, but I'm putting you at risk and you have a right to know. Senator Lodge contacted me Friday night and asked me to execute a special project. It didn't meet the established criteria, so I refused to approve it. Long story short, he called in a favor. I got an order from the President the next morning, directing me to plan and execute the mission ASAP. The Target Event was fifty years ago tomorrow night."

Tomorrow night. That's why the approval process was bypassed.

Drake continued. "I activated Doctor Wu for planning and Lieutenant Wheeler for equipment. Wheeler is already on location. Everything else, you'll be getting in a few minutes."

McKnight glanced at Wu, then back at Drake. "Permission to speak freely, sir?"

"Yes, what is it?"

"Is Senator Lodge here to see us off, sir?"

Drake turned to McKnight and smiled without humor. The elevator dinged, and the doors opened. "Captain, fifty years ago tomorrow, the Senator's father was murdered in an office down the street. Tonight, you're traveling back to 1985 to find out who did it."

CHAPTER 9

Drake turned and left the elevator, leaving McKnight standing with eyes and mouth wide open. Wu smiled as she passed, took him by the arm, and dragged him off the elevator. They followed the General down the hallway.

As they walked, Wu tugged at his sleeve. He turned toward her, and she went up on her tiptoes to whisper in his ear. "You know he did that on purpose, right?"

"What? Dropped that bomb before the meeting?" He thought for a second. "Yes, I do. He wants me to be sensitive to the Senator's motivation. He didn't want me to set Lodge off before I knew what was going on."

"Bingo." Wu said with a grin. "You rock, Captain."

Not for the first time, McKnight considered Kathy Wu might be the most valuable member of his team.

Drake stopped before a suite service door and moved an access disk across the scanner to open it. He led them into the kitchen, then through another door to a dining area.

Four men sat around a mahogany table that dominated the room. One of them was Senator Lodge. The others were strangers to McKnight. From the cut of their suits, two were carrying weapons. *Bodyguards?*

Lodge was speaking in a quiet voice to a man who nodded and typed on his pad computer. When he saw McKnight and Wu enter, Lodge dismissed the man with a wave and turned to face them.

Drake was the first to speak. "For those of you who don't know him, this is Captain McKnight. He leads the HERO Team. You've met

Doctor Wu earlier today." Wu stepped to the vacant chair at the head of the table.

Drake gestured toward the man nearest him. "Captain, this is Atlanta Police Detective Trevor George. He's a cold case investigator, and this is his case. He'll be providing the investigation summary."

George looked up from his notes, beamed without showing teeth and gave a little wave. His foot was tapping. *Excited to be here.* He was in his mid-forties, with a boyish face, twinkling eyes, dimples, and brown curls that spilled over his ears.

Pointing to the other man at the table, Drake said, "And this is Walt Matthews, head of Security for the NewT Telecommunications Company, who owns the building where the event occurred. He's our local liaison to ensure we have everything we need. And–"

"Whatever you need, I'm your guy," Matthews interjected. "My entire team is at your disposal and–"

"Yes, yes, thank you, Mr. Matthews," Drake said. "We very much appreciate it and I'm sure we'll be taking you up on your kind offer. And, Captain, you're acquainted with Senator Lodge, who's here to–"

"I'm here to make sure the objective is clear," Lodge interrupted. "And that you know what's expected of you and your team. Do you understand what–"

"He understands, Senator, or at least he will after Doctor Wu gives her briefing, which we'll get to in a minute. Would you please introduce your assistant? I like to know everyone who attends my briefings."

Lodge glared at Drake for a moment, then a cold smile crossed his face. "Fine. This is Mike Smith from my office. He's a security specialist. Let's get on with it."

McKnight studied Smith, whose posture and bearing suggested a military background. When the man smiled at him, McKnight realized Smith was studying him. *Uh-oh. Spook. Or mercenary. What the hell is he doing here?*

"Very good. Doctor Wu, you may proceed." Drake said. He chose the chair next to Lodge, leaving McKnight the chair between himself and Wu. McKnight sat, while Wu passed out a single sheet agenda and placed a small device in the center of the table.

Wu smiled, making eye contact with everyone. "First, these proceedings are being recorded into the official mission record, as required by the HERO Charter. They are confidential and may not be shared outside this group except under legal process. Does everyone understand?" There were nods around the table. Wu clicked the record button and announced the date and time, the reason for the meeting, and the names of the attendees.

From her briefcase, Wu distributed six numbered, sealed folders. "After the meeting, I'll collect these from you. Please unseal them and turn to page three. General Drake, since this is our first official mission, would you mind covering the Mission Authorization?"

Drake got out a pair of reading glasses and perched them on his nose. He scanned the document and read aloud. "The relevant information is in the first paragraph. 'The President of the United States, by Executive Order 15321, authorizes the mission described herein and acknowledges that standard protocol will be waived.' That's the gist."

McKnight glanced at Lodge. The Senator smiled at Drake, who didn't seem to notice.

"Thank you, sir," Wu said. "Now, for the Mission Statement and Objective. You have it in front of you, so I'll just hit the high points.

"The overall goal is to identify the unsub who murdered James C. Lodge Senior, without violating our prime directive of non-interference. I'll leave the details of the event for Mr. George to describe.

"At 2330 hours tonight, our traveler will go back to July 11th, 1985. We're looking for a good arrival location. He'll find or create an obscured base for himself and any gear he takes with him. Once that's achieved, he'll proceed to the murder scene, install a C-cam, and retreat to his base. Before the estimated time of the event which the record shows as being around 2200 hours, our traveler will position himself near the crime scene.

"We know this is a risk, but the traveler is back-up for the C-cam, in case it fails. Finally, he will retrieve the C-cam and engage the beacon no later than 0600 hours on July 13th to return to the present. Are there questions?"

"Yes," Matthews said. "What does unsub mean? Like, perpetrator?"

"Yes," George explained. "Unsub is short for unknown subject. I have a question, too. What's a C-cam?"

"Sorry, sir," Wu said. "It's the latest surveillance technology. A C-cam is a ceiling camera. A portable video camera that's about the dimensions of a credit disk and three times as thick. A tiny fiber-optic cable comes out with a lens at the end which is the only part that needs to extend below the ceiling. The chance of it being detected is slim, unless you are within two feet. The traveler will have the receiver in his possession. Mr. Matthews?"

"Yes, ma'am?"

"Today, companies routinely sweep their corporate offices for bugs. Was NewT sweeping their offices back in 1985? We don't want them to sweep this room and locate our device."

"Yes, they were. I'll check the records. I should be able to determine if there was an electronics sweep that day."

"Thank you, Mr. Matthews," Wu said. "Please let us know as soon as possible, so we can make alternate plans." Matthews nodded, pulled out his phone and tapped in a text message.

"If there are no further questions about the mission, we'll discuss the personnel," she said, scanning the room.

No one spoke, but McKnight didn't like what he saw. The Senator sat on the edge of his chair and leaned forward.

"Very well," she said. "The HERO charter dictates that the assigned planner selects the mission personnel. General Drake then approves the selection. I've selected Captain McKnight as the traveler. He's the natural first choice. He has the most time logged in training and was General Drake's pick to lead the team. Since this is our first mission, and it is off protocol, he is the best candidate for the mission.

"Lieutenant Wheeler and I will provide support. We'll be on site to monitor the Time Engine, the return beacon, and the travel event itself. Are there any questions?"

Lodge cleared his throat and spoke. "I'd like my associate Mike Smith here to go along to help. He's a former Navy Seal with lots of experience in combat and stealth operations. He'll be a good asset to the mission."

"Respectfully, Senator, this isn't a combat mission," Wu said. "While I'm sure Mr. Smith is capable, he isn't a member of the HERO team and is not eligible to participate."

"He's on my staff and I'm Chairman of the Oversight Committee. How much more a part of the team could he be?"

"He may be a great team player, sir, but he hasn't logged a single hour of time travel training. That introduces additional risk that–"

"Young lady, maybe you don't understand. This is my–"

Drake shook his head. "Not a chance, Senator. The HERO charter is specific on this point. Not on the team? No training? No way. I don't care who vouches for him. He's not going."

"Perhaps I should call the President and get her opinion," Lodge said. "I'm sure she'll see it my–"

Drake set his phone on the table in front of Lodge. "Be my guest," Drake said. "Speak her name. She's on speed-dial."

"I have a phone," Lodge said, his eyes fixed on Drake.

"Then use it. But make no mistake. One of these days, you'll run out of favors. Do you want to spend one on this?" Drake's expression was stony, his eyes narrowed to slits.

Lodge stared at him, then blinked. He pulled his phone out and spoke. "Wanda Taylor... Yes, Senator Lodge, calling the President...

Yes, I'll hold." Pressing the phone to his ear, he continued the staring contest with Drake.

After a few uncomfortable moments, Lodge said, "My man Smith is at least as capable as any member of your team, Drake. He can hold his own in any situation."

"I'm sure he can handle himself, Senator. Regardless, he's not going. He's not qualified. Besides, Doctor Wu, how many Time Engines do we have here?"

"Only one, sir," Wu said, glancing at Lodge.

"And how many return beacons do we have on site?"

"Only two, sir, but we need one for backup," Wu said, her voice stronger now.

Without taking his eye off Lodge, Drake said, "Thank you, Doctor. And how long does it take to calibrate the machine for the number of people on the mission?"

"Twelve hours. Lieutenant Wheeler has been working on it for…" She examined her phone. "About ten hours now."

Drake turned toward Wu. "And if we change the number of travelers, what's the impact on the calibration?"

Lodge lowered the phone from his ear, staring at the recording device on the table.

"We have to start over, sir. The number of travelers is integral to calibration."

Lodge's face twisted with anger. "Bullshit. We have a time machine. We can delay the jump and still go to the same time."

Drake turned back to face Lodge. "Senator, the power requirement goes up significantly when the time span is not exactly twenty-five years, increasing the risk of failure and insufficient power to send the traveler to the right time and place." Smith's head snapped up to look at Lodge.

McKnight smiled to himself. *Lodge never told Smith about the potential danger.*

Lodge pressed the hail button on his phone. After a moment, he spoke again. "Yes, Senator Lodge again. Please tell the President I'll call her back." Looking at Drake, he said, "You win this one."

Drake shook his head. "It's not a game, Senator. I'm thinking of the success of this mission. Your mission. Now, Doctor, shall we continue?"

"Yes, sir," Wu said.

She turned to McKnight and spoke in a firm voice. "Captain McKnight, let me be clear. You are to follow the first directive of time travel. No interference. Avoid detection and cause no impact while you are in 1985. Is that understood?"

"Yes, it is," McKnight said.

"Captain McKnight, is it understood that you will not, under any circumstances, try to prevent an established historical event, the murder of James Lodge? I ask this for the record."

Senator Lodge fidgeted, but said nothing.

It's one thing to agree that altering history is bad, but it's quite another thing to stand by while someone is murdered.

"I understand, Doctor Wu. I will not try to prevent the murder."

"Thank you, Captain." Wu smiled at him with what he perceived as empathy in her dark eyes. "Next on the agenda is Local Events to Avoid".

Wu paused and sighed before continuing. "Because of the short lead time, I had insufficient time to complete a full historical search. I managed to learn there's not much happening on this date back in 1985, except for a Southern Cuisine festival in Midtown Atlanta. That shouldn't impact us since the Captain will be inside the NewT building complex the entire time. As long as he stays indoors, there's no possibility of interaction. I didn't have time yet to execute a search on team ancestry. I haven't found any issues so far. Questions?"

McKnight raised his hand. "Lieutenant Tyler is from Atlanta. Is that why he isn't the planner for the mission?"

Drake spoke. "No, Captain. I excluded him. I have the utmost confidence in Lieutenant Tyler, but felt that Doctor Wu was the better option for this occasion and circumstances. Questions or reservations?"

Circumstances? He wants to shield the military members of the team from the shit storm if things go bad. "No, sir. Thank you, Doctor. That answers my question."

"Very good," Wu said. "Next is Local Terrain. Mr. Matthews, would you care to take it from here?"

"Absolutely. Thank you." He stood, donned a pair of glasses and peeked at his notes.

"The event took place on the forty-ninth floor of the office tower. The building is forty-nine floors of office space above ground, plus a two-story lobby and a two-story storage attic. There are three levels below ground, containing the loading dock, shipping, mail rooms, power and mechanical rooms, a paper shredding and recycling facility, and a small break area. There is an attached building that includes executive parking, data centers, meeting rooms, retail space and restaurants. We call it the support building. That's the view from ten thousand feet."

"Thank you, Mr. Matthews," Wu said. "Did you and Lieutenant Wheeler find a hideout for Captain McKnight?"

"We did. You needed a place where he can hide for a day as close as possible to the scene of the event. After reviewing the options, the logical choice is the office tower's storage attic. It's the top floor, right above the executive suites where the murder took place. Lieutenant Wheeler is already there. He toured the building this morning, designated the attic as the primary site and had equipment delivered there."

"Good," she said, glancing at Lodge. "But to fill out the details for the rest of us, sir, what's in the attic and what are its traffic patterns?"

"Yes, ma'am," Matthews continued. "The storage attic is only accessible by the freight elevator and the two stairwells. The other elevator requires a key to access the attic. There's a lock on the door from both stairwells to the Executive floor.

Wu was taking notes on her computer pad. "And the attic itself?"

"It's like any other attic except it's bigger and has more junk in it," Matthews said. "You should have no problem finding a place to hide. No guarantees, but it's a safe bet. Regardless, we'll provide you with a pair of work coveralls and a security badge. I have a team member researching and creating a 1985-style ID badge and we'll personalize it for Captain McKnight."

Matthews wiped his eyeglasses with his handkerchief and repositioned them on his nose. "As far as traffic patterns go, Security walked the attic four times a day back then. The schedule called for them to check it every six hours, beginning at three in the morning."

"Understood," McKnight said. "Thanks. What else?"

"Well, that's about it, unless there are questions." Matthews looked around the room. "Doctor Wu?"

Wu nodded and smiled. "Thanks for that excellent report. Captain," she said, turning to McKnight. "I suggest you use the stairs. There's less chance of meeting someone there than in the freight elevator, I would think."

"Yes, I agree," McKnight said.

"No need for you to go anywhere except the attic and the Executive floor," she said. "Use the stairwell. Make your hideout in the attic. Keep your head down when you're not executing mission tasks. Does anybody see it any other way? Questions?"

"Yes," McKnight said. "Mr. Matthews mentioned the security sweeps of the attic. But what about the schedules for security and the cleaning crews for the Executive floor? I don't want to run into a security guard or a janitor on that floor."

"Good segue, Captain," Matthews said, drumming his fingers on the table. "Sorry, but I can't offer a definitive answer. To keep their rounds unpredictable, they required the security team to walk the floors, twice a shift, but not always at the same time. Their logs didn't include notations about their security walks unless there was an incident. Your best tactic is to listen for the elevator bell. You'll have four to six seconds to get out of sight of the door. Sorry. Best I can do."

"Thanks, Mr. Matthews. At least I know what to expect," McKnight said. "That's all my questions for now."

"Okay. Any more questions about local terrain?" Wu asked.

No one spoke. McKnight shook his head and Matthews made his way back to his seat.

Wu stood again. "Mr. George, would you summarize your investigation for us?"

"Yes, ma'am," he replied with a smile. He strode to the front of the room and paused next to Wu. He glanced at each person around the table and stopped when he saw McKnight's profile for the first time.

He frowned and rolled his eyes. "Damn. I guess I have less information for you than I thought. Hold on a second."

He pulled out his phone and connected to the overhead projector. After a moment, a frozen image displayed onto the wall.

George pointed at the image. "One of the security cameras on the executive floor took this picture around midnight the night before the murder. I was excited because we had a picture of the unsub even though we didn't have a name."

The photo showed a dimly lit hallway. A man dressed in coveralls was in the foreground. He looked to the left and the camera captured his profile.

"Who is it?" Lodge said, as he lurched from his chair and glared at the screen.

"Shit," McKnight said. Wu groaned in sympathy.

"I believe that's you, Captain McKnight, isn't it?" George said.

CHAPTER 10

"Ordinarily," George continued, "that would make you a suspect."

"What?" Wu exclaimed.

"You're kidding, right?" Drake said.

George motioned for Lodge and Wu to sit. "Relax, folks. I'm not entertaining any theory related to it. All this tells us is Captain McKnight successfully travels back to 1985 and gets picked up by the camera."

He paused. "There's more. One of the security guards claimed she talked to this guy—you, Captain."

"What? That's not good." McKnight said.

"Yes," George replied. "When our investigator showed her that picture, she said she met you. But since they never identified a suspect, they doubted her story because of another guard's statement."

"What do you mean?"

"Well, he reported he found her unconscious in one of the conversation areas on the evening of the murder. I've always been curious about this. According to the guard on duty with her, she woke up shortly thereafter with no side effects. He vouched for her, but the investigative team suspected substance abuse."

"I see," McKnight said. "Did they test her?"

"No, they didn't. She quit on the spot when they suggested she submit to drug testing. They thought she resigned to avoid prosecution, but it looks different now, doesn't it? We owe that guard an apology if we can find her."

Wu waved at George. "Could you please get me a transcript of her statement? I want to know more about her."

"I'll get someone to forward it to you," George said, pulling out his phone and making a note to himself. "Now, where was I?"

"You said you didn't have much evidence," Wu replied.

"That's correct. We have very little surviving evidence. Plenty of DNA material was in the office, but it was new technology and Atlanta had no DNA processes until the next year. We didn't publicize the details of the crime because we didn't want to give away what information we had. Sorry, Senator Lodge, but I need to go into detail here."

"It's okay, Detective. It happened a long time ago," Lodge said.

"Yes, sir," George continued. "The cause of death was blunt force trauma. There was evidence of a struggle and someone struck him over the head with a heavy object like... Captain, could you help me demonstrate? You're about the same height as the victim."

"Sure. Where do you want me?" McKnight asked as he rose and turned toward George.

"Right here in front of me, please. Thanks."

McKnight moved into position.

"Okay, so if the Captain here is the victim, then the point of impact was..."

George swung both arms over his head like a club, slowing the arc to touch McKnight's forehead with the edge of his palms. "...here. Right where the forehead meets the hairline. That was the fatal blow, but it wasn't the only wound. He fell backward and the back of his head struck the corner of the desktop." He glanced at Lodge. "Sorry, Senator. Thank you, Captain."

"What else do we know?" McKnight asked.

"They didn't find a murder weapon. Lodge's assistant told us a figurine of the Greek god Atlas was missing, but nobody else remembered seeing it, so we can only hypothesize. If it exists, the unsub took it with him. And the evidence shows he or she was shorter than the victim. Five foot nine, according to the coroner's statement. That makes the unsub either an average height man or a tall woman."

"Do we have anything more?" Wu asked.

"Nothing consequential. We have more data, but none of it leads anywhere. Again, our questions will be answered when Captain McKnight returns. What else can I answer?"

Wu shifted in her chair. "I suppose that, being fifty years ago, computers didn't control the elevators? No usage records?"

"As a matter of fact, they were. They were state-of-the-art when installed. There are electronic logs that show every time an elevator moved or stopped on a floor."

"But no suspicious activity around the event time?"

"No, ma'am."

"Did the victim have enemies at work?" she asked.

"None of the executives said it out loud, but they weren't sorry to see him gone. My apologies, Senator."

"It's no secret he wasn't well liked, Detective. Office politics at this level are brutal," Lodge replied. "Please go ahead."

"To answer your question, Doctor, he had a few enemies. But every executive had an airtight alibi. All were questioned and cleared. They were with their family, at social events, or traveling. And before you ask, none of the cleaning crew or support staff had an issue with him as far as we can tell."

"And the security team?" McKnight asked.

"They were cleared, too. An event at the Fox Theater had just ended, and the security guards were all together in the support building lobby to manage the crowd.

"In short, the security team and cleaning crew have alibis. I might have asked additional questions if I'd been there. But the detectives probably asked those questions, and didn't consider the responses important enough to include in the report. Regardless, it is what it is. And it ain't much."

"Not very encouraging," McKnight said, tapping his pen on the table. "Anyone else who might have wanted him dead?"

"Possibly, but nobody we can place near the scene. We tied a long list of women to the victim. Most were secretaries who worked for him briefly. A few lived with no visible means of support after their association with him. None said anything negative about him."

Wu leaned forward at the table, her chin propped up in her hand. "Who stood to benefit from his death?"

"The victim's wife and his son, the Senator, were the only ones who gained monetarily–"

"That's ludicrous," Lodge said. "My mother was at a charity affair at the Ritz Carlton in Buckhead. A thousand people saw her there. It seems to me we could spend our time more productively if we focused on more reasonable possibilities."

"Excuse me, Senator," George responded, "but if you have other ideas, I'd love to hear them." He leaned forward, spreading his palms out on the table. "What do you consider more likely?"

McKnight detected no animosity or irritation in George's posture, only a desire to gather information.

Lodge leaned back and shrugged. "Well, how about a high-rise cat burglar or an industrial spy, for example? It'd be easy to climb up the building's exterior or land a helicopter on the roof. Did you look at that?"

"Yes, sir, we did, and we ruled them out. Would it help if I review our reasoning?"

"I'd like to hear it," McKnight interjected.

"Me, too," Wu said.

"Yes, Detective. I'd appreciate that," Lodge said, resting his hands on his stomach, his fingers interlaced.

"All right," George replied. "For the sake of argument, let's examine those two possibilities. First, the cat burglar scenario. The building's exterior is illuminated at night. Cat burglars shy away from lighted buildings. But leaving that aside, the exterior wouldn't be impossible to climb. But how would a burglar gain entry? Break a window, or pry open the access window? The detectives checked every window on the tower—2500 of them. None were broken or pried open. The evidence doesn't support this as a valid scenario.

"So what about the helicopter option? There is a helipad on the roof. There's a small steel shack there that houses the top of the southeast stairwell. The door has a massive steel deadbolt. It's designed to allow simple access to the roof from the inside, but you couldn't get in from the outside without tearing the shack apart. There was no damage to it that night."

George walked over to the coffee service and poured a cup. "So that's it, Senator. If you have other ideas, let's hear them. But here's the bottom line, sir. In forty-eight hours, this discussion will be moot. Captain McKnight will be back with the answer."

Lodge smiled and sat up straight in his chair. "Thank you, Detective," he said. "I underestimated you and I apologize." McKnight looked at Lodge. The politician had reappeared.

"No problem, sir. So, let's move on," George continued. "It's obvious how the unsub got there."

"The freight elevator," McKnight said.

"Yes," George replied, turning toward him and leaning forward, his knuckles on the table. "And how do we know that?"

"Simple," McKnight said, "but help me make sure my reasoning is on target. No window access, no roof access, and the other elevators had cameras in them. The unsub could use the stairs to the forty-ninth floor, but would have to pick the lock to get out of the stairwell. So, unless the unsub has lock-picking skills, I can't see any other way but the freight elevator." He looked to George for agreement.

"Great, Captain. You're on the right track. Or at least," he added with a smile, "you're on the same track as me. Okay, so what about lock-picking skills?"

"Yes," Wu said. "Could the unsub have been a thief? Could the murder be an attempted robbery that escalated? Was anything taken?"

"Great question, Doctor Wu. As far as we can tell, nothing except the missing figurine. No, this wasn't a thief. Any burglar with enough skills to break in and leave no evidence is smart enough to understand the executive offices of a company aren't worth the risk. If it was me, I'd burglarize the place where folks pay their bills."

George hesitated and looked back at McKnight. "I think I can follow the unsub's path to the office."

"I don't see it," Matthews said. "What am I missing?"

"Well," George began, "I didn't share everything I know yet. Let me lay it out for you." He sat back at the table, his forearms on the table and his fingers wrapped around his coffee cup. All eyes were on him.

"Courtesy of Mr. Matthews, I visited NewT Center earlier today. I wanted to try to get to Lodge's office undetected. If the unsub took the freight elevator, where did he board it? The answer is, from any other floor. But how did he get to another floor without an elevator and an ID? There are three floors you can get to without ID or an elevator—the basement, the tower reception lobby, and the bridge floor."

"Bridge floor?" McKnight asked.

"Yes. As you heard earlier, NewT Center comprises two buildings, a fifty-two-story office tower and an eight-story support building. A sky bridge connects the two, and the connected floor in both structures is called the bridge floor."

"Understood. You suggested there were three choices?"

"Yes," George replied. "But in the other two cases, the unsub couldn't avoid walking by a security counter. No, our best bet is the bridge floor. "If the unsub got on the elevator there, maybe we can find you a good place to watch from, Captain."

"Okay," McKnight said.

"The computer logs show that someone used the freight elevator several times that night. Lodge himself used it before his death."

George paused, looking up at the ceiling. "There's only one way to get on the bridge floor in the tower without using elevators--cross the bridge from the support building. Right, Mr. Matthews? By my count, there are two ways to access the bridge floor of the support building.

You can ride the main elevators, which are next to the security counter, or...." He stopped and looked at Matthews. McKnight followed his glance to Matthews, who was rolling his eyes, his lips a tight line across his face. "Do you have something to add, Mr. Matthews?"

"Yes," Matthews said, shaking his head. "I can't believe I didn't think of it myself. The unsub must have come up the support building's freight elevator from the loading dock. You need an ID to access and use that elevator, but you don't pass a security counter. That's the only way to get in without going past Security."

"Exactly," George replied, pointing at Matthews and touching his nose as if he were playing charades. He leaned back in his chair and held up his hands in a cautionary gesture. "Let's stop here for a minute. Mr. Matthews, have I missed anything? You know this building better than anyone else."

Matthews blinked twice before answering. "I'm embarrassed I didn't remember that elevator. To be honest, I was here a week before I found it. The unsub could have opened the loading dock door with an ID while the theater crowd distracted the security team."

Drake stopped typing on his pad. "The loading dock is accessible from the retail mall?" he asked.

"Yes," Matthews said. "It's across the food court from the security counter, thirty yards away. If Security was busy with a crowd, they might not see someone go through that door. At night, there's no other way into the loading dock without passing by Security." Matthews turned back to George. "No sir, I can't see any flaw in your logic, assuming the unsub had an ID."

"Yep," George said. "I think we can count on that fact. The unsub had an ID or access to one."

"Detective, you mentioned finding me a place to observe?" McKnight said. "Where did you have in mind?"

"Oh, I get where he's going, Captain," Matthews said. "On the tower side of the bridge, there's a social area. Several sofas and chairs.

Though they're not supposed to, people on the midnight shift go there to nap during their lunch hour or break. You could stretch out and pretend to be asleep. Or better, step into the meditation room and watch from there. That should be a perfect observation point."

"Sounds like the meditation room has potential. We can check it out when we get on site."

"Okay," Wu said, typing on her pad. "Is there anything else, Mr. George?"

"No, ma'am, that's it," George answered.

"Okay," she said. "There's one modification to the plan. At the proper time, Captain McKnight will go to the meditation room, hoping to witness the unsub getting on the freight elevator. This change is subject to Captain McKnight's review of the scene. And we're still waiting to find out about the security sweeps for that night."

"We should hear anytime now," Matthews said.

"Thank you," Wu said. "General Drake? Senator Lodge? Anything to add before we close the meeting?"

"Not from me," Drake said, rising from his chair. "Good plan, Doctor Wu."

"Let's get moving," Lodge said.

"Thanks, everyone," Wu said. "Please pass me your folders. Let's adjourn to the NewT Telecommunications building and complete the preparations. Two vans are waiting downstairs to take us there. If you will follow me, please?"

After gathering the folders, she stuffed them and her pad into her briefcase and left the room. The rest followed and took the elevator downstairs to the motor lobby.

While McKnight looked on, Lodge took Smith by the arm. "Looks like you won't be needed for this project. Come by my office tomorrow morning."

Smith nodded and left.

George fell in step with McKnight and touched his sleeve. "I wish I could go with you. I envy you, Captain. You have a great job. As a cold-case investigator, I've spent days trying to figure out what took place here. To be able to witness it... well, that would be like getting the keys to a candy store when I was six."

McKnight laughed. "It should be interesting, I wish you could come along, too. I need your case knowledge. It would be helpful."

"I do know the case well," George declared. "And I have my ideas about what happened. It's obvious."

McKnight stopped walking and faced George. "Really?" he asked.

"Yes. I didn't want to say in the meeting, but I need someone to know what I believe." He looked McKnight in the eye. "Bragging rights, you know?"

McKnight laughed. "I do. Okay, so tell me what happened. I won't mention it to anyone. If you're right, I'll be your proof after the fact. Deal?"

"Deal," George said. "Here's my theory."

He glanced around, then spoke to McKnight in a low voice.

CHAPTER 11

7:12 pm - Wednesday, July 11th, 2035 - NewT Center, Midtown Atlanta, GA

The vans entered the NewT Telecommunications complex through the delivery garage and rolled down a steep slope into the loading dock. The space was large enough to accommodate six trucks and trailers. There was a concrete platform along three of the walls for cargo to roll out of trucks and onto carts for delivery.

As they climbed out of the vans, Matthews took the lead and McKnight perceived a change in his demeanor. *We're on his turf now.*

Matthews led the group to a security station. He waved his company badge at the officer and received an envelope and a radio. The officer buzzed open the door to the Tower basement.

Matthews glanced at it and said, "Sorry, Bob, we aren't coming in this way. We're going across to the freight elevator."

The officer nodded. "No problem, Mr. Matthews. Have a nice day."

As they strolled along the concrete walkway to the opposite side of the loading dock, McKnight stopped to examine the security cameras at each cargo station. All cameras pointed at the loading stations instead of the doors. McKnight turned and hurried to catch up with Matthews.

"See the hallway there on the left?" Matthews said. "It goes back forty feet to the retail mall. That's the door the unsub may have used. It requires an ID."

At the corner of the loading dock, he stopped and pointed to the left. "There's the door." He turned right and walked thirty feet. "Now, the freight elevator's through here," he added, and pushed his way through a set of double doors. Inside was an alcove with two freight elevators.

He held the elevator call button. "Questions so far?" he asked.

"Mr. Matthews," McKnight said, "Pardon me for saying this, but security seems loose. Shouldn't we have signed in and gotten visitor passes or something?"

"What? Oh!" Matthews said, punctuated by a laugh. "Yes. But I pre-arranged entry for everyone to save time. Thanks for reminding me." He ripped open the envelope and pulled out a handful of security badges.

"Everyone, here are your visitor badges. Please wear them so they are visible at all times." He watched as each of them clipped on their badge. "Captain, each of you have full access to all offices, building areas and storerooms here in NewT Center."

The ID featured a photograph, McKnight noted with surprise. *Ah. Wheeler.*

"My apologies, sir," McKnight said. "Another question, if I may. I noticed the cameras in the loading dock don't point at the doors. Is that by design?"

"Yes, Captain. We use those cameras to prevent theft, not monitor access. They point at the trucks and we watch the unloading during deliveries."

"I understand. Did they have the same layout in 1985?"

"Yes. The layout hasn't changed since the building was constructed."

"Where's the monitoring station?" McKnight asked.

"Behind the security counter in the retail mall," Matthews answered. "Would you like to see it?"

"Later. I want to see the attic and the crime scene before I have to travel."

"Well, I would." George interjected. "I didn't get to review that area when I was here earlier."

"Okay," Matthews said. "After Captain McKnight travels tonight, Detective, I'll take you there."

"Great," George replied.

A man entered through the retail mall door and hurried toward them. Matthews stepped aside from the group to meet him. They couldn't hear what the man said, but he gestured and pointed toward the team. Matthews nodded and returned to the group. "We came in through the loading dock to tour this route, but also to keep a low profile. I've just been advised Chairman Crawford wants to meet with Senator Lodge and General Drake as soon as we arrive. He's waiting for you in his office. I'll have you escorted there and take Captain McKnight and the rest to check out the crime scene."

"Not without me!" Lodge exclaimed. "I will be involved in every aspect of this mission possible."

The elevator opened behind them. No one spoke. Matthews' mouth worked, but nothing came out. Lodge stood with his arms crossed, his posture daring anyone to argue with him. A long moment passed.

The elevator door began to close. McKnight pushed the safety bar and it opened. "Anyway, we have to go up, right?"

Wu turned to Lodge. "May I suggest an alternative, Senator? Captain McKnight and I need to brief Lieutenant Wheeler and set mission parameters on the Engine. Why don't you two go meet the Chairman while the rest of us continue to the attic to see Lieutenant Wheeler? Then we can meet you at the crime scene." She smiled at him and touched his crossed arms. "Senator, you've seen the machine operated during testing and training a dozen times, have you not? You don't have to be there for calibration, do you?"

Again, McKnight reflected on the value Wu brought to the team.

"No, I guess not," Lodge muttered as he uncrossed his arms. "Let's go. Chairman Crawford is waiting."

Matthews waved the new arrival to come forward. "Gentlemen and Doctor Wu," Matthews said, "Mike Kelley here is my second-in-command. Mike, please show Senator Lodge and General Drake to the

Chairman's office. After they meet with him, please escort them to forty-nine twelve."

To the Senator, he added, "Room forty-nine twelve is the crime scene, sir." Turning back to Kelley, he said, "Please radio me when you leave the Chairman's office."

"Yes, sir," Kelley said. "This way, gentlemen." He turned and headed toward the security desk.

"Thank you, Mr. Matthews," Lodge said, wearing a humorless smile and shaking Matthew's hand. "I appreciate your help in all this, and I'll make sure your Chairman knows it." He turned and followed Kelley across the loading dock.

Drake shook Matthews' hand and nodded at McKnight. "See you in a few," he said, and followed Lodge.

Wu, Matthews, George and McKnight filed into the elevator. Wu winked at Matthews as she passed and got a grateful smile.

"What floor, please?" George asked, taking position next to the elevator buttons.

"Bridge," Matthews replied, and George pressed the button.

At the bridge floor, the elevator opened to a small freight room, characterized by concrete block walls painted beige and a well-worn burgundy carpet. Empty cardboard boxes and well-worn computer monitors leaned against the wall. Another set of double doors lay ahead, each adorned with a crash bar and protective carpet beneath it.

"Follow me," Matthews said, as he led through the doors into a darkened hallway. "It's after hours. This part of the building is unused at night."

After several turns, they arrived at the bridge itself. Fifteen feet wide and forty-five feet across, the bridge was Plexiglas with a carpeted floor. Fifty feet below, McKnight saw a granite courtyard. As they crossed it, he glanced upward. The NewT tower rose another forty stories above the bridge.

On the other side of the bridge, they entered a dimly lit lobby with four conversation pit groups flanking a tiled walkway. In one massive chair, a young lady slept with a book in her lap.

McKnight stopped and looked around the room. To the right, there was a wooden door with slots cut in it, giving the subtle impression of a cross. He pointed at it. "The meditation room, I presume?"

"Yes," Matthews replied. "Want to check it out?"

"Yes. Give me a second."

McKnight pushed the door open and stepped inside. The room was twenty feet by thirty feet. Three pews dominated the space. A narrow table stood against the far wall. There were two small electric candles on the table and hidden soft lighting directed at the ceiling.

"Perfect," he whispered. He closed the door behind him and rejoined the group.

"Okay, let's ride the freight elevator to the forty-ninth floor," Matthews said. "Then we'll walk up to the attic where you'll find Lieutenant Wheeler."

They walked through double doors into the elevator alcove and Matthews pressed the elevator call button. He whispered into his radio while they waited for it to arrive.

The elevator was typical. Doors on both sides. Heavy duty stainless steel walls, with dingy moving blankets hung from hooks at the top of each side wall. Over fifty floor buttons were laid out by the door. Matthews pressed the forty-ninth floor button as they boarded. The elevator shivered as power was applied and then started upward. No one spoke as the floor numbers increased on the display.

After two minutes, the elevator door opened. "This is the forty-ninth floor," Matthews announced. "Follow me, please."

They left the freight alcove and entered a wide hall with thick carpet and wood paneling. After thirty yards, it opened into a lobby, dominated by a large, curved staircase on the right that went down to the next level.

A set of elevators dominated a passageway on the left. Through it, McKnight saw wood-paneled offices and secretary desks.

"The office Mr. Lodge occupied was back over there," Matthews said, pointing through the elevator lobby. "We'll come back after the Chairman's meeting."

They moved into another hallway and Matthews pushed through a door with an exit sign above it.

It was the stairwell, with steps leading up and down. Matthews bounded up the stairs and opened the door at the top. As they stepped into the attic, a slight musty smell assaulted them.

And music.

CHAPTER 12

7:30 pm - Wednesday, July 11th, 2035 - NewT Tower Attic

Fast-paced classic rock music filled the attic. McKnight knew the source. *Wheeler's here.*

To the right, a hallway led into darkness. They turned left and, after a dozen paces, they came to the main part of the attic. Much larger than McKnight expected, the interior was three stories tall.

He glanced around as they walked. There was junk everywhere. He saw old chairs and desks, stacks of drywall, plywood and metal two-by fours, paint buckets, and piles of ancient computer monitors and keyboards. The only lights hung from the ceiling far above.

They went along the edge of the building's central core to the east side, where a ten-foot high platform stood against the wall. Underneath it and enclosed by a chain-link fence was a forklift, a few generators and large toolboxes. A sturdy ladder provided access to the platform where Wheeler was working. He stood next to the Engine and typed on a small computer pad.

"Lieutenant Wheeler!" Wu called, as McKnight mounted the ladder.

Wheeler spun at the sound of her voice and muted the music. He snapped to attention and saluted as McKnight stepped off the ladder.

"As you were," McKnight said, returning the salute.

Wheeler grinned and shook McKnight's offered hand. "Evening, sir."

"Good evening, Lieutenant. How's it going?"

"Very well, sir, I've nearly completed the calibration. Three more sequences to go."

"Very good, Lieutenant. Do you know everyone here? Have you met Detective George?"

"I saw him downstairs earlier. He was talking to Mr. Matthews." He stepped toward George, offering his hand. "I'm Wheeler, sir. Pleased to meet you."

"Same here." George shook Wheeler's hand, but his eyes were on the Engine. After a moment, he looked at Wheeler. "Sorry, I'm somewhat of a time travel groupie. How does it work?"

Wheeler grinned at him. "Let me wrap up these last three sequences and I'll give you the grand tour." He pointed to the other side of the Engine. "Would you please stand over there for a few minutes? The Engine calibration is classified."

George nodded and retreated in the indicated direction while Wheeler tapped data into a handheld computer and conferred with Wu.

The Engine sat on a sturdy black table, resembling an antiquated gasoline engine for a muscle car, but twice the size. Constructed of a dull bluish-gray metal, a panel of red and green digital readouts covered the top. A metal shaft extended four feet from one end of the block. On the end of the shaft, a metal cap connected by cable to a stainless steel plate underneath it all. The plate was ten feet by ten feet square. A thick cable linked the other side of the Engine to a large power generator. Next to the generator, a portable table supported a road case, backpack and assorted electronic gear.

Matthews motioned for McKnight to follow him and went to the east wall where several plywood sheets leaned against it.

"This wood looks like it's been here since 1985," Matthews said with a chuckle. "Regardless, I suspect you'll find enough loose material around to create a hiding place. Just in case, I recommend you scrounge up tools and set them up so you look like a construction worker who stayed late to finish your work. I doubt you'll get challenged. But if you do, point to your badge and pretend you don't speak English. The cover won't hold up long, but might give you enough time to figure something out."

"Understood," McKnight said. "Thanks."

Matthews' phone beeped.

"Aha," he declared in McKnight's direction, "the response to our earlier question. There was no bug sweep scheduled for that day, so your C-cam should be safe. And someone's on their way up with the circa-1985 ID I had made for you. And... Rats."

"What?"

"Huh? Oh, sorry," Matthews said. "I was thinking out loud. I wish my other assistant April was here. She knows the history of this place, but she left right after her shift ended today. But no big deal—we can interview her during her next shift."

"Okay, I'm done," Wheeler called out, not looking up from the dials on the top of the Engine. Wu sat on the floor and read through Wheeler's notes. Matthews and McKnight engaged in a quiet discussion about the building.

"Still want to learn about this bad boy, Mr. George?" Wheeler asked.

George strode back over to the Engine. "Absolutely, Lieutenant. And please call me Trevor."

"Will do. I'm Mitch." He laid the handheld on the table. "So, what do you know about the Engine?"

"Well, I'm familiar with what they posted on the Net. What else can you tell me?"

"If it's not on the Net, it's classified," Wu interjected. "But you'll see it work soon enough."

Wheeler nodded at Wu, and looked back at George. "Okay, but I can tell you this – something new that's been cleared for publishing, but isn't up on the website yet."

He pointed at the shaft extending from the Engine. "See the cables attached to the shaft? Where they connect to the platform below?"

"Yes," George said.

"When first developed, you had to touch the shaft to travel. The platform is a new development from Doctor Astalos. The cable transfers the touch to it. If you're standing on it when I pull the trigger, you go. The point is, more people can travel together now.

"It's simple to use. Plug it in, release the safety, and pull the trigger. The power cycles up for fifteen seconds and then, bang! Lights, spatial distortion, a loud pop and the traveler is gone. He lands, or rather crashes, in the new time."

"Crashes?" George asked. "What do you mean?"

"Well, that's what I call it. We don't know why yet, but when you arrive at the new time, you're thrown off balance and you always fall backward."

"Weird."

"Tell me about it. So the traveler takes with him this little trinket." He held up a thin chain with a small medallion on it.

"What's that?" George said, stepping closer.

"This is the return beacon I mentioned previously. We sync it up with the Engine so the recall will work. It's hard to see by looking at it, but there's a pressure switch inside it. Squeeze the medallion between your thumb and forefinger and it signals the Engine to bring you back. You and everything within six feet of the beacon. We suggest you crouch, to make sure every part of your body is within six feet of the device. You'd hate to leave any important parts behind, wouldn't you?"

George chuckled. "You got that right."

"Seriously, though," Wheeler waved the beacon at George. "If you go without one of these puppies, you'd better hope somebody's coming after you, because you aren't getting home without it."

"Okay, different question. Is this the only place you can send someone to?"

"For now, yes," Wheeler replied. "For the first travel, we need a well-defined target location. But once a traveler has returned from another spot, I can send someone to that spot or a vector from it. You know, twenty feet due South or twenty feet below or whatever? The Engine logs the travel points as they occur. We can quickly calibrate the Engine to travel to a location relative to a known location."

"Pretty damn cool," George said. "What if the traveler is incapacitated? How do they get back? Is that a problem?"

"Not at all. As long as they have the return beacon on their person, we can start a return from here. We can't detect their condition, but we can find their beacon."

"Okay. So do you return to this exact time?"

"Not usually, because the Engine works best on an exact interval. Twenty-five, fifty, seventy-five years, or whatever. So if he spends two days in the past, he'll come back two days after when he left. This keeps the time interval the same and keeps the power requirement down to a reasonable level. There's nothing to force us to do that – you can override it – but the power can be an issue if the time interval is not the same."

"How much off the time interval can you travel or return before the power requirement is too high?"

"That's classified," Wu said, before Wheeler could answer.

"No problem," George said, putting his hands up in defense. "I was just curious." He stuck his hands deep in his pockets, then grinned. "But not anymore, thanks."

They heard the stairway door open and close with a clunk. A man dashed around the corner from the stairwell.

"Ah," Matthews said. "It's your ID, Captain."

"Great," McKnight said. "Let's get to it."

The man climbed the ladder and hurried toward Matthews, who pointed at McKnight. The man handed the ID badge to him, turned on his heel and climbed down the ladder. McKnight studied the ID while they waited for the man to retreat beyond earshot.

"Every night," Matthews continued, "the maintenance staff has a punch list of tasks they can't do during the day. Back in 1985, they worked the same way. The security staff reviews this punch list when they begin their shift. With any luck, anyone you run into will assume you're working an item."

"Okay. Dmitri Slovensky?" McKnight asked, reading the name on the ID. "Shouldn't I have an American name as a cover?"

"We thought about that, Captain," Wu interjected. "First, don't talk to anyone or let them see you. But if you can't avoid it, we wanted you to have a ready-made excuse for speaking differently. Languages and expressions change over the years. If anyone comments on your manner of speaking, you can say you're new to America. If nobody comments, then no problem."

"Is there a real Dmitri?"

"Nope. But it isn't likely anyone will check you out unless you do something suspicious. Most people will see your badge and not look closely. But it's a very thin cover. If anyone runs a check, you're toast."

McKnight considered this for a moment. "Okay. Makes sense. Thanks." He slipped the ID into his pants pocket. "Let's go downstairs and see the office."

"Yes, let's go," George said. "Thanks for the tour, Mitch. I'll see you later."

George and Matthews climbed down the ladder.

McKnight laid a hand on Wheeler's shoulder. "Helluva job, Mitch. I appreciate it."

"N-P, sir. Just holding up my end, sir."

"How's that baby doing?"

"He's growing like crazy, sir. Twenty-three months old now."

"And Lisa? She doing okay?"

"Yes, sir. Thanks for asking."

"Good," McKnight said, with a hand flourish. "Let's see the latest picture."

Wheeler pulled out his phone, called up the photo program, handed it to McKnight, and stood there, grinning.

The photo featured a stunning brunette and a toddler with Wheeler's hair and the woman's eyes.

"Great shot," McKnight said. "Keep them close and safe, okay?"

"Will do, sir. Thanks."

McKnight caught up with the others at the bottom of the stairs. Matthews produced a key and opened the stairwell door. Matthews led them through the elevator lobby to the executive office area. They saw Kelley coming from the other end of the hall with Drake and Lodge.

They met in front of an executive office. "Gentlemen and Doctor Wu? This is where it happened," Matthews said.

He unlocked the door, and they filed into the office where someone murdered the Senator's father.

CHAPTER 13

<u>8:00 pm – Wednesday, July 11th, 2035 - Forty-Ninth Floor, NewT Tower</u>

The doorway opened by the office's right wall. The room measured twenty by twenty feet. Mahogany panels covered three of the walls while the fourth was glass that reached from floor to ceiling. A credenza sat centered against the window with the executive's desk and chair in front. To their left a red leather sofa and coffee table stood, faced by two matching chairs.

A dozen pictures of celebrities and politicians adorned the wall to the right, each including a man McKnight assumed to be the office's current occupant. A built-in bookcase filled the left wall, flanked by a door. The wall behind them held three simple nature paintings with a wood grain filing cabinet in the far corner.

Matthews walked to the middle of the room, turned to face them, and spread out his arms. "Well, here you have it. Though the furniture is new, the layout of executive offices is standard. It hasn't changed since before the murder. You can expect the room in 1985 to be laid out like this."

George went to the window and looked through it at the Atlanta skyline. Wu followed him.

McKnight pointed to the door in the left wall. "Where does that go?"

"Private bath. Check it out," Matthews replied, gesturing in that direction.

McKnight entered the bathroom. It was reminiscent of a bath in a five-star hotel—brass fittings, various soaps and lotions, a medicine cabinet, a closet with a pair of suits and shirts, a tie rack adorned with three ties, a shower and a toilet. *Not bad.* He backed out of the room.

George stood by the window, his arms crossed as he studied the room. He walked around the desk and stopped with his back to it. "So, when he was killed, the victim was standing here," he said, glancing to each side and shifting to position himself accurately. Then he pointed forward. "The unsub came at him from there."

McKnight moved beside George and looked up. "Best place for the C-cam is in the ceiling near the window. That covers both doors and should give us a good shot of the unsub's face."

"About right here?" Wu asked, pointing at the ceiling tiles next to the window.

"Yes," McKnight agreed. "Two, three tiles over. How do we get above the tiles to install the camera?"

"Easy," Matthews said. "You push up on them. They're not connected. They're just resting in a metal frame. Makes it easier to replace them and access the wiring up above them."

McKnight moved to the credenza, climbed up on it, and pushed on one side of a tile. "Okay, I can set the C-cam on the next tile, thread the lens cable around the edge of it and point at the center of the room."

He replaced the tile and jumped off the credenza. Turning to Matthews, he said, "I have everything I need, except a nap. I may need to be alert for twenty-four hours straight."

"We can handle that, sir. On the bridge floor, we have an in-house clinic. There are two private rooms with beds. I'm sure I can arrange a place to nap."

"Good," Wu said. "I want to study the elevator and ID logs to see who went where and when, review the guard's interview transcript, and do more research. We still haven't had a chance to vet all the people who had access to the building then. Maybe we can turn up some useful information before the travel event."

"I'll join you," Drake replied.

"Me, too," George said. "I want to help if I can."

"Hmmph," Lodge said. "I'll be heading back to my office. Drake, can I count on you to call me if something develops?"

"Yes, Senator, I'd be happy to."

"Oh, one more thing. Something minor, actually," Lodge added with a dismissive wave of his hand.

"Captain, my father kept a personal ledger in his credenza. I often saw it in his office when I was a kid. Since they never found it, I presume the killer took it. But if you see it, I'd appreciate it if you'd bring it back. It's of no real value now, I guess, but it was my father's and I'd like to have it if possible."

"Senator, I can't promise anything, but I'll look for it."

"Thank you, Captain. Now if you'll excuse me?" Lodge left without waiting for a reply.

McKnight exchanged a glance with Drake, but there was no instruction there. It was against HERO policy to carry objects forward from the past. *I'll look for it, but no way it comes back with me.*

"Okay," Matthews said. "We're done here. Let's go."

They filed out of the room. Matthews turned off the light and locked the door on his way out.

"We need a base of operations. Where shall we set up?" Wu asked as they neared the elevator.

"In my office in the support building," Matthews said. "Let's get Captain McKnight situated first, then go down there." He switched on his radio and gave instructions to his assistant.

The old clinic was what McKnight needed. He picked the bedroom closest to the clinic's main exit, turned out the casual and stretched out on the bed.

But he was too excited to sleep. In a few hours, he would travel through time on the team's first mission.

****

The two low-hanging lamps created cones of light, leaving the rest of the corridor in deep shadow. McKnight tiptoed along without making a sound. But the hair on the back of his neck stood up—his instincts screamed something was wrong.

He stopped and pressed his back against the wall. He hyperventilated. *Calm down.* He closed his eyes and tried to slow his breathing.

"Focus, dammit," he whispered.

Escape was beyond the door at the end of the hall. The silence and the tension were palpable, as if he could reach out and touch them. A wave of fear washed over him. *Get moving! Now or never!* He opened his eyes, balled up his fists, and thrust himself from the wall.

He ran for the door, but he was too late.

A man's silhouette appeared before him. Previously unnoticed doors burst open to admit more men who grabbed McKnight and pinned his arms behind him.

The man facing him ambled forward until an overhead lamp illuminated his business suit, but a fedora cast dark shadow over his face. The ancient Webley revolver in the man's hand demanded McKnight's complete attention.

"You are under arrest," the man said. British accent. *Just like before.* He reached forward to McKnight's breast and snatched off the return beacon medallion. "I'll take that," he said. "We'll have no mysterious disappearances."

McKnight struggled against the men holding him as he felt handcuffs being slipped around his wrists.

"Take him, lads," the Brit commanded. The others dragged McKnight back down the hallway, away from the door he struggled so hard to reach. They pushed through a door behind him into the dark.

CHAPTER 14

<u>11:15 pm – Wednesday, July 11th, 2035 – NewT Center Infirmary</u>

McKnight awoke with a start. *That dream again! Where the hell am I?* He blinked twice.

Oh. The infirmary in the Tower. Shit.

Not sleeping would have been okay. Training taught him how to rest and gather strength without sleeping. But having that nightmare again exhausted him.

He sat up and checked the time. *Wu will be here any minute.*

He was as ready as he would ever be, but the recurring dream underscored the danger as nothing else could. There's always a chance a mission will fall apart and become a disaster.

The time travel didn't bother him. He had traveled before, but this was their first mission. It's zero hour, the real thing. Soon, he would be on his own, back in the year 1985. In real time, he wouldn't exist yet.

He recognized a certain irony to his situation. Though the captured scenario made up an interesting intellectual exercise in training, he was now face to face with the realization his mission could end badly due to circumstances beyond his control.

If the authorities in the past detained and questioned him, he couldn't claim he was from the future. No one would believe him.

If he lied, his cover story was superficial. Anything more than a casual investigation would blow it. They would take the beacon along with everything else and he'd be unable to return to the present without a rescue attempt.

Saying nothing was the best course of action, but the consequences would be the same. They expected the authorities to detain the traveler because they couldn't identify him. No fingerprints on file and no discernible past was reason enough to raise suspicions. But possession of advanced video technology and tools for breaking and entering would remove all doubt.

Most of the potential endings for the mission were negative and potentially deadly.

So why had he taken the job?

He had to admit the excitement and danger were a big draw as was the opportunity to serve his country in a significant and unique way. Still, he expected this job to test him in ways he hadn't considered.

McKnight's logical mind understood the nightmare represented his worst fear—that he would fail his command and let his team down. Intellectually, he knew he could depend on his training, but this did little to reduce the apprehension and fear. Some fear was desirable. It made you careful and gave you motivation to prepare. But too much fear made you stupid and prone to mistakes.

Relax. He pushed the fear away, took a few deep breaths to calm himself and recalled the astronaut's prayer. "Oh, God," he said. "Please don't let me screw up–"

The door opened. Wu stood there, a silhouette framed by the lights behind her.

"I'm sorry. Did you say something?" she said.

McKnight shrugged. "No, just a little positive self-talk. Are we ready?"

"Yes. We're waiting for you. Here," she said, handing him folded clothes and a pair of running shoes. "Your maintenance uniform showed up while you slept. You ready? Everything okay?"

"Perfect," he said. "Let me change and we can get moving."

She stepped out and McKnight stripped off his clothes and pulled on the Coveralls, shrugging to adjust them on his shoulders. After slipping on the shoes, he retrieved the ID from his pants pocket and attached it to his breast pocket. He checked his appearance in the mirror and left the room.

McKnight and Wu made their way through the dim hallway to the executive elevators. Wu slid an access card into the security slot and selected the top floor. The elevator doors closed.

She waved the card at McKnight and smiled. "Courtesy of Mr. Matthews."

"But of course," McKnight said, shaking his head. "Kathy, are you and the rest of the team getting everything you need to get the job done?"

"Yes, we are. Don't worry about that, not while the General is here. But I doubt it would be a problem, anyway. I think Mr. Matthews wants to help. Besides, I could still manage." She threw a sly smile at him.

"I'll bet," he said.

"They're in the attic, waiting for us, including Mr. George and Mr. Matthews," Wu said.

"George and Matthews? Is it okay for them to be there? I mean, is it a security issue?"

"I wondered about that, too, but the General invited them. He said they had contributed to the project and deserved to witness the travel event. He said they'd have to stand back so they couldn't watch Mitch run the engine, but otherwise it was okay. I'm not concerned—the General is a great judge of people." She tapped the ID against her open palm a few times. "Besides, I started and expedited a security clearance request for both. Matthews has a top-secret clearance from an earlier security position with DLA and George passed at least the preliminary review for the same clearance."

"Good to know. Thanks, Kathy," McKnight replied.

The elevator chimed, the door opened, and they stepped out into the lobby of the executive floor. Moments later, they climbed the stairs to the attic.

****

George vibrated with excitement. He hadn't expected to see the time travel event itself and was looking forward to it. Standing on the platform with the others, the detective in him observed the people around him. Matthews looked nervous, but Drake and Wheeler looked calm. *Must be the training.*

He heard the stairwell door close and turned to see McKnight and Wu approaching. He watched as Drake strode to the top of the ladder and took Wu's hand to steady her as she stepped onto the platform. Drake took McKnight's hand as he came up and turned it into a handshake. "Are you ready, Captain?" he said, looking McKnight in the eye.

McKnight straightened into that posture reserved for talking to senior officers. "Yes, sir," he replied. "One hundred percent."

"No reservations or questions?"

"No reservations," McKnight said. "But lots of questions, sir. We'll know more when I get back."

"Understood. Good luck."

George watched as McKnight approached him. "Well, Mr. George, soon you'll have the answers to your mystery. And I have a question for you."

"Oh?" George said, raising an eyebrow. "And what would that be?"

"This has been a case of high interest for you. After it's solved, what will you do to occupy your spare time?"

"Oh, I'll find a puzzle somewhere. The City of Atlanta has a lot of unsolved cases." He glanced over at Wu, now engaged in quiet conversation with Wheeler at the Engine console. He turned back to McKnight and winked. "Or maybe I'll apply for a government job."

McKnight nodded. "Good luck with that. I'll see you soon."

"And good luck to you, Captain. Remember my theory."

"I will. I haven't forgotten."

McKnight turned to Matthews. "Sir, I wanted to thank you for the help and support you've provided my team."

Matthews raised his hands, palms out. "Don't thank me yet," he said. "Doctor Wu and I are still doing research, looking for issues. Hopefully, we won't find any problems. Good luck and God speed."

"Thanks. I'll see you when I get back."

Wheeler beckoned McKnight over to the table, opened the backpack and pulled out a black pouch. "Okay, Captain. Standard issue, by the checklist. Ready, sir?"

"Ready."

Wheeler reached into the backpack again and produced a small satchel with a shoulder strap. "Forty-eight hours' worth of MREs and a water bottle. I'm presuming you'll be able to find water there, so no need to carry it."

"Check," McKnight said.

Wheeler handed McKnight items from the pouch.

"One return beacon."

McKnight slipped the chain and medallion over his head. "Check."

"One C-cam and receiver, tested and confirmed operational, two sleep bulbs, one packet of anti-nausea serum, and a penlight."

"Check." McKnight stuffed the sleep bulbs in his pocket and the rest of the gear in the satchel.

"That's it, Captain. Do you need anything else?" Wheeler asked.

"Nothing I can think of, Lieutenant. Thanks." He slung the shoulder strap over his head and positioned the satchel on his left hip.

"What's that stuff for? Or is that classified?" George asked. He grinned at McKnight.

"I think I can share this," McKnight said. Despite himself, he smiled back at George. "The C-cam you know about and the rations and penlight you can guess. Sleep bulbs are standard issue in case we get cornered by someone and can't escape any other way – squeeze it in their face and they're out cold. The nausea serum is for people who get nauseated by the travel."

Drake touched Matthews and George on the shoulder. "Gentlemen, please come stand over here with me for the travel event." He led them to a position several yards from the Engine console.

McKnight strode to the Engine where Wu and Wheeler stood. "Everything ready?" he asked.

"Yes, sir," Wheeler said. "Ready to jump?"

"Affirmative."

The sense of calm exhibited by the team impressed George. His own heart beat so loudly he could hear the blood rushing in his ears.

Wheeler turned to the Engine and plugged the heavy cable into the power generator, checked the lights, and switched on the Engine. George felt more than heard the resulting low-pitched hum.

Wheeler turned back to McKnight. "Sir, may I have your return beacon, please?"

McKnight handed it to Wheeler, who detached it from the chain and inserted it into a slot in the console. The console beeped and the beacon popped out. Wheeler reattached the chain and handed it to McKnight, who draped it around his neck.

"The traveler has the return beacon in his possession," Wheeler said, as Wu stepped to his side.

"Check," she responded.

Wheeler picked up the trigger and plugged the cable into the Engine console.

"Trigger connected."

"Check."

He lifted a small cover over the trigger and switched off the safety. "Trigger safety off."

"Check."

"All set, sir," he said to McKnight. "Ready when you are."

"Understood," McKnight said. He waved in the general direction of George and Matthews and knelt on the steel plate. Leaning forward and placing both palms on the plate in front of him, he nodded at Wheeler and looked down at his hands.

"Traveler acknowledges ready."

George saw Wheeler look to Drake for final approval. Drake nodded back with a short, curt motion.

"Roger," Wheeler announced over the hum of the Engine. He turned to face Wu at the Engine console and said, "Target time is Thursday, July 11th, 1985 at 2330 point zero-zero hours."

"Check," responded Wu, her eyes scanning the console. "We are green across the board, Lieutenant. All systems GO."

"Copy. We are GO for travel," answered Wheeler. "Good luck, Captain."

"Be careful, Captain," Wu added.

McKnight nodded without looking.

George looked on as Wheeler held up the trigger. "Starting time jump in five... four... three... two... one... mark."

As Wheeler squeezed the trigger, the volume and pitch of the Engine hum spiked up and continued to climb. The lights in the room dimmed.

George watched in awe. A noticeable increase in static electricity caused the hair on his head to stand up. The plate glowed and the air above it sparkled with energy. The machine hum grew louder and higher in pitch. A globe of shimmering light formed and spun around McKnight, his hair blowing around as if he were kneeling in the middle of a tornado. The light from the globe grew so bright, it was difficult to see him inside it.

George stared in amazement. "Almighty God!"

As he watched, the globe of air and light bulged to double its size and vanished with a loud crack. It took a moment for George's eyes to adjust back to normal lighting.

McKnight was gone.

"Damn!" George said.

"No shit!" Matthews said. "I don't think I grasped what would happen until now. Now that I've seen it, I might be too scared to try it myself."

"Not me, man. I'd do it in a second. But I'll tell you what—Captain McKnight ain't no wimp."

"You got that right," Matthews said. "Jeez!"

Wu approached them from the console. George tried to read her face, but couldn't. She spread her arms with palms up and said, "That's the end of the show, gentlemen. We still have research to do, right? We need to keep checking, in case there's an issue that might cause a problem for our traveler. Shall we adjourn to your office, Mr. Matthews?"

"Yes, ma'am," Matthews said. "Let's get to work."

Wu pushed past George and headed for the ladder. He quickened his pace and caught up with her near the stairwell door.

"Are you worried, Doctor?" he said.

Her expression softened.

"I am," she said. "I can't help it. It's the first mission and we don't know what to expect. Captain McKnight is a big boy, but who knows what he'll find when he gets there? For example, we've got no way to check the landing point to make sure it's clear. There are just too many things that can go wrong."

"I see." George hadn't considered the jump itself might be dangerous. What if something obstructed the landing place? He wanted to ask, but this wasn't the time.

CHAPTER 15

<u>11:30 pm - Thursday, July 11th, 1985 - NewT Tower Attic</u>
The attic at NewT Center was dimly lit by security lights, hung fifty feet above the dusty floor. A light, musty smell permeated the room and its unpainted concrete block walls. It was dead quiet.

A gray mouse scurried along the edge of the raised platform. It stopped, stood on its hind legs, and sniffed the air, its tiny pink nose vibrating with the effort.

The lights dimmed and the air in the room crackled with static electricity. The mouse scampered away. In the center of the platform, a white silhouette of a kneeling man materialized. The surrounding air formed a pulsing globe of spinning light. The globe bulged outward, then vanished as the man sprawled backward.

McKnight rolled into a crouched position and listened. All he could hear was the sound of his own breathing. *No one here. So far, so good.* Before moving around, he stood and turned around, surveying his surroundings. A water fountain stood against the central core wall. A bandsaw, sawdust and two by four wood scraps lay on the attic floor. *There's my excuse for being here.*

A few four by eight plywood sheets were leaning against the wall. McKnight smiled. *My God. Matthews was right. Those sheets of plywood really have been here that long. That's my hideout. Okay, first things first. Water, then hideout.*

He descended the ladder to the floor. After filling his bottle from the water fountain, he climbed back up and headed for the plywood sheets. Behind them, he noticed a plastic paint drop cloth covering a pile of... something. He lifted the edge of the drop cloth and almost laughed out loud. There, beneath the cloth, was a roll of thick carpet.

He chuckled. *Well, at least I'll have a comfortable place to hide. I can sleep.*

He stepped back and looked up at the top of the plywood, gauging the effort required. After memorizing the scene before him, he went to work. He shifted the plywood to cover a larger area of the wall and draped the drop cloth over the top to create a makeshift tent. It took a few minutes, but the results were worth it. *Not bad.* No one could see behind it unless they walked over and lifted the drop cloth.

McKnight slid his body sideways into the hideout and sat on the carpet. He ate an MRE from the satchel, took a few swallows of water and settled in to wait.

In his mind, he ran through the mission plan. It took less time than he expected to set up his hideout. If he allowed fifty minutes to set up and test the camera, he still had ninety minutes before the scheduled attic check at 0300. His phone read 2340. He had time for a brief rest before setting up the camera.

He programmed himself to wake in twenty minutes, leaned back against the wall and closed his eyes.

****

<u>Wednesday, July 11th, 2035 - 11:40 pm—NewT Tower hallway</u>

They were still on the elevator when Matthews' radio squawked. He held it to his lips and answered, "Matthews here."

George recognized the radio's tinny voice as Matthews' assistant. "Sir, we have the transcript of the security guard's interview for you. Are you coming back downstairs?"

"Thanks, Mike. We're on our way there now. Lay it out on my desk, would you, please?"

"Yes, sir, no problem." The radio squawked again.

Matthews hung the radio back on his belt and turned to the others. "Seems like a good place to start."

"Yes, it is," Wu said.

"I'll help if you don't mind," George said. "I've already seen it, but I wouldn't mind a refresher."

"Thanks. Two heads are better than one."

They arrived at the security office a few minutes later.

"It's going to be a long night. I'll put on some coffee," Matthews said. He picked up a folder from his desk and handed it to Wu. "You two want to read the guard's file?"

"Yes, thanks," she said. She slipped the folder under her arm.

"You can work in our conference room." He strode ahead of her to a door and pushed it open. Drake got a ping on his phone and waved everyone to go in without him, so Wu and George slipped past Matthews into the room.

The windowless room was empty except for a large conference table and an electronic whiteboard. Wu sat at the conference table, but the far wall attracted George's attention.

"What's this?" he asked, walking over to examine it. The wall was covered with framed newspaper clippings and memos.

Matthews grimaced and stepped into the room. "That, sir, is our Wall of Shame."

"You're kidding," Wu said. She rose and joined George at the wall.

"Nope. The first security chief here created it and every chief since then has maintained it. I thought about getting rid of it, but just couldn't bring myself to do it. Respect for tradition, I guess."

Matthews moved over to the wall, removed his glasses, and scanned all the framed artifacts. George could sense determination and pride coming from the man. "The idea is to remind us how important security is. Corporate security teams are perceived by many as next to useless. And some are...but not us," he said, jabbing a thumb into his chest. "Anyway, we use this wall to remind ourselves of the cost of failure and the result of a casual attitude."

George stood in front of the largest of the newspaper hangings. He pointed at it and looked at Matthews.

"Yep," Matthews said, his eyes downcast. "That's the granddaddy of all failures. The murder of Senator Lodge's father. There isn't a worse failure for a security team. Someone in their building gets murdered, and they didn't even know how the perpetrator got in the building, let alone who did it."

"Wow," Wu said. "Mr. Matthews, you have my respect. I see the pride you take in your work."

"Well, thanks," Matthews said, letting out a long breath. "Let me go get that coffee going. I'll be right back."

As Matthews left the room, Wu and George sat together at the conference table, and she positioned the folder in front of her.

George cleared his throat to get her attention. "Doctor Wu, is there any way I can convince you to call me Trevor?"

She looked at him. If he blundered and she needed to ask him to leave, being more familiar would make it awkward. Was she confident of his abilities and professionalism? He hoped she was.

The serious expression on her face turned into a genuine smile. "Absolutely." she said. "Thank you, Trevor. And you may call me Doctor Wu."

"Okay…"

She laughed and patted his hand. "Just kidding. I'm Kathy. So let's get to it." She opened the folder to the summary page.

"What's her name?" George asked.

"McAllister, Meredith April."

Wu froze, her face paled as she hunched over the folder, her eyes racing across the pages before her. When she found the one she was looking for, she scanned it. George saw concern on her face.

"What's wrong?" he asked.

"Shit! General Drake!" she yelled. She pulled out her phone and touched a speed dial. Under her breath, she cursed again and stood, knocking her chair over. She paced by the table. When she stopped and spoke into her phone, the calmness in her voice did little to hide the urgency underneath.

"Wu here. Where are you?" she demanded. George replaced the fallen chair and stood next to her.

"How far is that from NewT Center on Peachtree Street?" she said.

Drake and Matthews came running into the office and George raised a finger to his lips.

"That close? Okay, good. We need you there ASAP. Go to the security counter in the retail area, identify yourself to the guard, and ask for me. Got it?... Good. I'll see you in ten." She disconnected the call.

"Report," Drake said.

She held up a finger to Drake, looked over his shoulder and called out. "Mr. Kelley? Could you please go out to the security counter and meet our associate there and bring him up here? He'll be here in ten minutes. His name is Tyler and he will ask for me."

Kelley spun on his heel, tossed "Yes, ma'am" over his shoulder and trotted out of the office.

Drake stood in front of her with his hands on his hips. "Doctor Wu, may I have a report, please?"

"Yes, sorry, sir." she paused before speaking. "We have a risk. And a stroke of luck. He was out with friends and less than ten minutes away. He's on his way."

"Tyler?" he asked.

"Yes, sir. The security guard is his grandmother. And she's about to meet Captain McKnight."

CHAPTER 16

Thursday, July 11th, 1985 - 11:58 pm – forty-ninth floor - NewT Tower

Meredith April McAllister's radio squawked as she stepped out of the elevator on the forty-ninth floor. "April, you copy? What's your twenty?"

"I have you five by five, Ed. I'm on the Exec floor. I'm starting the doorknob lap."

"Ten-four. Don't be too long. It's time for the theater drunks to arrive."

"Ten-four. Out."

She sighed as she holstered her radio. She disliked the nights when the Fox Theatre had events. The theater patrons who drank all evening during the show sometimes caused problems. By the time they shuffled through the Tower's retail mall on the way to the train station, most were feeling no pain. Sometimes, they had to be asked to leave the premises.

For Merrie, the problem never changed. Emboldened by liquid courage, a patron or two would hit on her and hang around for a while, wasting her time and distracting her from her duties. She politely declined their invitations. If they were persistent, she rewarded them with a phony telephone number.

Her uniform included a name tag. On her second day on the job, she received a call from a stranger who found her home number in the phone book. The next day, she had her name tag changed to show her middle name instead. The guards she worked with and everyone else knew her as April.

Well, might as well get this done and get back downstairs. What a way to spend your birthday!

The executive floor was dimly lit at night. A few fluorescent ceiling fixtures provided enough light to safely navigate the floor. Executive assistant desks stood in the middle of each office area, while executive offices lined both sides.

Tonight, she would go clockwise around the window offices and then counterclockwise around the interior offices. She tried not to be predictable in her rounds.

At the first office, she twisted the doorknob and found it locked. She sighed again. *I don't know why I worry about predictability. Who would be up here?*

The next door was unlocked. Following procedure, she walked through the office. After determining the room was empty, she locked it and moved on to the next door.

****

<u>Thursday, July 12th, 2035—12:00 am–NewT Center Security Office</u>

When Kelley entered the room with Tyler, Wu stood and gestured toward them. "Mr. Matthews, Trevor, this is Lieutenant Tyler from our team. I asked him to come here, because the guard who met Captain McKnight in 1985 is his grandmother, as I'm sure you've gathered."

"What?" Tyler said. "What about my grandmother? Is she all right?"

"Yes, she is," Wu said. "Sorry if we alarmed you, but we called you here because she met Captain McKnight during the mission he is on, back in 1985."

"May I ask why you didn't include me in the mission? I mean, I think being from the area might be an advantage, right?"

Drake spoke. "Lieutenant, my decision, my responsibility. We are where we are. Now we determine the risks and take prevention steps. Doctor Wu, could you please brief the Lieutenant on the mission?"

"Yes, sir," Wu said, motioning for Tyler to sit. "I'll tell you everything about the mission. But first we need to know anything you can tell us about your grandmother and her history, specifically around this date back in 1985."

Tyler sat and stared at his hands as he talked. "Okay, let me think. Today is her birthday. She's seventy-two years old. 1985? She would be twenty-two years old. I talked to Captain McKnight about this today."

He looked up and smiled at Wu. "That was the day she met my grandfather. At NewT Center. He walked by the security counter where she worked and that's how they met." Concern flashed across his face as he looked back and forth between the people at the table. "The event is here at NewT Center?"

"Yes, Lieutenant. Do you know anything else about their meeting?"

"That's all. They got together a month later. I'm not sure why it took so long for them to... No, wait. There is more. There was a murder. Someone killed an officer of the company. To my knowledge, the case was never solved. She thought she might have bumped into the killer, but no one believed her, so she quit." He looked up at Wu. "That's the event? Captain McKnight traveled back to witness the murder?"

"Yes, Lieutenant," Wu said. "It was Captain McKnight she bumped into, not the killer. Most likely, they had a brief contact. You know Captain McKnight will cut it as short as possible without arousing suspicion. I'm sure everything will be okay. I'll brief you on the rest of the mission. You've heard the story from your grandmother, correct?"

"That's right."

"Well, if something strange happened, she would have mentioned it, right?"

"Maybe. She's smart—she doesn't let on everything she knows or suspects. But you're probably right. So what about the murder?"

"The murder doesn't happen until tomorrow by the Captain's timeframe, so everything today will be routine. Let's talk about the mission."

****

<u>Friday, July 12th, 1985–12:00 am – forty-ninth floor - NewT Tower Attic</u>

McKnight awoke and checked his watch. *Right on time.* He pulled the water bottle from his satchel and took a long sip.

He leaned his head back against the wall and tried to remember what he had been dreaming. *What was it?* After a moment, he remembered. He dreamed of Merrie Tyler. But she was much younger in his dream.

In his dream, she wore a blue summer dress that matched her eyes and set off her honey-blonde hair. They sat in her gazebo, drank Blue Moons, and watched the sun set. They talked about anything and nothing, solving the problems of the world, as only good friends or perfect strangers can do. He'd never felt so comfortable around any woman, let alone one as beautiful as she.

McKnight willed himself back to reality.

What the hell is wrong with you?

He dreamed of a relationship that was ludicrous. She was married, forty years older than he, and, worse, his best friend's grandmother. Tyler's words from earlier in the day echoed in his ears. "Jeez, Marc! Are you hitting on my grandmother?"

Get your head back in the game!

He peeped out of his hideout. *No one around. Time to get going.* After doing a quick equipment check, he crawled out and headed for the ladder.

The old metal chair had stood on the platform for years. People had pushed it here and there. Tiny vibrations moved it millimeters at a time. Over time, it crept across the plywood platform to rest on the edge.

Perhaps it was the vibration of McKnight walking by, or maybe it was just the end of a long miracle of balance. As he passed it, one of its wheels slipped off the edge with a thud.

He spun at the sound and saw the chair tip away from him. He leaped toward it, but it was too late. The chair fell off the platform and hit the concrete floor ten feet below with a loud crash.

He couldn't have made more noise if he'd tried.

CHAPTER 17

Friday, July 12th, 1985 – 12:07 am – forty-ninth floor - NewT Tower

Merrie finished the doorknob lap and was on her way to the elevator when she heard the crash.

What the hell was that?

The sound came from the stairwell door. She pressed her ear against it and listened for a full two minutes, but heard nothing more. She pushed away from the door as a tiny thrill of apprehension ran up her spine.

She leaned against the doorjamb and tried to recall the maintenance list for tonight. *Was there an item for the attic?* She didn't remember seeing one, but it didn't matter. She had to investigate.

Get a grip. It's your job. Radio your situation and get your ass up there!

She snorted, angry with herself for her tentativeness. She gripped the doorknob and pulled her radio from her belt. As she raised it to her lips, she stopped. This time, the thrill up her back tinged with fear.

She heard soft footsteps on the staircase behind the door. The doorknob moved slightly in her hand as someone tried to turn it from the other side.

She recoiled from the door. If she had been a second faster, she would have opened a locked door for them. She took a deep breath and pressed her ear against it again. Now she heard metal rubbing against metal. *They're picking the lock.* She chose caution and pushed away from the door. She would observe the subject and radio Ed.

She dashed down the corridor on her tiptoes and paused at the elevator lobby. *Now where?* A small alcove adorned with an artificial plant and pedestal stood to her right next to the elevators. *No good. Too close and no escape route.*

She ran through the elevator lobby and crouched behind a desk in the Executive area. At least from here, she had escape options and a decent observation point. She scanned the immediate vicinity. Office 4912 was ten feet behind her.

She tried to remember everything she knew about being silent. She turned off her radio so a call from Ed wouldn't give her away.

She checked the time on her watch. It had been two minutes since she'd stood at the stairwell door. She was about to risk a peek over the top of the desk when a man passed without a sound, not five feet away, headed toward the office behind her.

Startled, she caught her breath, and the man changed direction as if he heard her. He wore a maintenance coverall and carried a small satchel over his shoulder. She stood and tapped the desk with her radio.

The man spun and landed in a fighting stance underneath a security light.

She had the advantage—he stood in the light and she in the dark. If he saw her at all, she was a silhouette against the lights behind her.

The man craned his neck, peering into the dark. "Who's there?" he said with a slight tremor in his voice. He sounded scared, but his posture didn't support that assessment.

She wasn't a martial artist, but she knew a skilled fighter when she saw one. He looked ready. But even as she considered this, he relaxed his stance and lowered his guard somewhat. She decided to diffuse the situation.

"Sorry if I startled you," she said. "What are you doing here?"

The expression on his face changed. His eyes widened and his guard dropped more. What did she see in his face? *Surprise? Recognition?*

She stepped forward and stood at the edge of the light.

"I said, what are you doing here?"

The man stared at her. He dropped the fighting stance and his hands hung by his sides. His mouth moved, but nothing came out.

No doubt now. Recognition.

"Merrie?" he said.

What the hell? She brushed an errant lock of hair away from her face with her free hand. She couldn't imagine where she might have met this man. He was tall and handsome. She would have remembered him.

She cocked her head to one side and studied his face. "I'm sorry, do I know you from somewhere?"

A brief flash of panic, then composure washed across his face. "No, sorry," he stammered. "For a moment, I thought you were someone else."

"But you called me by name. How did you know? Nobody here knows me by that name."

"Did I? I'm sorry. I thought you were my friend Mary. Mary McKnight. Is your name really Mary?"

"My name is Meredith, but my close friends call me Merrie."

The man smiled. "Oh, Merrie, like M-E-R-R-I-E? My friend's name is Mary, M-A-R-Y. The two names are a lot alike." The smile seemed genuine, but she thought she detected nervousness.

"It sure sounded like Merrie," she said.

Something still didn't feel right.

"You look a lot like her. Her hair is blond, like yours, and you're the same height." He paused and pointed up. "The lighting here isn't so good. When you stepped into the light, it was an easy mistake to make."

He's trying too hard to explain himself.

Remembering his fighting stance, she changed the subject.

"Tell me something," she said. "When you turned around, you took a fighting stance. Not many members of our maintenance staff are into the martial arts and that looked pretty automatic."

A charming smile took over his face. "Oh, thanks. I'm new at it, but I've been working hard. I had class tonight, and I must have jumped to it a hundred times. I must be getting it down."

"I'd say you're getting pretty good at it," she said. "So what are you doing here?"

"Oh, I was up in the attic, cutting studs for next week's construction. I was nearly finished, but I... well, I had to use the bathroom, so I came down here to, you know, save time." Her face must have shown disapproval because he rushed to continue. "Look, I'm sorry. I know I shouldn't be on this floor, but my work was almost completed and I didn't want to go all the way to the basement. I'm sorry, but I really have to pee."

For the first time, Merrie noticed he was shifting his weight back and forth.

Has he been fidgeting all along?

"The bathroom is back that way," she said, jerking her thumb back over her shoulder toward the central hall. *Maybe he's telling the truth. Maybe he's just an idiot, trying to cut corners a little and use the Executive bathroom to save time and get off work earlier.*

"Really? I was working up here two weeks ago, and I thought the bathrooms were in the offices."

"What? And you were going to just pick one?" *How could he not know this if he works here?* "The offices are supposed to be locked. And they are. I checked them."

"Okay, thanks, I didn't know. I'll go back down the hall." He edged his way in the direction she showed. He pointed over his shoulder with his thumb. "Back this way, you say?"

"Yes."

"Okay. I'll go there now. Thanks." He walked toward the central hall.

She fell in step with him. "I think I'll come along and show you where so you don't get lost..." She inclined her head to read his security badge. "Dmitri? You don't sound like a Dmitri."

"I know. I grew up in the US, out west. My parents came from Poland. But my brothers and sisters and I were born here and never spoke Polish at home. It pisses my Dad off, but hey, what can you do?" He shrugged.

"Ah, here's the Men's Room." He turned to her and flashed that smile again. "Thanks for pointing me in the right direction. I'll be a few minutes and then I'll get back upstairs to finish the job."

"Good." she said, smiling. "Have a great night."

"Thanks. You, too," he said and pushed through the door.

After he disappeared into the bathroom, her smile faded. She stood there for a moment.

He was hiding something, no question. But what could it be? There was no cash or other valuables on this floor, any intelligent thief would know that. He didn't seem stupid to her. To her emotional mind, he felt right. But her logical mind rang alarm bells.

She decided to go downstairs to check the schedule and confirm the construction work order. She reattached the radio to her belt, turned on her heel and headed for the elevator.

****

McKnight counted off thirty seconds and pulled the door open a tiny crack. He saw Merrie walking toward the elevator lobby. He waited until he heard the elevator arrive and leave again. He let the door close, leaned against the wall and closed his eyes.

He thought of the gear and technology in his pockets and satchel. If they searched or scanned him, he would be in big trouble. *What else can I screw up tonight?*

He shook his head, stepped to the washbasin and turned the cold water on full blast. He plunged his hands under the stream and splashed it up into his face. His reflection in the mirror didn't look it, but he felt disoriented. He had time. He would stay in the bathroom for five minutes before venturing out.

****

The elevator door closed as Merrie pushed the button for the Bridge floor. Her logical mind gnawed at the back of her consciousness.

What was it about that guy? She replayed the scene in her mind. When she first saw him, he was walking toward one of the Executive offices. He changed direction when he heard her. She was convinced of that now.

And the professional fighting stance. What else?

The elevator stopped on the Bridge floor and the door opened. Merrie didn't leave the elevator.

He was carrying a satchel. He didn't seem the type to carry a personal satchel unless...unless it contained tools of the trade. Like lock-picking or safe-cracking equipment.

She pressed the button to return to the forty-ninth floor. Things were coming together now in a bad way. The fighting stance, the satchel, the nervousness, and heading for an executive office? Did he recognize her because he had been casing the place? The man's demeanor didn't match that of a construction worker.

And there wasn't a trace of dirt on his Coveralls.

The elevator door opened again and Merrie stepped back onto the forty-ninth floor. She became angry, convinced she had been manipulated.

Who the hell are you really, Mr. Dmitri Slovensky?

She pulled out her radio and pushed the call button.

****

Downstairs, Churchie Tyler pushed his way through the revolving door and rode the elevator to the ground floor of the retail mall. The area was crowded with people who were headed home. He was only a few steps from the entrance to the MARTA train station.

He passed the security counter on the left and waved to the middle-aged man in a uniform sitting there. As he passed, the man's radio squawked, and he whispered into it. Churchie Tyler entered the MARTA station, just in time to catch the last train home.

****

Thursday, July 12th, 2035 – 12:18 am – NewT Center Security Office

George sat in on Tyler's briefing with Wu and Drake. It was over and Tyler asked questions about the project.

As the discussion turned technical, George let his attention wander. Out of the corner of his eye, he saw movement. He looked at the Wall of Shame. *No, not movement.* The framed news clipping of the murder was glowing.

He stood and walked over to investigate.

"So, what can I do?" Tyler said. "Can I help with research or something? How about, uh…? What if I…? Wow, I feel really dizzy…"

George spun around and looked at Tyler. Drake and Wu stared at him across the conference table. Like the clipping, Tyler was glowing.

Drake recovered first. "Recall McKnight! Now!"

Wu punched a speed-dial number. "Lieutenant, recall the Captain now on the General's orders… Yes, now! We'll be right up."

"What?" Tyler said. "What's wrong?"

George looked at him. He was Tyler all right, but not Tyler. The glow persisted and Tyler's visage changed. Like the TelExtraVision commercials where one face morphs into another, his blue eyes darkened to brown, and his hair darkened from blond to almost black. His face became fuller, his complexion darker, and he grew two inches taller. Then the glow faded.

"Follow me," Wu said. As they hurried past the security counter, she paused. "Mr. Kelley, could you please find and pull the security logs for this evening, fifty years ago and take them to the conference room?"

"Yes, ma'am, no problem."

"Thank you." Turning to Tyler, she said, "Let's go, Lieutenant." She entered the elevator and pressed the button for the Bridge floor.

To George, it was clear something had altered Tyler's family tree. McKnight somehow changed the past with immediate and personal consequences.

CHAPTER 18

<u>Friday, July 12th, 1985 – 12:22 am – forty-ninth floor - NewT Tower</u>

"Ed? April here. You copy?"

"I have you five by five, April. When are you coming back down? Over."

"In a few minutes. I ran into a guy up here who claims to be maintenance, but he's behaving suspiciously. Can you confirm the work order for me? What's on the attic schedule tonight? The maintenance guy is Dmitri Slovensky, spelled S-L-O-V-E-N-S-K-Y. Thanks. Over."

"Let me check. Stand by. Over."

She stood next to the elevators, listening. All she could hear was the sound of silence, that soft hiss of white noise when there is little sound. She edged over to the hallway and looked toward the men's bathroom. She could hear water running.

Her radio squawked. "April, you copy? Over."

"Yes, Over."

"April, there is *no*, repeat *no*, maintenance scheduled for the attic tonight. And Dmitri Slovensky is not on the maintenance team list. What's your status? Over."

"Ed, we have an intruder, possibly a professional burglar. Call Atlanta PD right now. Over."

"April, do not confront. You don't know who you're dealing with. I repeat, do not confront. Do you copy, April? Over?"

She ignored his transmission. She shut off her radio so it wouldn't give her away and walked down the hallway towards the bathroom.

And I thought he was cute. Son of a bitch!

Her anger boiled over and she walked faster. A bright light spilled out underneath the bathroom door.

What the hell? Has he started a fire?

She broke into a run. A blinding light flooded the hallway from under the door.

She was ten feet away when the light went out.

"Oh, no, no, no!" she cried, as she reached the door. She threw her shoulder against it and crashed into the bathroom.

Nothing. The light inside was normal and water was running in the sink. She checked every stall, but he was gone.

Damn! He slipped out while I was on the elevator. But what the hell was that light?

She turned her radio back on and keyed the transmit switch. "Ed, you copy? Over."

"Five by five, April. I called APD. Are you okay? Over."

"Yes. He's disappeared. But he's got to be here somewhere." She walked back toward the stairwell. "I'm going up to the attic to search for him. Over."

"You are not, dammit! Stay put. The cops will be here any second. At this time of night, you can hear everything. If he's in the attic, you'll hear him if he comes down the stairs. If he doesn't, we'll search the place. But you stay put! Got it? Over."

"Copy. April out," she said, with little enthusiasm.

She was furious. An intruder walked the halls that were her responsibility. She stopped at the stairwell door, took a deep breath and opened it.

****

12:30 am – Thursday, July 12th, 2035 –NewT Tower Attic

When Wu called, Wheeler ran the recall procedure. As he flipped the switch, the Engine hummed to life again. The white silhouette of McKnight appeared. The spinning globe of light formed around him as his form became more defined. The brilliant sphere around him bulged outward, and the light went out. He fell backward on the floor.

He jumped to his feet and hurried over to Wheeler. "Why did you bring me back?"

"Orders, sir," Wheeler said. "Doctor Wu said to recall you immediately, on the General's orders."

The doors from the freight elevator around the corner banged open. Both turned in that direction as the rest of the team came into view and climbed the platform ladder.

"Captain," Wu said. "You changed the future by what you did in the past. We had you recalled to assess and fix the problem."

"What do you mean?" McKnight asked.

Meeting Merrie must have caused it. What else could it be?

He searched the faces of the team, trying to find a clue. He didn't recognize one of the men. Puzzled, he stared for a moment.

The man looked familiar, but he couldn't place him. "Who's this?" he asked.

The man looked shocked. "What?" he said. "You're kidding, right?"

"That," Wu said, gesturing toward the man, "is Lieutenant Tyler."

McKnight was stunned into silence. His best friend, changed.

Probably my fault.

Wu touched his arm. "It's how we knew something happened," she said. "He changed right in front of us. We need your report right now so we can figure out how to fix it."

She turned to Wheeler. "Lieutenant?" He nodded and tossed her a small audio transcriber. She sat on the floor, Indian-style. "Please join me, Captain. I need to record what we saw before the memory fades, then we need your story."

McKnight sat beside her and closed his eyes to focus while she described Tyler's physical change for the record.

A new past affected the present. Wu saw it happen and now she has two sets of memories—the old Tyler and the new Tyler. The old memories will fade and soon she won't remember the old Tyler. She had to record the events before the new memories overtook the old.

Time isn't forgiving. You can't fix your timeline mistakes if you don't move quickly.

Wu related into the recorder Tyler's story about how his grandparents met. McKnight would remember it because he and Tyler talked about it—not twenty-four hours ago.

McKnight somehow interfered with that event. He opened his eyes and looked around. Tyler was across the room talking to the General.

He's got much of the same personality on the inside, but he's not the same man. He's forgotten himself already.

McKnight lowered his gaze to stare at his hands in his lap. *I'll get you back to normal, no matter what else happens.*

Wu continued to record her experience. She covered how Tyler changed before her eyes, and how they ordered McKnight's recall. Next, they'd analyze the problem. By the time they got to the analysis, McKnight would be the only one who remembered Tyler before the change because he was the traveler. George and Matthews would be the first to forget since they had only known Tyler for a few minutes.

"Okay," Wu said, switching off the transcriber. "Let's go to the office and work on the solution." She led the way down the ladder and to the elevator. No one spoke on the freight elevator ride. Tyler hummed quietly to himself.

Once in the office, they filed into the conference room. While the others found a place to sit, Wu set the transcriber on the table and plugged it into the A/V link. At the touch of a button, a transcript of her experience appeared on the wall.

"Okay," she said. "Captain, let's hear your report. We already have the time frame since we witnessed the transformation."

"Yes, ma'am," McKnight said. "I traveled as scheduled. When I arrived, there was no one in the attic. I set up my hiding place as planned and catnapped for a while. Then I proceeded downstairs to set up the camera. The stairwell door was locked as expected, so I picked the lock and entered the forty-ninth floor, after listening for a few moments to make sure there was no one around. I walked down the hall as quietly as I could. She was waiting there for me near Lodge's office. She heard me coming."

"Who?"

"Merrie. Tyler's grandmother."

Tyler shifted forward in his chair. "What? You must be mistaken, sir. Neither of my grandmothers are from Atlanta. And neither of them is named Merrie–"

Wu turned and held up her hand to silence him. "Lieutenant, remember what we do for a living. You've been the victim of a history change. For now, I need you to relax and accept that we know what we're doing. You'll get the whole story in a few minutes, okay?"

Tyler looked confused, but nodded in acceptance. "Yes, ma'am."

She turned back to McKnight. "Please continue with your report, Captain. Any idea how she heard you?"

"She might've heard a chair fall off the platform right before I came downstairs."

"A chair fell off the platform?" she replied, taken aback.

"Yes, ma'am. I never touched it. When I arrived, I noticed it was near the edge. I walked within ten feet of it. Maybe the vibration of my footsteps? I don't know. But it fell off and she might have heard it from downstairs. I don't see how, though, unless she was in the stairwell or close to it."

"So she was waiting for you there?" Wu said.

"Yes," he said. "I was quiet coming down the stairs. After I opened the door, I stopped to listen for sounds of activity. I didn't hear anything. When I walked down the hall, I was in quiet mode. She couldn't have heard me in the hall. So she knew I was coming, or she heard me upstairs. I walked right past her before I was aware she was there."

"I see. Tell me about the interaction with her."

McKnight repeated the conversation, word for word, with practiced precision. He related how she walked him to the men's room where the recall occurred. He said, "She left the floor while I was in the bathroom. How did I disrupt time?"

Wu paused. She shook her head and looked up at the transcript. "I..." she stammered. She looked at Drake, then back at McKnight, confused.

She's losing the memory. "Doctor Wu?" When she looked at him, he said, "Focus on the exercise." He pointed up at the transcript. She followed his gaze back to the writing on the wall.

"Okay. Sorry. Let me get my bearings here." She scrolled through the transcript. After a moment, she spoke again. "We hypothesize, because she stayed so long upstairs, she didn't get back to the security counter in time to meet Tyler's grandfather. Consequently, they never found each other, Tyler's grandfather married someone else, changing the family tree."

"Okay," McKnight said. "I need to fix this. I need to tell myself what to avoid so I don't disrupt the past. Let's get moving."

"Not so fast," interjected Drake. "We don't go without a plan. Let's don't make things worse."

"I agree," Wu said, checking the time. "We have time, so let's make sure we get it right."

****

Trevor George's mind was in overdrive.

What's the deal here? Why can't he just go back and tell himself not to knock over the chair?

It took a few minutes for the problem to register in his brain.

If McKnight traveled back to warn himself and returned, there would then be two McKnights, one in the past and one in the present.

How would they avoid it? He couldn't see a way. No matter what, the result would be more than one McKnight.

Then what?

Drake and Wu stared at each other. Though they said nothing, they were communicating. Wu raised her eyebrows, and he responded with a single nod.

They've reached a decision. What do I not understand?

Matthews spoke up. "Can I ask a question?"

"Sure," Wu said.

Matthews looked around the room. "How come we remember any of this? Since it happened fifty years in the past, why do we remember the old Tyler?" He looked at Tyler. "No offense intended, sir."

The others looked at Drake. He leaned back in his chair and steepled his fingers. "Okay. We can take time to explain that. Besides, you two can't contribute if you don't understand. It's not a secret, though we haven't published it. Doctor, would you explain, please?"

"Yes, sir." She looked at the two men. "We don't understand how it works, but I can describe what our hypothesis, based on our experience and evidence." She paused. "A perception about time travel has persisted for years and it comes from science fiction literature, not science fact. The basic premise is that, when something changes in the past, it affects the future and the original past is lost forever. That's only partly true.

"We say time is folded because of the impact on the power needed to travel. But that's not all. During a travel event, the times are linked and what happens in one time manifests itself in the other immediately, but memories of the original history will persist for a while after it changes. We don't understand why, but that's how it works.

"You'll remember what Tyler looked like, but your memory will fade. For us who have known him for a while, we now have a new set of memories of him that conflict with the old. The new memories will soon crowd out the old ones."

Matthews pulled on his lower lip. "I think I get it. I'm sure I'll have more questions later. But, let's press on. We have an emergency here and I'm wondering how you will fix it."

"Well, it's simple," Wu said. "Captain McKnight is right. He has to fix it."

"So do you send him back again to warn himself about it?"

"No," George said. "Then you'll have two McKnights, right? What do you do then?"

Matthews stopped to consider that. "I see what you mean. Like Professor Astalos and his other selves. Then what do we do?"

George looked at Drake and then at Wu. "I think Doctor Wu has something up her sleeve. It's written all over her face."

Wu looked at him with new respect. George saw her smile at him, then look to Drake, who nodded his permission.

"Recombination," she said, still looking at Drake. McKnight nodded. Wu turned back to George and repeated. "Recombination."

"What?" George asked. "Recombination? What does that mean? It sounds downright dangerous."

"Well, it isn't common, but we don't think it's dangerous. It's...well, it's under-tested and under-documented."

Drake spoke. "Okay, we need to get moving, but I'll try to explain. If multiple individuals with the same DNA travel to the same place and point in time, they're recombined into one individual. The result is much like temporary multiple personality disorder. The intellect of the individuals end up in one body--that of the oldest personality. They're aware of each other and can communicate. The oldest personality is the strongest and the others will recede. The human mind is an amazing instrument. After the recombination, it begins to cope with the multiple consciousnesses. Over a short period, it eliminates redundant memories and what remains is permanent. The shorter the time interval between the events, the sooner the additional consciousness recedes."

"Let me get this straight," George said. "So, you send Captain McKnight back to the exact same time again and he gets recombined with himself?"

He looked at McKnight. "I know I'm a civilian here, but are you okay with this?"

McKnight considered the question. "I'm not crazy about it," he said. "But it's my job and my screw-up. My responsibility. I have to fix it."

He turned to Drake. "Sir, I'll fix it. Send me back and I'll take care of it."

"Thank you, Captain. I know you will," Drake said.

George nodded and sat back.

Must not be as important as I thought.

He rose and stood by the Wall of Shame, his eye caught by the murder clipping.

"It's been a little more than an hour," Wu said. "There'll be little difference between the intellects. The younger consciousness will fade within a matter of hours if not minutes."

"I'm sorry to interrupt again," George said. "But may I ask two more questions?"

"Okay," Drake said, drumming his fingers on the table. "Then we need to get moving."

"Thank you, sir. How did you find out about recombination? I think I can guess, but I'd like to know."

"Really?" Wu said. "I'd like to hear your guess."

"Well," George said, collecting his thoughts. "I've been reading about Doctor Astalos and his two other selves. Rob Astalos hasn't appeared in public for a while. The story is he's off somewhere, writing a book. I'm wondering now if he is still around. Or is he recombined with Robert or maybe Robby Astalos?"

Drake and Wu looked at one another and reached another unspoken agreement.

Wu turned back to George. He basked in the warmth of the smile she gave him.

Drake spoke. "We found out by accident. It was a routine test run and the two Doctors Astalos wanted to take part. They traveled to the exact same time, and Rob disappeared. At first, we thought the Engine malfunctioned, killed him and created emotional problems for Robert. But, then we discovered Rob's intellect was alive and well inside Robert's body, along with Robert's consciousness."

"So he's gone now?" George said.

"No, he is still coexisting with Robert Astalos. Both consciousnesses are in the same body."

"But I thought the younger consciousness fades after a short time?" Matthews said.

"They do," Wu said. "But Robert and Rob Astalos worked together for twenty-five years as separate entities. That's a lot of history and memories to assimilate. It'll take a while for the Rob intellect to fade. The last we heard," she glanced at Drake, who nodded. "He's still active."

George said, "So I guess the jury's still out on the whole phenomenon. I have more questions, but they can wait.

"Here's my second question. Did anyone else notice that the framed newspaper clipping about the murder also changed after it glowed?"

CHAPTER 19

Wu and Drake looked surprised. Wu rose and hurried over to examine the article. "We noticed Tyler was glowing, but what else happened?"

"I saw it when I came over here. The article has changed. Before, the article said there were no clues to the murder. Now it says there were unsubstantiated rumors of an intruder who disappeared."

"I didn't notice that," Wu said. Her knitted brow and down-turned mouth betrayed her irritation with herself.

"Of course, you didn't," George said. "You were focused on Lieutenant Tyler, and rightly so. And now something else occurs to me."

"What's that?" asked Drake.

"Well, if something glows, that means it's changed, right? If that's true, then we can use that to give us clues about what's happened in the past, or at least, know when something has changed."

"Yes, I think we can accept that as a fact," Wu said. "We'll keep an eye on it and Lieutenant Tyler. Good catch, Trevor. I'm glad you're here. Now, we need to start the ball rolling here. Captain, are you ready?"

McKnight was standing by the door. "Yes, ma'am. The sooner, the better."

"Okay," she said and leveled her brown eyes at McKnight. "So please walk me through your plan. How do you plan to prevent a recurrence of the interference?"

"Yes, ma'am. Upon arrival, I should perceive my younger personality in my consciousness. I may have to explain who I am and negotiate. Then I plan to go to that chair and secure it. Next, I'll do the same routine as before, except I'll go downstairs a little later, say about twenty minutes later. That should give her a chance to go downstairs, meet Tyler's grandfather, and be out of my way."

Wu looked at Drake and then back at McKnight. She placed her phone on the conference table, leaned forward, and clasped her hands in front of her. "Okay, Captain. The plan is fine."

She looked down at her hands and then back at McKnight. "However...you need to be extra cautious. You don't want to take any chances on meeting her again. We should be able to fix it this time, but meeting her twice would be courting disaster, don't you agree?"

"Yes, ma'am. I agree," McKnight said. "Am I cleared to travel?"

"Yes, of course you are," Wu said, as she picked up her phone and touched the speed dial.

After listening a moment, she spoke. "Lieutenant, get ready for another travel for the Captain. Target the original delivery point and time... Yes, the exact same time... Yes, Lieutenant, that's correct. It'll be a recombination attempt...Affirmative."

She disconnected the call and looked at the others. "Let's get upstairs."

They left the conference room for the elevator. George fell in step with McKnight. "Captain, may I ask a question?"

"Sure," McKnight said.

"Traveling through time. What does it feel like?"

"Well, there isn't much to it. There's the wind in the beginning, then a mild electric shock at the moment you go, you feel like you're falling through a star field, and then you're there. It doesn't take long."

"I'd like to try it sometime. It's a lot more interesting than what I do for a living."

"I can't help you there. Only a few people are trained to travel. And they're all on my team."

"I understand," George said. "I think I need to apply for a job with your team." He grinned from ear to ear at McKnight. "Got any openings for a resource with a detective skill set?"

McKnight stopped and looked George in the eye. Then he smiled and walked again. Over his shoulder, he said, "Send the General your resume, Detective. He might be open to it."

They reached the freight elevator and stepped inside with the others.

Wu stood next to Tyler, watching him. After a moment, he realized she was staring at him.

"What?" he said. "Do I look funny or something?"

"Are you okay?" she said.

Tyler had a new set of memories and might not be excited about exchanging the life he remembers for a life he knows nothing about. The Tyler McKnight knew would work hard to set things right and make light of it.

But what is this new Tyler be thinking? He glanced at Tyler.

Tyler was looking at the elevator ceiling and rubbing his chin with his thumb and forefinger. Abruptly, he glanced at Wu and spoke. "I'm sorry, were you talking to me?"

Wu frog-punched his arm. "Ow!" he complained, then laughed. "Of course, I am. Why wouldn't I be? Just because I've changed my DNA doesn't mean I'm not still adorable."

Wu looked at McKnight. "That, at least, sounds familiar."

McKnight winked at her. "Yup. Some things never change."

"I might kill him before you get him changed back." she said and frowned at Tyler.

The elevator stopped at the attic. They all stepped out and walked around the corner and climbed up the platform. Wheeler was there, waiting for them.

"I'm ready to start when you are, Captain," he said.

"Thanks, Lieutenant. I'll be ready in a second. Doctor Wu?"

"Yes, Captain?"

"Let's get this fixed. Anything else I need to know before traveling?"

"No, sir. You're good to go."

"Thanks." McKnight turned to Wheeler. "Lieutenant? I'm ready. Let's do it."

****

McKnight was a stickler for process and preparedness, and Wu was glad. He would miss nothing and would be prepared for whatever happened.

She sighed and glanced at the others. Matthews was talking to Drake about travel and George was watching McKnight and Wheeler.

She smiled. George was an interesting study. She sized him up as mature, but with a youthful enthusiasm and a strong intellect. She surmised he was the type who found something interesting in everything he encountered.

And not unattractive, either. She shook her head. *Don't get defocused.*

"Doctor Wu?" Wheeler said, looking at the calculator in his hand. "Power requirement is up six percent, but still well within acceptable limits." He looked up at her. "We're ready."

"Okay," Wu said. She dashed to the bench and picked up the checklist.

"It is 1:28 am, July 12th, 2035. Captain, you will have almost two more hours of experiences than your target self. I'd like to record how long the other self persists."

"Yes, ma'am," McKnight said, as he stepped onto the travel plate.

"By the book and from the checklist. The traveler has the return beacon in his possession?" Wheeler said.

"Check." responded Wu.

"Trigger connected," Wheeler said.

"Check."

He switched off the safety.

"Trigger safety off."

"Check."

"All green, sir," he said to McKnight. "Ready when you are."

"Roger. Let's go," McKnight said. He knelt, leaning forward with both palms on the plate in front of him, and nodded.

"Traveler acknowledges ready."

Wheeler glanced at Drake for his approval and got the nod. "Go for travel," Wheeler announced. He turned to face Wu at the Engine console and said, "Again, target time is Thursday, July 11th, 1985 at 2330 point zero-zero hours. This is a recombination attempt."

"Check on the recombination." Wu said, her eyes scanning the console. "We are green across the board. All systems go for travel." She checked the item off.

"Copy. We are GO for travel," answered Wheeler. "Good luck, Captain."

McKnight made no sign he heard. He was already deep in concentration.

"And... we jump in five... four... three... two... one... mark."

Wheeler pulled the trigger. The Engine hum got louder and the audible frequency of the hum glided up.

Again, the air above the plate and around McKnight seemed to be alive with energy and swirled around him. The globe of spinning light formed around him and the hum from the Engine rose in volume and pitch. McKnight's hair blew around as before and he disappeared in the glare of the light. The globe bulged out and, with a loud bang, he was gone again.

The others blinked their eyes, trying to adjust again to the lower light of the attic. They all stood in silence together, except for Wheeler, who scanned all the dials on the Engine. Satisfied, he wrote notes on his clipboard and set it down.

"Okay," Wu said. "I think now we should go back to the office, go over the original plan, and wait for the Captain to return. And bring you up to speed, Lieutenant Tyler." She turned to him. The face grinning back at her was not the one she remembered.

She laughed. "So this is what you look like. Well, the first part of the mission has been accomplished."

"How did he get it done so fast?" asked Matthews.

"He didn't," George said, with a sideways glance at Wu. To her, he said, "Can I take a whack at explaining it?"

"Sure."

Turning back to Matthews, George said, "Remember? We're about fifty years plus two hours since he landed in the past. We are living in parallel with fifty years ago. The two hours have already occurred, so the problem has already been fixed. In the last two hours, he avoided the woman and her original actions were restored. She went back downstairs and met Tyler's grandfather. Right, Kathy?"

"Are we working an exercise?" Tyler asked.

Matthews and George burst out laughing.

Wu turned to Tyler and said, "Yes, Lieutenant, we are." To the others, she added, "Let's go back downstairs."

As they started down the ladder, Wu touched Wheeler's arm. "Better get some sleep, Lieutenant," Wu said. "You might not have time later."

"Yes, ma'am. Will do."

In the walk from the elevator to the Security Office, George fell in step with Wu. "Were you worried?" he asked.

She looked at him. On his face, she could see both concern and curiosity.

And sensitive, along with everything else.

"Well, yes, I was. I have confidence in Captain McKnight, but dozens of things could go wrong. But, he'll do it if it can be done. He's resourceful, and I'd bet on him, even if the odds are against him."

"I sensed that," George said. "And he's worried about his friend. I got the impression he would crawl fifty miles over broken glass for Lieutenant Tyler."

"You're wrong," she said.

He stopped walking. She continued on a step or two, then stopped and turned back towards him.

She smiled and said, "He'd do that for any of us. You, too, if he thought you were in trouble. That's who he is."

CHAPTER 20

Thursday, July 11th, 1985 - 11:30 pm - NewT Tower Attic

The attic at NewT Center was lit by the security lights, hung fifty feet above the dusty floor. A light, musty smell permeated the room and its unpainted concrete block walls. The room was dead quiet.

A gray mouse scurried along the edge of the raised platform. It stopped, stood on its hind legs, and sniffed the air, its tiny pink nose vibrating with the effort.

The lights dimmed further, and the air crackled with static electricity. The mouse scampered away. In the center of the platform, a white silhouette of a kneeling man materialized. The surrounding air formed into a globe of spinning light. The globe pulsed as the man became more discernible. Without warning, the globe bulged outward, then vanished as McKnight sprawled backward.

He crouched and listened. All he could hear was his own breathing. He looked around. No one there.

Well, sort of.

He froze. *What the hell?*

You're not going crazy. It's just me. Or you, rather.

Huh?

We're in a recombination. A successful one.

A recombination? So you are me? Like what happened to Rob Astalos?

Yes.

How come? What happened?

Long story, but I screwed up.

What does that mean?

It means I screwed up history on the first try, so now I'm back to fix it.

What do you mean? How did you screw it up?

It was an accident. I ran into her.

Who?

You know who. Don't you? You're me. What have we been thinking about?

A pause. Merrie? How in God's name?

Back in 1985, she worked as a Security Guard at NewT. Nobody knew except Tyler, who wasn't involved in the planning. He's here now, though.

What?

He's here, and he was changed by my screw-up. He looks completely different. Same personality and sense of humor, but everything else is different. I somehow prevented his grandparents from meeting. We didn't know they were close by.

Damn. Is he okay?

He's fine, but not himself. Since his grandfather met and married someone else, Merrie's influence in his genetic makeup and environment isn't in him.

Shit. We've got to fix this. That asshole Lodge! If he hadn't rammed this mission down our throats, we'd have done enough research and avoided this.

I agree. Nothing we can do about that now, though. We have to fix it.

Understood. What do we need to do different?

First, we secure this damned chair. He walked toward the teetering chair on the edge of the platform.

Why?

Because if we don't, it'll fall and give away the fact that someone is up here. Or, at least, that's our theory.

Okay. No problem.

As he reached for the chair, it teetered and tipped over the edge. He dove after it, landing with his head and shoulders hanging over the edge and catching the chair by one of its arms. He pushed himself up into a sitting position, lifting the chair back onto the platform.

Ouch. I see what you mean.

McKnight pulled the chair back three feet from the edge and walked over to his hiding place.

Where are we going?

On my first trip, I found a perfect place to hide. You'll like this.

Hmm.

What?

I just realized... I won't be here much longer, will I?

I don't know. That's the theory. Then again, we haven't heard much about the event from Robert Astalos. He constructed his hiding place as he had before.

Yeah, he's a private person. He acknowledged that Rob was there in his mind with him so everyone wouldn't freak out, but was close-mouthed about the details. I guess we'll find out soon enough, eh?

Yeah, I guess so. Sorry.

Can't be helped, though. The alternative is to leave Tyler in an altered state. Not an option. My responsibility to fix it.

Yeah.

Hey, how come we don't have on two sets of clothes?

I don't know. Maybe because I didn't change clothes. Maybe it got re-combined as well? We should catalog that one and bring it up to Kathy and Doctor Astalos.

Yep. Agreed.

McKnight stepped back from the hideout to admire his handiwork. *Okay, that should do it.*

He stepped inside the hideout and sat on the carpet again. *Feels like home.*

He unwrapped an energy bar and ate it. He deposited the wrapper back in the satchel, opened a water bottle, took a few swallows and placed it back in the satchel.

How do you like our hideout?

No answer. He waited for a few seconds.

Are you still here?

No response. He checked the time. It was 2340. His other self was gone after ten minutes. Two hours of difference, and it took ten minutes to assimilate. Was that a death? Or is he still in there somewhere? McKnight shook off that train of thought. *No time to think about that now.*

Discipline clicked in. He ran through the mission activities again. The hideout was set up, and he had time to rest before he positioned the camera.

He could afford to rest a little longer and reduce the chances of meeting Merrie again. The time was 2345. He willed his subconscious to wake him in forty minutes and closed his eyes.

There was a rush of images.

Wu, Drake, the old and new Tyler.

The Tyler home in Atlanta.

The gazebo.

Merrie as Tyler's grandmother.

Merrie as he saw her on the Executive floor. She smiled and said, "Marc."

He awoke with a start. Was it a dream or had someone spoken? He peered out of the hideout. There was no one in sight. He waited five minutes, barely breathing.

Nothing. Now she's in my dreams. I've got to get a grip.

McKnight leaned back against the carpet and executed a breathing regimen to calm himself. Then, without a sound, he crept out of the hideout. He made his way across the platform, generating only light creaking sounds from the plywood flooring. He climbed down the ladder and went to the opposite stairwell, away from the one he used the previous time. This one was near the freight elevator. He stepped through the door and descended the stairs.

The stairwell door was locked as expected. He placed his ear against the door and listened for a full minute.

Nothing.

In his mind, he checked off the sounds he heard. The air conditioning system, the hum of the lights, the remote sound of an elevator moving between the floors far below. And his beating heart. Otherwise, the silence was deafening.

He pulled out his lock-picking kit and worked on the lock. In that intense silence, the sound of the pick against the metal of the lock sounded louder than it was.

In thirty seconds, he had the lock open. He stowed the kit, took a deep breath and twisted the doorknob. It made no sound.

He pushed the door open a crack and peeked out. The hallway was as he remembered it—areas of darkness interspersed with low light from the security lights. He took a breath and pushed the door open. It creaked so loudly, he jumped and almost laughed out loud. He started down the hall in quiet mode, making for Lodge's office. The Executive floor was dead quiet.

A security camera recorded his image. He was aware of it, but didn't avoid it. No one would identify him for fifty years.

As he expected, Lodge's office door was locked. McKnight pulled his kit out again, defeated the lock and opened the door. As expected, the room was dark except for the lights from the streets outside. He closed the door behind him and locked it.

Once inside, he ran through the checklist.

Lift the tile, place the C-cam, replace the tile, check for tile dust, clean up, get out. No sweat. There was enough ambient light coming from the window. He checked the time again. The scheduled security check for the attic was at 0300 hours, plenty of time to get the job done.

****

<u>Friday, July 12th, 1985 – 12:33 am - NewT Security Office</u>

"April?"

Merrie turned to see Ed Bailey standing at the edge of the security counter. An older guard, he was kind person and a perfect gentleman. She always felt relieved when the manager paired her with Ed for a shift. With him, she wouldn't have to cope with a coworker more focused on her than building security. The current schedule called for them to be here tonight and tomorrow night.

"Yes, Ed?"

"Who was that guy? A friend of yours?"

"Nope. Just another drunk trying to find his way home."

What was his name? Churchie? He was cute and interesting, but I'm not sharing that with anyone from work. I doubt he'll call, though. He'll probably lose my number on the way home.

"Some things never change, do they?" He walked behind the security counter and back into the security office. Merrie knew he was heading for the coffee machine inside the office door.

"Not that I can tell," she said. A few moments later, Ed reappeared with a steaming cup in his hand. "What's next on the schedule? Anything interesting?"

He picked up the duty clipboard and read the top page. "Nope. Looks boring tonight."

He shifted his weight, took a cautious sip of the hot liquid and looked towards the Tower. "Well, I guess I'll go do a doorknob check on the Executive floor."

"I just did that," she said.

"Yes. It's about being unpredictable," he said with a grin. "I'll be back in a few."

"Okay, I've got the fort here. Call me if anything interesting happens."

"No problem. I'll be back in thirty minutes, tops. I have my radio if you need me." He laid the clipboard on the desk, turned on his heel and walked down the hallway toward the Tower.

Merrie smiled as she watched Ed tread the long hallway. He made this little trip every workday. He told Merrie he liked to walk the halls of power. But she suspected the real reason was to see the spectacular view of the city lights from the forty-ninth floor. She went with him once. He liked to open one of the executive offices, step in with the light off and enjoy the city lights while he drank his coffee.

****

Friday, July 12th, 1985 – 12:38 am – Suite 4912, NewT Tower

McKnight assessed the options. He could move a chair over and stand on it to set up the C-cam, or he could stand on the credenza. No decision, really—too many things could go wrong while standing on a chair. He climbed onto the credenza. He was close enough to the ceiling to carry out the task. He lifted the tile and slid it aside so he could place the C-cam behind it.

He heard a faint sound. *What was that? The elevator bell?*

He resisted the temptation to keep working. Murphy's Law had worked against him once today and he didn't want to tempt fate. He replaced the tile and jumped off the credenza. He walked to the door and opened it a tiny crack.

Through the crack, he could see a uniformed man walking toward him. Silently, he closed and locked the door.

Nowhere to hide.

CHAPTER 21

McKnight heard a key being inserted into the lock. With no place to go, he pressed himself against the wall behind the door.

No way I can claim to be lost this time.

Glancing at the window, he realized what would happen in the next few seconds.

When he turns on the light, he'll see my reflection in the window. No choice. I'll have to take him out.

He pulled a sleep bulb from his pocket.

The door opened and dim light spilled into the office. The guard entered and walked to the window. McKnight was ready to dose him, but stopped.

He didn't turn on the lights.

The man didn't close the door which, so far, saved McKnight from discovery.

McKnight shrank back into the tiny space behind the door. He inclined his head enough to see around the edge. With a cup in one hand and the other hand in his pocket, the man stood at the window.

Relaxed posture. He's here for the view. If he turns on the light, the room's reflection will spoil it.

The guard sighed and leaned against the credenza.

The air conditioner clicked off. McKnight noticed the sound of his own breathing. Training kicked in and he took slow, shallow breaths.

After a moment, the guard set down his coffee and turned to face the room. The guard apparently didn't hear him, but noticed something was different. McKnight tightened his grip on the sleep bulb. He might still be forced to use it.

Don't move.

The guard stood in silence, listening. The man was doing what McKnight would in the same situation—check off the sounds he heard and see what's left. The hum of power from the hallway lights, the occasional elevator hum or bell and the gentle bubbling of the filter in the aquarium in the hall. Traffic sounds from the street below. His own breathing.

After a full minute, the air conditioner clicked back on, obscuring most of the sounds again.

The guard shrugged and turned back to the window. After one last look at the Atlanta skyline, he turned and left the office, pulling the door closed and locking it behind him.

McKnight stood motionless, not daring to breathe. After ten seconds, he slipped the sleep bulb back in his pocket, stepped forward and placed his ear against it. As he did so, he heard footfalls outside the office. He sprang away from the door to better cover in the bathroom.

The door opened. The guard walked to the credenza and picked up the coffee cup he left there. He took a sip and stole another long look out the window. Then he left the office and locked it behind him.

McKnight waited a few seconds, then tiptoed from the bathroom to the door. He stood there listening. The elevator bell rang again, the doors opened and closed, and the lift rumbled as it started its descent back downstairs. He leaned back against the door, closed his eyes and exhaled softly.

Damn, that was close!

He got back to work. He climbed back onto the credenza and moved the tile out of the way. He extracted the C-cam and receiver from his pocket, switched them on and confirmed they were dialed to the same channel. He pointed the hair-thin fiber cable at his face and confirmed the image was getting to the receiver.

Satisfied, he placed the C-cam above the ceiling and replaced the tile he moved. After two adjustments, the C-cam was positioned to capture the unsub's face.

He stepped off the credenza and moved over to the spot where Lodge's body was found. A quick glance at the receiver screen confirmed the C-cam would capture the murder.

I need to risk a little light to make sure the fiber cable is virtually invisible.

He retrieved a bath towel from the bathroom and pushed it against the crack under the door. He examined the edges of the door, then switched on the overhead light. The C-cam fiber cable was hard to see, even when he looked for it. If he didn't already know it was there, he wouldn't have noticed it.

He switched off the light and hung the towel up in the bathroom. With a damp washcloth, he wiped down the credenza and the carpet to remove any fallen dust.

He ran through his mental checklist again.

Done. Back to the attic.

He took one last look around the office, then left and ran up the stairwell. Within seconds, he was back in his hiding place in the attic.

All I have to do now is witness a murder.

CHAPTER 22

2:47 am – Friday, July 12th, 1985 –NewT Security counter

"Well, I guess it's my turn for rounds, Ed."

"Yup, April. I believe it is. So…"

"Attic first, this time. I haven't started there first in a while." She picked up the log clipboard and noted the time on the attic check log. She stood and handed the clipboard to him. "I'll be back in an hour. I'll hit a few other floors as well, and then it'll be near the end of my shift."

"Sure, no problem."

She went into the office and returned, carrying a gym bag. "I'll change clothes before I come back. It's a long drive home and I want to be comfortable."

"I know what you mean," said Ed. "See you later."

She walked up the inactive escalator and into the Tower lobby. She walked past the reception desk and pushed the call button for the Executive elevator. The door opened as expected—there wasn't any elevator traffic since Ed's earlier tour. She entered and made playful attempts to press the Executive floor button by swinging her gym bag at it. After missing and pressing the buttons for two other floors, she laughed and used her finger instead.

****

Friday, July 12th, 1985 – 2:55 am – NewT Tower Attic

McKnight knew he was dreaming, but his body was not ready to wake. In his dream, he sat across an unfamiliar dinner table from Tyler. At least, he knew it was Tyler, but the figure before him was short, rotund, and bleached blonde. Not at all like Tyler. He laughed and ribbed McKnight about his inability to find a date. McKnight swallowed hard. *It's my fault he's changed.* He closed his eyes, hoping Tyler would be his old self again when he opened them. He heard something beeping. When he looked again, the real Tyler sat before him and the beeping came from his mouth.

He woke. The beeping sound in his ear buds was the alarm he set to be awake during the guard's rounds at 3:00 am. He turned it off, unplugged and stowed the ear buds, and took another sip of water.

A faint noise caught his attention. Was the guard coming? He looked out through a small peephole he had created between the plastic sheet and the plywood of the hideout.

Nothing yet.

He breathed easier and leaned back against the carpet roll.

I wish he'd come on and get it over with. I hate waiting.

As if on cue, the stairwell door opened and footsteps approached. The acoustics of the attic were poor, making it difficult to guess the source or direction of a sound. He peered through the peephole again. He expected the guard to make a quick circuit around the floor and leave. From his vantage point, he couldn't see much of the attic floor.

He listened, trying to use the sounds to visualize where the guard was on the floor. The footsteps stopped.

He's listening to the attic.

Again, McKnight reminded himself not to underestimate the training of these guards. He slipped into quiet breathing mode.

The footsteps started again after a moment. They moved a few steps and stopped. A click, followed by a high-pitched whine.

The water fountain.

McKnight shifted his position for a better view of the platform and the area beyond.

He heard more footsteps, but the guard didn't appear in the open stretch of floor. He craned his neck to see more floor space and almost jumped when a head and shoulders appeared at the top of the platform ladder.

Merrie!

Why didn't he consider she might be the guard who made the attic inspection?

She reached the top of the ladder and stepped onto the platform. She turned and stared down at the floor. As she stood there, he noticed she carried a small bag.

What's that for?

She stood still.

She's listening again.

Seeing her there, he admitted she was attractive, even in a frumpy, ill-fitting guard uniform.

She plopped into the rickety office chair with her back to him, dropping the bag next to it. As before, her honey-blonde hair was pulled back into a bun, but now it had slipped and strands of her hair hung loose, floating free behind her.

She reached up behind her head with both hands, pulled something from the bun, and it fell apart, her hair cascading across her shoulders and back. A shake of her head removed any trace of the bun.

She dropped the object into the sport bag and pulled out a white, long-sleeved shirt and black heels, which she dropped on top of the bag. She stood, pulled out her shirttail and unbuckled her belt. Then she stepped on the heel of one shoe with the other and slipped her foot out. She repeated the action with the other foot.

Her movement mesmerized McKnight. He should have looked away, but he couldn't take his eyes off her.

She dropped the uniform pants to the floor, stepped out, and stooped to pick them up. She folded them and set them on the chair, then leaned over the bag, searching for something.

He stared at her. She exhibited such grace and poise, just executing this little task. He liked the way her hair draped around her face and the curve of her bare legs under the blue uniform shirt.

She pulled a pair of jeans from the bag and dropped in the uniform pants. She sat in the chair again to pull the jeans on past her feet, then stood again and hopped once to pull them up to her waist. A thin black belt was threaded into the belt loops of the jeans, but not buckled.

McKnight held his breath.

Why is she changing clothes up here? Why not downstairs in a bathroom?

He felt his heart beating faster and commanded it to slow down.

I've seen this before. What's the big deal?

She unbuttoned her shirt and removed it. Facing the chair and McKnight's hideout, she reached up behind her back to unhook her bra.

McKnight closed his eyes and leaned back against the carpet roll. Everything male about him urged him to watch, but... *not like this.*

He reined in his emotions. *You're an officer and a gentleman. Act like it.*

After a few seconds, he opened his eyes. The shirt was on and she was tucking in the shirttail. When she finished, she buckled the belt and slipped on the heels.

She pushed the clothes into the bag and picked it up. She hurried over to the ladder and stopped. The bag slipped from her hand and she stood there with her hands on her hips. Her head tilted to one side.

Listening again.

He held his breath. Now he couldn't look away. The pose she struck there on the edge of the platform captivated him. She was a vision in the dim light. His eyes traced her body from the ground up. The heels, the slim line of her legs in the tight jeans, the shape of her hips, her tiny waist, her erect back in the white tailored shirt, and the golden hair tumbling off her shoulders onto her back.

To McKnight, every photon of light in the attic was pulled into play to illuminate this vision.

Then, she moved. She turned her gaze upward and lifted her eyes toward the ceiling. She raised her arms, palms turned upwards.

He wanted to call out to her, inexplicably desiring to respond to this phenomenon. With effort, he resisted the impulse.

He sensed something else, too. An energy release. And it radiated from her. The room seemed lighter somehow.

She dropped her arms, then suddenly thrust them up hard, as if trying to blow the roof off the building. She held that position, straining and trembling, for a few moments, then relaxed, dropping her hands by her side and resting her chin on her chest.

Then she picked up the bag, purposefully stepped over to the ladder and slid down it. She ran across the floor and around the corner. McKnight heard the stairwell door open and close. She was gone.

What the hell was that?

He replayed the scene in his mind. Could it be the recent travel activity in this room had an effect on the environment? Or maybe heightened my sensitivity to emotions? Or the power of her emotions? Both?

There was no doubt energy was released–he experienced it. But what was it? He made a mental note to add the incident to his report when he completed the mission. Every unusual event had to be reported.

He reminded himself he would need sleep to function well later today, so he closed his eyes and tried to empty his mind for sleep.

But sleep wouldn't come.

The vision of Merrie in his mind refused to go away.

CHAPTER 23

7:30 pm – Thursday, July 12th, 2035 –NewT Security Office

The HERO Team, George and Matthews sat around the table in the NewT Security conference room.

"Okay," Drake said. "We're coming up on the event time in 1985. Soon Captain McKnight will make his way to his observation point and wait for the unsub to go by if - and it *is* a big if - we've guessed right about what happened. What time is he going down?"

"At 2115, sir," Wu said.

"Is that cutting it a little close? The event will occur around 2200. Is there not a risk he'll run into the unsub on the elevator?"

"Oh, no, sir," spoke up George, looking tentatively at Wu. She nodded and he continued. "We worked it out with Captain McKnight before he traveled. There are two reasons. First, the more time he spends in the open, the more chance of him having contact or being seen. Second, there's an attic check at 2100. We agreed it made more sense for him to lie low until after that check."

"And there's little chance he'll run into the unsub, sir," Wu added, "because he plans to take the stairs to the bridge floor. Very little chance of encountering the unsub or a guard. According to Mr. Matthews, they would use the elevators."

"The stairs? That's forty-five floors, right?" Drake asked, scanning the faces before him.

"Yes, sir," Wu said. "The captain's in tip-top shape and should be fine. The only real issue is he'll be sore tomorrow, but he'll mitigate that by stretching first. Shouldn't be a problem."

Drake considered that. "Okay. Now, what can we do to support if something goes wrong?"

"I've thought of that," Wu said. "When we recalled the Captain earlier, I had to communicate with Lieutenant Wheeler first. Why don't we move our command center to the attic so we can react more quickly? If there's a problem, we're in the same room."

Drake looked around the room. "Anyone see any reason not to?" No one spoke. "Okay, let's do it."

"May I suggest we take the newspaper clipping with us?" George added, pointing to the framed story on the wall. "It changed when the Lieutenant did a little while ago—maybe it will give us a heads-up or something, if something else changes?"

"Good idea," Wu said. She lifted the frame off its hook and slipped it under her arm. "Let's go."

****

Friday, July 12th, 1985 - 8:46 pm – NewT Attic

McKnight sat in his hideout in the attic. He managed a little sleep, but mostly remained in a semi-meditative state so he would know if anyone came into the attic.

Overnight, there were three attic inspections by security. Every hour, he crept out of the hideout and stretched his muscles. Twice, he hammered out fifty pushups to keep the blood going, reduce his boredom and stay sharp.

He waited for the guard's attic tour at 2100. They knew how the unsub entered the building and that he must pass by the meditation room, but it was still an assumption. It was possible the unsub was already in the building, which would change the whole game.

What if he's already upstairs?

What if they were wrong and the perpetrator was an employee? A new thought hit him.

It could be Merrie. Why not?

He shook his head in denial and chided himself. He was dwelling on possibilities when he should be resting.

It is what it is. Wait for the facts.

He ended that line of logic and started a new one.

About ten minutes now. The guard will make his or her round. I'll wait six minutes after that and hit the stairs.

In the meantime, he cleared his mind, but not without one final thought. An emotional, hopeful thought.

It can't be Merrie.

****

Friday, July 12<u>th</u>, 1985 – 8:56 pm – NewT Security counter

"Ed, I'll take my break now. Anything I need to address first?"

"Nope, April. You're good to go. Bob's coming by to relieve me and I'll make my rounds, including the attic check."

"Shouldn't he be here already?"

"Yeah, but I'm sure he'll be along anytime. Go take your break."

"Okay," she said. "You sure? I don't want to leave you unsupported."

"Get out of here," he said, with a casual wave of his hand. "I might be able to manage."

"Okay, okay," she said. "I'll be back." She turned and walked into the support building elevator and pressed a button.

Merrie rode the elevator to the bridge floor. Usually, she took her break on the thirty-seventh floor break room, drinking a Coke and looking out the window at the night lights. But tonight, she wasn't thirsty and didn't care about the view.

She crossed the bridge and stopped to look at the outside world. The Plexiglas walls and ceiling of the bridge offered a view of Peachtree Street and the Fox Theatre on one side and West Peachtree Street and Georgia Tech on the other.

As she stared into the night, her thoughts returned to the young man she met the previous night.

What was his name? Something unusual. Clarkie? No, Churchie.

She recalled his face. He was cute.

If he calls, maybe I'll meet him for a drink or something. She frowned then. *He probably won't though. He had a few drinks last night. Ha! He probably lost my number on the way home.*

She inhaled deeply and let it out with a sigh.

Another one will come along.

Merrie tapped the window with her forefinger to punctuate that thought and her own reflection in the window caught her eye.

Damn.

Try as she might, she had trouble keeping her hair up in a bun. She took a moment to rewind and pin it, turning her head from side to side to inspect her handiwork. Finally, she nodded at her reflection and continued across the bridge.

When she reached the tower side she stopped and stood for a minute with her hands on her hips. She sometimes found night shift workers on break or asleep in the lounge chairs there, but tonight it was deserted and dead quiet.

To her left was the meditation room. She always felt drawn to it, and tonight she succumbed. She stepped inside and sat in the front pew.

Like many Southerners, she grew up in the Baptist faith. She believed in prayer and miracles. As she did so many times before, Merrie bowed her head and prayed.

At first, she prayed for the things she always prayed for—forgiveness, wisdom and strength.

Tonight, a new emotion flooded her mind with an urgency she had never experienced before. She prayed for the man God intended for her. And she prayed that she not waste her life, but instead have the wisdom to recognize and follow the path He had laid out for her.

Now, overcome by this emotion she didn't fully understand, she reclined on the pew to think. She laid on her back, stared at the ceiling and thought of the man God intended for her.

I wonder what he's doing right now?

****

Friday, July 12th, 1985 – 9:05 pm - – NewT Attic

For the fifth time in the last ten minutes, McKnight checked the time. The guard was late for the attic check at 2100. He couldn't wait any longer, so he grabbed his bag and slipped the strap over his head. He crept out of the hideout and, with a glance at the rickety old chair, hurried across the platform, down the ladder and to the north stairwell.

Descending forty plus stories was certain to tax his leg muscles, so he stretched against the wall. When he finished, he pressed his ear to the door. Satisfied there were no sounds of entry from the other side, he opened it.

Almost simultaneously, he heard the stairwell door on the opposite side of the floor open, followed by the sound of footsteps. He slipped through the door, smiling.

Figures. Well, at least I know where the guard is.

He closed the door behind him and began the long descent to the Bridge Floor. He reached it in fifteen minutes and picked the lock in less than thirty seconds.

The stairwell door was across the hall from the freight elevator. This was the tricky part because it crossed the path they expected the unsub to take. There was no sound, so McKnight didn't hesitate. He entered the hallway, looked both ways and dashed across the common area to the meditation room. He pushed the door open and stepped inside.

The room was unchanged. It looked the same as it would in fifty years—still six pews in three rows lit by two electric candles.

He slipped the bag off his shoulder and laid it on the floor behind the back pews. He peeked out at the common area through one of the slots in the door.

Yep, this should give a decent view of anyone who walks by.

He looked around. The curtains were open.

If I stand by the window, I might see the unsub cross the bridge.

He moved across the back of the room to the windows, looked out, then walked to the front. As he rounded the front pew, he saw her out of the corner of his eye. She was lying on the first pew next to the far wall, her feet towards him. He tried to pretend she wasn't there, but she didn't cooperate.

At the sight of him, she sat up. With that motion, her hair fell out of the bun again and cascaded across her shoulders. In that soft light, she was beyond beautiful.

"Hi," he mumbled.

"Hi," she answered. "I wasn't asleep. I'm on break and came here to think."

"Me, too," he said. "I didn't think you were asleep."

If she leaves now, she might run into the unsub. How do I keep her here?

He sat on the pew next to the window, trying to be as non-threatening as possible.

There was a thick book laying on the pew. He picked it up and said, "Is this your book?" He turned it over. It was a copy of 'The Lord of the Rings.' He tried to speak, and nothing came out at first. "Oh, my God," he said.

"What?"

"This is my favorite book in the world. Is it yours?" As he spoke, he recalled their discussion about this book. Fifty years in the future for her, less than thirty-six hours ago for him.

"No, it was here when I came in. I tossed it over there. What is it?"

He handed it to her. "It's a classic. I've read it several times. Hey, I'm sorry if I disturbed you."

"Not at all," she said. She looked at the title page, then laid the book down. "I probably should get back to work." She straightened her blouse and pushed her golden tresses back into a bun.

He gave her his most charming smile. "Whatever suits you just tickles me plumb to death. But I was hoping you'd hang around for a minute."

She laughed as she wiped her eyes and said, "What did you say?"

"I said, I was hoping you would hang around for a while."

"No, before that... Something about 'plumb to death?'"

"Oh. I said, whatever suits you just tickles me plumb to death. It's something I heard in an old movie once."

"It's funny. I like it." She searched his face. It occurred to him she was trying to memorize his features–training was kicking in.

Distract her.

"Well, it stuck with me, " he blurted. "I'm Dimitri. What's your name?"

She paused and then smiled. "April. Nice to meet you... so why did you come in here?"

Got to come up with something that'll get her attention. Something to keep her here.

An idea struck him, and he hoped it would appeal to her feminine instincts and entice her to stay in the meditation room.

He smiled at her and made sure he had eye contact. "I came here to pray to find the girl of my dreams." He turned toward the table and the candelabra before him.

Her silence was deafening. He ventured a look at her. She looked stunned. He saw a tear run down her cheek. She brushed it away. More tears followed.

McKnight felt ashamed. His cheap flirtation had pierced her heart. Of all people, she was the last one he wanted to hurt. And now, there was nothing he wanted more than to comfort her.

"I'm sorry," he said. "I didn't mean to..." He stopped.

Are my emotions out of control?

"No, it's not you," she said. "I..."

She stood abruptly. "I've got to get back to work." She rose and walked around the pews toward the door.

McKnight stepped into the aisle between the pews and rushed to intercept her. Why was he acting like this? Was it her or a side effect of time travel?

He didn't care. The only thing that mattered was to console her.

****

Thursday, July 12th, 2035 – 9:20 pm – NewT Attic

George stood on the edge of the platform, away from the others. A pile of computer monitors and cabinets on the floor had captured his attention.

He turned back toward the team. "Hey, Mitch. Check out these…"

From his removed position, he saw what no one else did. "Kathy? Lieutenant Tyler is glowing."

All eyes returned to Tyler. He was still himself, but the aura around him was unmistakable.

Drake turned to Wheeler. "Lieutenant?"

"On it, sir," Wheeler said with a glance at Tyler. He punched the recall button. He had already programmed in McKnight's beacon signature.

****

Friday, July 12th, 1985 – 9:20 pm – NewT Meditation Room

They reached the meditation room door at the same instant. In her haste, Merrie didn't see McKnight's bag on the floor.

She tripped over it and fell forward, into his arms. He took in the scent of her hair. He lifted her back to her feet, and she buried her face into his shoulder and sobbed once. His heart broke.

After a few seconds, she turned her tear-streaked face up toward him.

"I'm so sorry," she said softly. "Could we please just stand here for a minute?" Her eyes searched his face.

"Sure," he said, his voice hoarse. He couldn't think of anything else to say. She buried her face back in his chest.

They stood there holding each other for a full minute.

"Are you okay?" he asked. Her proximity and touch filled his senses and blotted out the universe.

"No," she said. "But I think I will be. I..." She raised her face to look at him and her eyes darted across his features. She closed her eyes and spoke again. "Are you... him?"

He sensed the first tingling of static electricity. The room got brighter. He started to push her away, but reconsidered.

If he pushed too hard, she would be clear of the travel sphere, but she might be injured and certainly would see him disappear. If he pushed too gently, she might be killed by the travel sphere.

He made the safest decision he could think of. He held her close and said, "Yes, I am."

As the intensity of the light flared, she opened her eyes wide. She struggled to push him away. He lifted her off her feet and stepped away from the meditation room door, making as much space around them as possible. Her hair stung his face as the wind in the travel sphere buffeted them.

"Oh, my God!" she cried, and the light sphere bulged and they plunged into a field of stars.

****

The shadowy figure on the bridge saw a bright light blaze from a window to the right.

"Let's wait right here for a few minutes, shall we?"

CHAPTER 24

Thursday, July 12th, 2035 – 9:21 pm – NewT Attic

From the moment the travel sphere appeared, they knew there was trouble. It contained two figures, not one. George glanced at Tyler. The tall dark version of him was back, and the dimples had disappeared.

We got problems, all right.

Drake's face looked like stone and Wu looked worried. He looked back at the spinning light globe. The second figure was a woman, and she was struggling against McKnight. When the light winked out, the two fell to the floor.

McKnight threw out a hand to break their fall, holding her close to prevent injury. He loosened his grip, and she tried to twist away from him. He pulled out a sleep bulb and squeezed it in her face. Her eyes registered surprise, then rolled back. He gently lifted her limp body and carried her off the plate.

George turned to the table and picked up the framed newspaper clipping. As he expected, the clipping glowed. His eyes flew across the page, then he handed it to Wu. He rubbed his eyes with the heels of his hands. Wu looked up from the paper and their eyes met. "Oh, crap," she said.

"Captain, I need a report," Drake said.

"Yes sir. I had no choice."

"Why did you bring her back to the present with you?"

"For her safety, sir. When the recall began, I had the choice to push her away from me or bring her. Bringing her looked safer than pushing her away."

"I don't understand," George said. "What do you mean? Was she in danger from the unsub?"

"No," McKnight said. "From the travel sphere. She was too close. I started to push her away, but I was afraid she wouldn't get clear of the travel sphere. In my judgment, I had no other option. Besides, she isn't likely to remember any of this."

"How come?"

Wu spoke. "Because, by design, the sleep bulb causes a small amount of memory loss. She won't remember the last five minutes. If she does, it'll seem like a dream. She should be out for thirty minutes."

"Correct," McKnight said. "Which should be enough time to return her to the past and into one of the lounge chairs. Isn't that where the report said they found her?"

"Yes, I like that idea," Wu said. "But we need to do a review before we lose this timeline." She clicked on her hand recorder.

"Understood," McKnight said. "But why did you recall me? She already met Tyler's grandfather. I couldn't have interfered with that."

Without turning or looking, Wu pointed at Tyler. "We don't know," she said. "But when Lieutenant Tyler started glowing again, we knew something was wrong."

McKnight looked at his friend, who was again the dark-complexioned person he had become before.

Tyler looked confused. "What?" he said.

McKnight shrugged. "I'm clueless. Here's what happened. I went to the meditation room as planned. I walked in and there she was. I had no idea she would be there and in such an emotional state."

"A what?" Wu said.

"She was upset. At least, she was towards the end of the encounter. Now that I think about it, she seemed very… what's the word? Fragile, maybe? Preoccupied? Not like our first meeting. She was confident and assertive then. This time, she appeared vulnerable and distracted. I'm not sure what happened in the meantime, but she was in a different emotional state."

"Were you the cause of that?" Wu asked. "Wait. Hold that thought. Let's do the review before too much time passes."

McKnight nodded. They sat on the plywood floor as before and Wu reported what she saw. When she finished, she nodded to him and he related the details and filled in the blanks.

When he completed the story, he nodded at Wu and she projected the notes up on the wall.

"A pretty pickle," she muttered under her breath. "Okay, it's obvious to me. She was attracted to you and never hooked up with Tyler's grandfather. Let's call him Tyler One."

"My grandfather's name is Churchie," Tyler said.

"Okay. Churchie, then. Let's surmise she got interested in you and, even after you disappeared, she hoped you'd show up again. She couldn't know you wouldn't be back. So she blew Churchie off when he called because she wasn't interested."

Drake spoke. "That makes sense. If we can get her back to a point before she connected with Captain McKnight, history might revert to its original course. If she doesn't remember the last five minutes, she may only remember meeting him in the meditation room."

"It's worse than that—we have another problem," George said.

"It is," McKnight said. "I left my bag there. I need to get back pronto to secure it."

"Okay, that, too." George said, "but that's not what I meant."

"Oh, yes," Wu said. "There's more."

All eyes turned toward him. He sat on the floor, the framed newspaper clipping in his lap. He looked up at them. "According to this newspaper clipping, Lodge wasn't murdered."

CHAPTER 25

"What does it say?" McKnight asked.

"Tell them," Wu said.

George held up the framed clipping. "It says here, and I quote: 'At some point over the weekend, an unknown person broke into the executive offices of the NewT Communications Corporation and vandalized one office. Several plaques and pictures were destroyed and books were torn off the shelves. The police have the details, but no additional information has been released, pending the investigation.' Unquote. Looks like we have more problems to fix."

"No mention of a murder," McKnight said. "Anything about Lodge?"

"No, but he's not dead. He was the spokesman who released the information." George held up the article for them. "See, there's a picture of him talking to reporters."

"Interesting," Wu said. "So, instead of being killed, an office—maybe his—was vandalized. Puts everything in a new light, doesn't it? Sounds like industrial espionage gone wrong. Or a jealous lover."

"Yeah, so what happened differently?" George asked. "My guess is the unsub was delayed and arrived after Lodge left the office. Missed him by minutes or even seconds."

"Well," Wu said, "let's try to put things back like they were. So, what do we need to fix? I see two things. Number one is Lieutenant Tyler. Number two is the murder must happen. Something Captain McKnight must have screwed up the timing. It either delayed or sped up the unsub."

"Wait," George said. "Let me propose something else. It's obvious the Captain's actions affected Lieutenant Tyler, no argument there.

But our recall might have caused the unsub to deviate from the original course."

"What do you mean?" Wu asked.

George turned to McKnight. "Captain, were there any blinds or curtains in the meditation room? If so, were they open or closed?"

McKnight closed his eyes for a moment, then opened them.

"There were heavy curtains, and they were open. Before I ran into Merrie, I intended to stand by the window and see the unsub come across the bridge."

George turned back to Wu. "I think," he said, then paused. "Let me gather my thoughts." He closed his eyes for a few seconds.

McKnight tried to visualize the relative locations of the meditation room, the bridge, the hallway and the angles.

"Yes, it makes sense." George began again. "What if the unsub was on the other side of the bridge when we recalled Captain McKnight? There would have been this bright light in the meditation room that would shine through the window. Anyone across the bridge would notice it. If you're the unsub and you don't want to be seen, you'd be put off by a bright light you didn't expect. Lights mean people, and people are witnesses. Perhaps it wasn't something the Captain did at all."

Matthews spoke. "You may have something there, Detective. I've been on the bridge at night and noticed a light in the meditation room. Very plausible."

"There's another good theory," Wu said.

"I know where you're going," George said. "The Captain kept Ms. McAllister from being in that timeline. It's still possible she's the unsub."

Everyone looked at the sleeping figure on the floor.

Drake spoke. "Captain, you've talked to this woman twice. You have the most experience with her. What do you think?"

"Sir, I don't think she's capable of it. When I met her—and it was only a few minutes ago for me—she was in an emotional state, but not murderous. Besides," he continued. "If she was the unsub, who trashed the office upstairs? No, it's not her. I'd bet my life on it."

"Oh, I'd say more than your life depends on it," Drake said. "Still, you make a good point about the office damage. Okay, so what's our plan of action? Doctor Wu?"

"Okay, remove the light from the recall to fix Lieutenant Tyler and return Ms. McAllister to her time, right?" She looked around the room for any dissent and, finding none, continued.

"We can't be sure what to do to fix Lieutenant Tyler, but we can send Captain McKnight back with the sleeping Ms. McAllister. Have him place her in the lounge chair where she was found. We know that was tried because he saw himself and Ms. McAllister outside the meditation room. Right, Captain?"

"Yes, ma'am."

"Uh-oh," she said. "Their travel back generates another problem, though. They'll create the same bright light when they go back."

"I didn't notice a light," McKnight said, "but I was inside the meditation room with the door closed. But shouldn't I have seen something?"

"No," Wu said. "You were in the middle of a time jump, remember? I doubt you'd have noticed any light from outside the time sphere."

"I agree," Matthews said. "There's a conference room next to the meditation room. The door has no window. The conference room doors are weighted to swing shut. I'll bet the captain and the lady can jump into the conference room without being seen. It's 9:00 pm on a Friday night. There's zero chance anyone is in that room."

"So, they go back into the conference room instead of the meditation room?" Wu asked.

"Yes."

"That's consistent with what you saw. Right, Captain?"

"Yes, ma'am."

"Okay. Lieutenant Wheeler, can you travel them to that new location?"

"N-P, Doctor. I need a distance, a vector and a time. How far and which direction from the earlier point, and what date and time."

"The time is the same as the recall time." Wu said, and Wheeler typed in the data on the Engine keyboard. "What's the power requirement, Lieutenant?"

"About standard plus three percent, Doctor," Wheeler said. "Well within range."

"Great," Wu said. "Mr. Matthews, can you get a precise distance from the recall point to an open place in the conference room? As near to the meditation room as possible to reduce the margin of error? We need the vector, too."

"I'm sure I can. They kept the area next to the door clear to allow access for refreshment carts. No problem with the measurement. But the vector is another story. I don't know what that is."

"Not a problem, sir," Wheeler said. "Here, catch." He tossed a small device to the security chief. "Stand where the Captain stood in the meditation room and point it parallel to the wall towards the conference room. Press the red button and it will calculate the vector. Piece of cake."

"Sure thing," Matthews said. "Captain, where were you were standing when Lieutenant Wheeler recalled you?"

"I was in the meditation room, directly in front of the door, and five feet away. That should get you close enough."

"I'm on it." The security chief slid down the ladder and ran to the freight elevator.

Wu glanced at the sleeping woman on the platform.

"Captain, you should dose Ms. McAllister again. She'll wake up soon and we don't want that."

"Agreed," McKnight said. He stooped over her and gently lifted a lock of blonde hair away from her face. She stirred.

"Sorry, kiddo," he said under his breath.

He took a breath and held it as he squeezed a bulb in her face.

"Hold on a second," George said. "I'm confused. General Drake, didn't you tell the Senator it took a long time to reset the Engine to accommodate multiple travelers? Don't we have to do that?"

Wu grinned from ear to ear.

Drake smiled. "I lied."

CHAPTER 26

George laughed and Drake fought off a smile.

Drake waved his hand at the group and spoke. "No way I would allow a mercenary to go on a mission without a thorough background check and psychological screening. Especially someone I don't know. By the way, the mission is still classified. No one is to discuss the issues we've experienced or our solutions, is that understood by everyone?"

"Yes, sir," the military team said in unison.

"Agreed, sir," George answered.

"I'm in," Wu said.

"Very well. Doctor Wu, please cover Chief Matthews on this when he returns."

"My pleasure, sir. Okay, next problem. How do we fix the recall light problem?"

"There's only one way I know of," Drake said.

"Yes," Wu said. "Someone has to go back and close the curtains. That's an easy decision. The question is, who goes and to what time do they go back?"

"Right," Drake said. "Go back way before the event, and you risk someone opening the curtains afterward. Go closer to the event and you might run into Ms. McAllister in the meditation room. So what's the time frame?"

"I can do it," McKnight said. "She said she was on her break, right? I could go back to Recall minus thirty and we should be golden."

"No, I don't think it should be you," Wu said. "If we're mistaken and you run into her again, it's liable to make things worse. We don't need to risk complicating the timelines again. No, it needs to be someone else."

"How about me?" Tyler said. "I can go, no problem."

"Thanks, Lieutenant, but no," Wu said. She waved her hand at him when he looked offended. "You're not yourself because we moved off the original timeline. If something else happens, there's a real chance we'll never be able to fix it. Sorry, but until you're changed back, you're on the sidelines." She looked at Drake, who nodded agreement. "If we can get you changed back, the next travel is yours."

Tyler didn't look happy, but he nodded.

"What about Mr. Matthews? Or me?" George said. "He knows the place like the back of his hand and should be able to present a credible story to anyone who asks a question. And I have been studying this place for the last few years."

"Thanks, but no," Drake said. "No training means no time travel. Besides that, the President's order for this mission reeks of Senator Lodge's self-interest. There are members of Congress who are against time travel and they'd love any excuse to question our judgment and beat up the Senator. If I allowed a civilian to travel and the mission went south, they'd skin us alive. No, it must be a member of the team. So our options are Doctor Wu, Lieutenant Wheeler, and myself. I'm inclined to do it myself."

Wu shook her head. "No, sir. It has to be me. Someone has to be here in command and with authority to handle outside contingency. That's you, sir. Given the choice between me and Lieutenant Wheeler running the Engine, well, you know I can do it and so could the Captain or Lieutenant Tyler. But nobody knows the Engine better than Wheeler. If I were him, I'd be more nervous with me running it for him than with him running it for me, if that makes sense. I'm the best choice. Do you agree, Lieutenant?"

Wheeler looked at Wu and back to the engine console.

"You go," he said quietly.

"Damn," she said. "I was hoping you'd tell me there was a flaw in my logic. Okay. So I'll jump to the conference room, agreed?"

"That's the best option," Drake said. "Little chance of running into anyone. Get in and out. No muss, no fuss. Anyone see a problem with that logic?"

No one spoke.

"Okay. Lieutenant Wheeler?" Drake said. "Let's send Doctor Wu back as the Captain suggested, maybe forty-five minutes earlier, but let's return her to the exact time she left. That'll give us immediate feedback and a good sign it worked."

"Yes, sir. No problem. All I need now is Mr. Matthews' data to calculate the landing place."

"Speak of the devil," George said, as Matthews came in from the freight elevator. He bounded up the ladder and ran to Wheeler with the device in hand. Wheeler keyed in the data, plugged a token into the synchronizer, and turned to Drake.

"Who goes first, sir?"

"Doctor Wu. I want that problem addressed first." He turned to Wu and his expression softened. "Are you ready, Doctor?"

"As I'll ever be. Lieutenant, got my token programmed yet?"

"One second." He referenced her profile and imported the target location and time. "Yes, ma'am, I do," Wheeler said.

He punched the release button and handed the token to her. She grinned and curtsied to him. Then she hung it around her neck and stepped onto the travel plate.

She struck a pose with her hands on her hips and her chest thrust out. She spoke in a loud voice with a heavy accent. "I'll be back!" With a grin, she said, "I always wanted an excuse to say that!"

With a flourish, she pulled out the rubber band that held her hair in its ponytail. "If I have to do this, I want the full experience." She shook her head and all suggestion of the ponytail disappeared.

"Wait a second," George said. "I have an idea. Paper! I need paper."

"Oh, I get it," Wu said, as she stepped off the plate. She pulled a paper pad from her briefcase, tore off a sheet, and handed it to George. He scribbled on it and held it up. Written on the paper was the text 'Please leave curtains closed'.

"Brilliant," Wu said, taking it from him.

"You need a safety pin or something to attach it to the curtains," George said.

Wu looked around. All eyes were on her.

"Oh, yeah!" she said. "Everybody looks at the woman when they need a safety pin. How sexist is that?"

She glared at them for a moment, and no one dared make eye contact with her.

Matthews walked toward the ladder.

"Wait," she said, giggling into her hand. "I can't get too upset with you guys when I do have a safety pin and I'm sure none of you do." She pulled a pin out of her bag and stuck it in her pants pocket along with the note and stepped onto the travel plate again.

"Be careful, Kathy," George said.

"I will. Thanks."

Wheeler ran through the checklist assisted by McKnight, got the nod from Wu and Drake, and pulled the trigger.

The low hum started and glided up in pitch. Static electricity crackled and the surrounding air glowed. Wu's raven hair shone and floated around her head. The light globe formed and intensified. The winds of time travel blew her hair furiously about her face.

There was a loud crack, a flash of intense light, the globe bulged and faded. Wu fell forward as the light winked out.

"Dammit! I forgot about the falling part." She rose and turned to Drake. "It's done."

She turned to McKnight. "Captain, now you have one more thing to do later. Retrieve that paper and pin and open the curtains before you travel back to the present."

"Yes, ma'am. Will do," McKnight said. "Damn. Is there anything you can't do?"

"Nothing so far," she said, and winked at George.

"Anyone around?" asked Drake.

"Not a soul, sir," Wu said. "Oh, I need to give my report!"

She assumed an exaggerated posture of attention and saluted the room. With a grin on her face, she came to parade rest. "I landed in the conference room as planned. I peeked out and saw no one. I left the room and entered the meditation room. The curtains were open as expected. I closed them and pinned the note to them." She glanced at George. "That was a stroke of genius, Trevor." She tapped the side of her temple as she spoke his name.

She resumed the parade rest posture. "Then, I retreated to the meditation room door and squeezed the beacon. Piece of cake, sir." She snapped back to attention posture and executed another salute.

Drake laughed despite himself. "Superb, Doctor Wu. Thank you," he said.

She grinned and stepped behind the Engine console to stand with Wheeler.

Wheeler leaned toward her. "Only you could pull that off," he whispered. "Nobody can drain off tension like you can."

Wu nodded, the smile still on her face. "It takes practice."

Drake turned to McKnight. "Ready?"

"Yes, sir," he said. He took off his token and handed it to Wheeler for synchronization. He knelt, gathered Merrie in his arms, carried her to the travel plate and set her on it. Anticipating the fall backwards, he knelt beside her and lifted her torso so he could cradle her head and shoulders against his arm and chest. Wu stepped up to reposition the unconscious woman's legs underneath her to ensure all of her was within five feet of the token.

Wheeler stepped over with the token. McKnight slipped it around his neck with his free hand and then nodded to Wheeler. "I'm ready. Let's do it."

"Yes, sir," Wheeler said. He looked at Wu. "Will you help me with the checklist again, Doctor?"

"Sure," Wu said. They walked to the Engine console and she picked up the clipboard and pen.

"The traveler has the return beacon in his possession," Wheeler said.

"Check." Wu said, marking her checklist.

He picked up the trigger and plugged the cable into the Engine console. "Trigger connected."

"Check."

"Trigger safety off."

"Check."

"All set, sir," he said to McKnight. "Captain, I'm ready when you are."

McKnight looked at Merrie's face. She was still unconscious. Then he looked toward Wheeler. He nodded and pulled her closer for stability.

"Traveler acknowledges ready," Wheeler said.

"Remember, Captain," Drake said. "If Mr. Tyler doesn't change back to himself right away, we'll be bringing you back and looking for Plan B."

"Understood, sir. Thanks."

Wheeler looked at Drake, who nodded his silent approval.

"Roger," announced Wheeler. He turned toward Wu at the Engine console and said, "Target time is Friday, July 12th, 1985 at 2120.25 hours. This is fifteen, one-five, seconds before last recall."

"Check." responded Wu, her eyes scanning the console. "Green across the board. All systems go!" She checked the item.

"Copy that. We are GO for travel," answered Wheeler. "Good luck, Captain!"

"God speed," George said.

McKnight nodded without looking.

"Initiating Jump in Five... Four... Three... Two... One... Mark!"

He pulled the trigger. The Engine hum got louder and rose in frequency.

A globe of glowing air swirled around McKnight and the woman. The bright light and time wind turned Merrie's hair into shimmering waves of gold around their faces. The frequency of the Engine hum rose in pitch faster and faster.

Then came the loud crack, the outward surge of the light sphere, and they were gone.

CHAPTER 27

All eyes turned to Tyler. They watched him for a moment, but nothing changed. After twenty seconds, Drake turned toward Wheeler and spoke, "Okay, prepare to bring them back. It was a good idea, but–"

"Wait!" George exclaimed. "I see a glow."

Drake turned back to Tyler. At first, he couldn't discern it. But then the glow was unmistakable and Tyler's face was changing.

"Scratch that order, Lieutenant. Looks like it worked. Mr. Tyler, are you all right?"

"Yes, sir, I'm fine. Why do you ask?"

Drake addressed the others. "We have a good start at least." To Tyler, he said. "Any dizziness or confusion?"

"No, sir. I'm five by five."

"Good. Now, we wait again. It's nearly time for the event. Let's hope we don't have any more complications."

"Amen," George said. "Kathy, tell me about your Jump. I want to hear everything. Or, at least, what you can tell me."

****

Friday, July 12th, 1985 – 9:21 pm – NewT Conference Room

McKnight laid Merrie on the floor and stood to inspect the room.

It was a typical conference room. The entire west wall was glass and faced west, overlooking the Atlanta downtown connector and the Georgia Tech campus. A residual glow from the summer sun illuminated the horizon. The conference tables were pushed together to make one massive table near the windows.

McKnight opened the door a crack and peeked out. *Not a soul in sight.*

He stepped back to Merrie and lifted her gently as though he were a groom carrying his bride across the threshold.

He pushed the door open with his foot and hurried to the closest pit group. He glanced at the meditation room door in time to see a flash of light.

So far, so good.

He laid Merrie in an oversized lounge chair, brushed a golden lock from her face and smiled at her sleeping form. He stood to walk away, then leaned over and lightly kissed her lips. "Too bad I wasn't born fifty years earlier, Merrie," he whispered. "Sorry for all the trouble."

As he stood again, his peripheral vision picked up a shadow.

Someone is crossing the bridge.

He considered the meditation room, but it wasn't close enough. He ducked into a crouch behind the huge chair. The sound of footsteps came from the bridge. They slowed, then drew nearer.

McKnight didn't dare move. He held his breath and listened. He heard shallow breathing.

Then the footsteps started again and moved away from him. He heard the freight elevator doors open and close.

Damn! I missed my chance to observe the unsub. What else can I screw up tonight?

Something was unusual about the footsteps. Something itched in his subconscious mind.

What am I missing here?

He peeked around the chair. Nothing moved in the room.

Voices!

There were people talking on the other side of the bridge. He dashed to the meditation room and stepped inside. To complete the illusion, he scooped up his bag, sat in the front pew, and pretended to pray. He willed himself to relax and counted to one hundred.

The voices were faint, but it was clear they had reached the common area. He risked a look.

Two women and a man, all wearing coveralls, stood outside the door.

Probably the late shift from the data center on break.

They were arguing. And the subject was Merrie.

"Well, I don't know about you, but I'm not above waking her up. She's not supposed to be sleeping here or anywhere else." She leaned over and shook Merrie's shoulder. When she didn't respond, she shook her shoulder again, harder.

"Y'all, I think she's unconscious."

The man spoke. "Well, of course she's unconscious, you idiot. She's asleep."

"Shut up, Hank, you dumbass! No, I mean like drugged out or sick."

"What?" the other woman said. They gathered around the sleeping woman. The second woman grasped Merrie's lower jaw and turned her head back and forth. Then she placed her hand on Merrie's forehead and used her thumb to pull back her eyelid.

"Oh, sweet Jesus," she said. "This child is completely out of it. Hank, run down to the security counter and let Ed know one of his folks is up here and unconscious. Do it now!"

Hank hurried off across the bridge.

The speaker continued, "Shouldn't be this hard to wake up someone who's sleeping."

The first woman spoke again. "Charlotte, she's either drunk, or drugged, or both–"

Charlotte spoke again. "Shut up, Vonelle! You think everybody acts like you. Now go to the bathroom and get some paper towels. Wet 'em down, wring them out, and we'll make a rag out of it."

"Charlotte, she'll probably be okay. We should leave her there like she is."

"We will not!" shouted Charlotte. "You get your ass down the hall like I told you. Get me them towels!"

Vonelle walked toward the central hall where the bathrooms lay—slowly, but not daring to refuse. Soon, she returned with the towels and Charlotte applied them to Merrie's forehead.

And so it was that Ed found her when he came upstairs with Hank. "Oh Lord, child! Did anybody see what happened to her?"

"We think she got drunk or did some drugs," Vonelle said.

"Oh, shut up!" retorted Charlotte. "Don't go making up stuff when you don't know. Ed, we just found her like this. We don't know what happened to her."

Ed looked at Vonelle. "Girl, you don't know what you're talking about. She was downstairs talking to me thirty minutes ago. Something's wrong."

Ed stood and his eyes darted around the room. McKnight recoiled from the door. Now, here was a threat. The security people he had seen so far were well trained.

If Ed came into the meditation room, he would question McKnight. The last thing he wanted to do was sedate another security guard.

I might not have a choice.

He pulled a sleep bulb from his pocket.

Merrie moaned and stirred. Ed knelt by her, picked her up and carried her back across the bridge, followed by Charlotte and Vonelle. Hank shrugged his shoulders and stretched out in one of the lounge chairs. He was asleep and snoring in two minutes.

McKnight stood at the door for a full three minutes, watching the sleeping man.

I doubt I'll wake him if I'm quiet. He's making more noise than a train.

He walked to the curtains and slipped the pin and note into his bag so he wouldn't forget them.

Wait a minute! I can view the video feed from here. I missed my chance to see the unsub come by, but I can still see the event live.

He pulled the receiver and ear buds from his bag. But before he could switch on the device, he heard voices again. Charlotte and Vonelle were returning.

He stuffed the receiver and ear buds back in his bag. Until the workers left, he couldn't watch the video feed without the display light attracting attention. And he couldn't leave the meditation room without being seen.

Think!

He checked the time again.

The murder could be happening right now. I might have missed it already.

Out of options, McKnight resigned himself to wait until the workers left.

It was the second shift and Friday night. The workers didn't hurry back to work. It was thirty minutes before they woke their co-worker and trudged back across the bridge to the elevators. As soon as they cleared the room and started across the bridge, McKnight dashed out of the meditation room and silently ran down the west hall to the elevators. The time was 2155.

CHAPTER 28

9:55 pm – Friday, July 12th, 1985 – Bridge Floor

The Bridge Floor of NewT Center was a conference room floor. The rooms on the east, south and west sides of the building were conference rooms, with a perimeter hallway around the central core for access to the rooms. McKnight trotted along the west side of the perimeter hall, desperate to find a secure place to view the C-cam's output. Once out of earshot of the common area, he twisted doorknobs, hoping to find an unlocked, empty room.

After a few failures, he decided to pick a door lock. He stopped and considered the options. he stood at a corner of the building, where the west and south halls intersected.

Good visibility.

He looked down both hallways, then knelt by a door on the west hall. As he examined the lock, he heard a light footfall behind him, so he looked down and began tying his shoe.

McKnight took his time with the laces, setting them just right and hoping the footsteps would continue down the hall. They didn't.

A melodious voice came from behind him. "Well, hi there."

McKnight rose and turned. Before him stood a petite female security guard with short blonde hair. She wore a brilliant smile. He smiled back.

"Can I help you find something? Are you lost?" she asked.

"No, I... I am Dimitri. I am on construction team."

"Um-hmm. Shouldn't you be somewhere else, constructing something?"

"No. Umm... yes. But I was looking for the toilet."

"Of course. And here I thought you might be trying to get into a locked conference room. What's wrong with the toilet in the attic?"

McKnight was certain she didn't believe him. There wasn't a toilet in the attic and he was sure she knew it. She took a step closer to him and placed her hands on her hips.

McKnight tried to look surprised. "I did not know there was a toilet in the attic," he said. "I came here instead of going to the basement. It was wrong but I was in need. I'll go to the basement."

The woman smiled, her mouth twisting in amusement.

She's not buying it.

"I see," she said. He turned to leave, but she held up her hand and said, "Not yet."

McKnight shrugged and stuck his hands in his pockets. The tip of his fingers touched the sleep bulb in his right pocket. He assessed his chances for subduing her. It wouldn't be hard. She was much smaller than he. He didn't want to, but he might not have a choice. She acted too suspicious to let him slip away.

She glanced at his hands in his pockets, then back to his eyes.

Did her smile just get bigger?

"I don't think I've seen you here before," she said. "Have you been with the company long?"

"No," McKnight said. "Only a short time. I began work here a month ago. I was in the attic, cutting studs for next week's construction. This is new work for me, but I am getting better every day. I have been in the United States only two months now."

"Your English is good for coming here so recently."

"Yes, ma'am. I learned before I came here. I work hard to learn."

"So I see." She smiled, turned and walked to the bend in the hallway. She turned back toward McKnight and smiled. "You'd better get back to work."

"Yes, ma'am, I will."

"Good. Oh, and... Dimitri, is it?"

"Yes, ma'am?"

She grinned at him. "You don't look like a Dimitri to me. You look more like a Marc." She turned and disappeared around the corner.

McKnight stood there for a full five seconds, stunned.

What the hell?

He sprang after her and, as he rounded the corner, saw her disappear around the next corner. He dashed to it and peeped around it. She was gone.

He pressed his back against the wall and closed his eyes.

What just happened? Am I hallucinating?

It made no sense. How could she know who he was? He peeped around the corner again. Still nothing. Could prolonged visits to another time have mental and emotional effects on you? Paranoia? Hallucinations? His heart and mind were racing.

Calm down! Think!

He closed his eyes again and focused on slowing his breathing and his heart rate.

He remembered his bag. He left it in his haste to follow the woman. He ran back to the west hall and turned the corner. It remained where he left it.

Better look around before going any further.

He picked up his bag and tiptoed to the edge of the elevator lobby to see if anyone else was nearby.

Nothing. So far, so good.

He crossed the elevator lobby and ventured down another hallway. At the end of the hall, he peeked around the corner and saw a male security guard checking conference room doors.

Damn! It's Grand Central Station here.

He backed up a few steps and realized he was next to the stairwell door.

Good grief! I have fifty floors to choose from. Let's get off this one!

He opened the door and raced up the stairs.

McKnight passed five floors before he let himself consider stopping. The guard might walk up a flight or two for his next set of rounds, but not five floors. So he chose the next one.

Kneeling before the door, he pulled out his lock kit and defeated the lock. Once on the floor, he was relieved to find it dark except for the night lighting. It was a standard layout, with an inner hallway that surrounded the central core which in turn was surrounded by a sea of cubicles. Ringing the cubicles was a perimeter hallway, which gave access to the window cubicles, offices and conference rooms.

He listened for a moment, then searched the inner and perimeter hallways, ensuring there was no one working on the floor. Satisfied, he looked for the best place to set up and view the C-cam output. He chose a conference room far from the elevators, but not out of earshot.

After propping the door open, he sat at the conference table, facing the door. He inserted one of the ear buds in his left ear and switched on the monitor. It glowed a dull green as he checked the time again.

Damn! It's 2205.

He looked back. The monitor showed a view of Lodge's office.

Whatever had happened was over. Lodge lay on the floor, partially obscured by the desk. There was no movement on the screen. He cursed under his breath as he pushed the download button on the monitor to capture the contents of the C-cam's buffer.

Let's don't risk losing the video.

He saved the recording to the internal disk.

He stopped and listened again. Satisfied he was still alone, he pressed the rewind button, then the play button. Now, he was in the right place on the recording. Lodge sat at his desk. McKnight watched the man read and write in a ledger for five minutes. Impatiently, he pressed and held down the fast-forward button, watching the man's last moments alive at high speed.

After a moment, the figure behind the desk leapt up and disappeared. McKnight pressed the rewind button for a second and replayed the scene at normal speed. Lodge was back at his desk. After a moment, he rose and walked into the bathroom.

Oh, he's stopping to use the john.

He allowed himself to relax and settle back in his chair when a shadow moved on the left, near the door. "Hello," he breathed, leaning forward again. The shadow moved into the field of light at the desk.

Well, I'll be damned. George was right.

He watched the rest of the scene, trying to memorize every detail. He checked the time stamp on the recording.

I missed the event in real time by seconds. Okay. Time to collect my gear and get the hell out.

He stowed the monitoring gear in his bag and made for the stairwell. Another long climb was in store for him.

On the way to the stairwell, he had an epiphany.

No reason to avoid the freight elevator now.

Fifteen minutes had passed since the killer had left the room, going in the opposite direction.

He ran to the elevator and pressed the call button. While the elevator ascended, his mind focused on the next steps. Get into Lodge's office, don't disturb the evidence, get the C-cam, find the ledger, get to the attic, dismantle his hideout and activate the recall beacon.

Anything else?

He reached the Executive Floor and walked along the row of offices. The hallway wall was mahogany paneled, radiating success and position. Tonight those decorations had death for a companion.

He reached Lodge's office and stood at the door for a long moment. He took a long breath, stepped inside and closed the door.

Something's wrong.

The room didn't feel right. He stood there for a second, trying to figure what was different. The body position didn't match what he remembered from the crime scene photos. Then he listened.

No way. He's still alive.

Lodge was breathing, but with effort. McKnight knelt beside him, careful not to disturb the blood or the body itself. He saw where Lodge's head hit the corner of the desk as he fell. Based on the spatter and the blood on the floor, he knew the man's head had struck it full force.

He whispered to the unconscious man. "I'm sorry, sir. I wish I could help you, but I can't."

He walked around the desk and looked at the ceiling where he had placed the C-cam. As he pushed the desk chair out of the way, he noticed the ledger on the desk. Something gnawed at the back of his mind and finally surfaced to his consciousness.

The ledger is still here?

They didn't find it at the scene, so they assumed the killer had taken it.

Why is it still here?

He rounded the desk and reexamined the body. There was something next to it. As he looked closer, understanding crashed into his brain.

The figurine! The murder weapon is still here.

This could mean only one thing.

The killer is coming back. But when?

The answer came to his ears. The sound of hurried footsteps came from outside the office. McKnight dove under the desk just before the door opened.

CHAPTER 29

McKnight drew himself into a ball under the desk.

Footsteps moved around the room. There were other sounds, and it took McKnight a few seconds to understand—the killer returned to clean up the crime scene. The desk and sofa were being wiped to remove fingerprints and any other trace evidence.

The footsteps came to his side of the desk. He held his breath and there, twelve inches from his face, were the hemline of a red evening dress and matching heels. He heard the ledger being closed and picked up. The dress and shoes moved away.

More sounds caught his attention—a groan and clothing rustling.

Lodge is moving!

A raspy feminine voice said, "Stay DOWN!" A sickening thud punctuated the last word.

After a moment, the voice spoke again with a cold calmness.

"Fuck you."

The door opened and closed. The footsteps receded into the night. He waited a full minute before venturing from beneath the desk. Lodge's body position now matched the crime scene photos and the ledger and figurine were gone.

He completed the tasks of retrieving the C-cam and removing all evidence of being there in three minutes.

McKnight looked again at the body and sighed. He had seen death before, but not like this. You expected to see death on the battlefield. But blood and death was out of place in this peaceful office tower in downtown Atlanta.

He listened at the door, then stepped through it. Reaching back in, he locked the door from the inside and closed it.

Okay. Let's get the hell out of here.

He retraced his steps to the stairwell, walked up to the attic and climbed the ladder to the platform. Now he had to remove the evidence of being in the attic.

He searched behind the plywood that formed his hideout. He placed the plastic sheet back over the carpet and moved the plywood sheets to their original positions. Satisfied, he walked back to the center of the platform to do a three-sixty check.

He spotted the old rickety chair.

Well, hello, old friend.

He grabbed the chair and positioned it at the edge of the platform, with one wheel on the edge. He smiled and tiptoed back to the spot where he first landed.

McKnight took a deep breath, knelt and grasped the return beacon on the chain around his neck.

He turned it over in his hand and read the engraving. "Bis vivit qui bene vivit." He lives twice who lives well. He smiled.

I could have done better. I will, next time.

He squeezed the beacon between his fingers. He sensed the static electricity growing in the surrounding air. There was no sound here, but the Engine was starting up in the year 2035. He felt a breeze start up from below him and turn into a fierce wind that whipped his hair back and forth. The surrounding air grew brighter until he could scarcely make out the room's features. He placed his hands on the platform before him. He thought of the blonde security guard.

Was she real or part of my imagination?

The light flashed, the bubble surged, and McKnight left the year 1985 through a field of stars.

Darkness again covered the attic. A gray mouse scampered to where McKnight had knelt. It stood on its hind legs and sniffed in every direction. Apparently satisfied, it ran to the platform edge and down the ladder.

****

Friday, July 12th, 2035 – 11:07 pm – NewT Attic

Drake stood like a statue, watching the team. Matthews stood next to him, jingling the change in his pockets and shifting his weight from side to side. Wheeler and Tyler stood over the dials of the Engine, cataloging the jumps for the mission records and final report. Wu and George sat together, laughing and talking about old movies.

Everyone appeared casual and relaxed, but Drake sensed the tension in the room. The mission was drawing to its conclusion, and each team member was coping with waiting in the best way they knew how.

They jumped to their feet when the Engine started humming.

"Is that what I think it is?" George asked, raising his voice over the hum of the Engine.

"Yes," Wu said. "He's early, though. Well, he's ahead of schedule. It could be he has everything he needs and is coming back right away. I guess we'll see."

The light bubble formed. Drake crossed his arms and then tugged on his lower lip. He saw McKnight's figure materializing inside the light globe. He was relieved McKnight was returning safely. Hopefully, he accomplished his mission.

The globe pulsated, then bulged. There was the characteristic crack of sound, and the light winked out. McKnight sprawled forward, but sprang to his feet. Wu and Wheeler rushed over to him, with Drake right behind them.

McKnight slipped his bag off over his head and handed it to Wheeler, who carried it back to the desk for an inventory.

"Are you all right?" Wu asked.

"Fine," he said.

"Report. Who killed Lodge?" Drake said, as the group approached McKnight on the travel plate.

McKnight pointed at George and grinned. "You were right."

"Thanks for that." George said and looked at Wu. Her radiant smile warmed his heart.

"But, with a twist we didn't expect," McKnight added, and turned back to Drake. "I'm ready, General. We still have a couple of things to check to confirm we have the whole picture. But can we find a place to sit? I'm beat."

"We can manage that, Captain. Mr. Matthews? Where's the best place? Your office?"

"Yes, sir," Matthews replied. "Right this way." He strode to the ladder and descended. McKnight and Drake followed him.

At the bottom of the ladder, McKnight stood with Matthews and Drake while the others made their way down.

"By the way," McKnight said to Matthews. "I ran into your other female guard in the building."

"I beg your pardon?"

"Yes, after I took Ms. McAllister back, I got delayed and couldn't get back upstairs right away. So I decided to find a room where I could watch the event live on the recorder. While I was looking for a place, she appeared out of nowhere and asked me a few questions. She acted suspicious, but then she just walked away."

"What guard?" Drake said.

"Another guard?" Matthews said.

"Yes, sir. She was approximately five foot two, with short blonde hair."

Matthews shook his head. "I'm confused, Captain. In 1985, Ms. McAllister was the only female guard on our staff."

CHAPTER 30

8:20 am – Friday, July 13th, 2035 –NewT Center

Drake looked across the table at McKnight. The huddle room they occupied was small, featuring two chairs, a table and power and communication ports. They normally used rooms like this one for a private discussion and this conversation fit the profile. Drake wanted to talk to McKnight about the mysterious female security officer.

"Captain, now that we have privacy, I'd like to hear the details again about the second security guard you met."

"Yes, sir."

Drake thought McKnight looked anxious, but not upset. He softened his tone to set him at ease. "I'm trying to sort this out and, to be honest, I'm perplexed. Maybe you can help me get it straight. Do you mind stepping me through the story again?"

McKnight relaxed. "I'm not going crazy and I'm sure she was real, but I have no proof to offer. I'd prefer to have a reason that explains it."

"Yes, I would, too. First, let's consider another option. You've made more trips through time than anyone else on the team."

"Yes, sir?"

"Jumping back and forth in time, that's not something anyone else has done. I'm wondering if there is a cumulative effect on your system? Plus the stress and responsibility of the mission. What do you think?"

"No, sir. I'm tired, but I've never felt better. To be honest, I considered the possibility of emotional or mental effects, but I don't buy it. I'm sure she was real."

"Okay. I'm not ready to rule that out, but let's set it aside for now. So run through the story again and let's brainstorm."

"Yes, sir."

McKnight walked through the events. He covered the woman's approach, her language, her posture and body language, and the words she spoke. Drake watched him as he spoke, noting his care and deliberateness as he repeated the story.

When he finished, Drake spoke. "Thank you, Captain. Did she have a name tag on her uniform blouse?"

"That's it, sir. I knew something was different about her, but I couldn't put my finger on it. No name tag. Her uniform was like the ones worn by Ms. McAllister and the other security personnel. But they had name tags, and she didn't." He rolled his eyes. "Why didn't I notice that? Do you have a theory, sir?"

"A couple of ideas come to mind. A spook conducting industrial espionage, or an employee on a power trip. But they don't fit the evidence."

"Yes, sir," McKnight said. "I agree."

"If it were one of the two scenarios I mentioned..."

"Yes, sir?"

"There's no way she could know your name. And she *did* know your name. It wasn't a wild guess, and it wasn't an accident she was there."

"I'm glad you're saying it and not me, sir. I agree with you."

"I think... and I'm having trouble saying this, but there's only one explanation that fits."

"Yes, sir," McKnight agreed. "Okay, I will say it first. She's a time traveler, too."

Drake leaned back in his chair. He didn't want to admit this was true, but no other explanation was supported by the evidence.

Drake shifted in his chair. "Tell me, Captain. When she said your name...What did her eyes tell you? Was she innocent? Was she toying with you? Or did you see something else?"

McKnight leaned back in his chair and studied the room's ceiling. He leaned forward again and caught Drake's eyes with his. "I saw recognition and satisfaction that she caught me by surprise. It was as if... as if she was flirting with me." He rolled his eyes. "Does that sound nuts?"

"Yes. And no." Drake pulled at his chin. "But you saw no surprise or compassion there?"

"No, sir."

"I'm not ready to buy into this unknown time traveler idea, but if it's true, we have bigger issues."

"Yes, sir, we do."

Drake leaned back and crossed his arms. "Let's assume for a minute she *is* a traveler. What does that tell us? For one thing, she knew where you were going to be and when."

"And she couldn't know that unless she has access to the records of our mission. How does *that* work?"

"Good question. She has our mission records. That's the only way."

McKnight leaned forward again. "Our records are classified. No public access. So how did she get access and a Time Engine?"

"Another good question. The records are classified now, in 2035. Who knows what happens in our future?"

"You think she might be from *our* future?"

Drake shrugged. "I don't think anything yet. We're brain-storming, right?"

"Yes, sir. But this experience is very real for me. I'm sure it wasn't a dream or a hallucination."

"Okay. But if she came from our future, she violated our mission protocols and directives, didn't she? Why present herself to you and reveal she knows who you were? No, there is something more to this. Maybe she was trying to push you off track? Or trying to change history? Or was she trying to warn you off another time path?"

"I don't know, sir. I couldn't tell from her actions. Or her eyes."

"I don't doubt it, Captain. And here's another big question. Was she trying to help or hinder you? Is she a friend or an enemy?"

McKnight shook his head. "I'm getting a headache."

"Yes, I don't blame you. But I think we can count on her to show up again."

"Yes, sir."

"Okay. We've beat this dead horse enough for now. Let's get back to the mission at hand. We'll come back to this later, with Doctor Astalos, Doctor Wu and Lieutenant Tyler. And let me know if you remember more details or you get new ideas about this whole thing."

"Yes, sir."

They rose and Drake opened the door, but then stopped. "So, write up your notes and I'll do the same. Don't leave out any details. We have more questions than answers, but we can't solve this without more information."

"Yes, sir."

"And, Marc?"

"Yes, sir?"

"I believe you saw what you think you saw."

"Thank you, sir."

"Don't mention it. We need to figure out the rest. I'm not comfortable with the idea of an unknown traveler looking over our shoulder."

****

10:25 am – Friday, July 13th, 2035 –NewT Center, a small conference room

"General Drake?"

Drake turned to the man at the conference room door. "Yes, Mr. Matthews?"

"Senator Lodge is on his way up. My man downstairs says he's really pissed. Thought you might like to know."

Drake smiled at the security chief. "Thanks for the heads-up. No problem. Show him in when he gets here."

"Yes, sir, I will."

"Would you mind asking Doctor Wu, Captain McKnight, Lieutenant Tyler, and Mr. George to join us, please, and have someone keep the lady in Room 4D company?"

"No problem, sir. My pleasure," Matthews drawled and left the small conference room.

"Thanks," Drake called after him and returned to his review of the ledger before him. The more he read, the more reasons he found to dislike the murder victim. The elder Lodge made meticulous notes about his business dealings. He tracked his money transactions religiously. He even tracked bribery payments, blackmail receipts, prostitute transactions, and drug buys.

In most cases, he used company money as if it were his own. Every illicit transaction was correlated in the ledger to the transaction description he used in his company expense reports. He routinely misused the millions entrusted to him by NewT Telecommunications.

But the information in the ledger didn't stop with financial records. Elder Lodge also used it as a diary. Many of the entries were tirades against others—racial slurs, sexual innuendos, and other unsavory passages. He documented his many trysts with women and recounted them in steamy detail. Some bordered on rape. He rewarded some women with drugs, but most were drawn to the money and power and the prospect of marriage.

He intentionally and systematically used the women. Of this there was no doubt. Many were young. Some were new to the business world. He pulled them out of secretarial pools and minor management positions, brought them close to the seat of power at the company, and seduced them. When the affairs were over, he pushed them away, paying them well for their silence. One even committed suicide, and he expressed relief in the ledger that he didn't have to worry about her talking and it didn't cost him "even one red cent."

Drake wondered why the Senator was so eager to find the ledger. He was only a kid back then. Did he have some idea, even then, of its value? Or maybe he assumed it was valuable because it was taken?

Someone knocked on the door. He turned to see Wu peeking in. "Come in, please."

The team walked in and picked out seats in the conference room. "Save that one for the Senator," Drake said, pointing to the chair across the table from him.

McKnight eyed the ledger on the table in front of Drake. "Sir, is the ledger as important as you expected?"

Drake grimaced and raised a gray eyebrow. "Oh, it's perfect. Please review it and discuss with Doctor Wu and Lieutenant Tyler before you create your final report. It's still confidential. Not to be shared outside the team."

"Damn," George said. "I wanted to see it. Based on your excitement, I'll bet I could solve a cold case or two if I did."

"It's a possibility, Detective," Drake said. "At some point, I'd like to talk to you about a position on the HERO Team, if you are open to new opportunities. I am required to have civilian team members and Doctor Wu is the only one I have so far. Until this weekend, I haven't met anyone I considered qualified."

George beamed. "Sir, I'd be delighted to have that conversation." He glanced at Wu, who smiled back.

The door burst open as the Senator came in, followed by his security specialist Smith.

Lodge glared at Drake, bristling with anger. "Drake, I'm told the mission ended hours ago. Why wasn't I notified?"

Drake remained calm and formal. "Good morning, Senator Lodge. It's true the traveler has returned. But the mission isn't complete. I've received verbal reports from the team and the paperwork is being executed. But you've arrived at an opportune time, sir, as the team is ready to give a readout on the mission. Please sit down. Oh, but not you, Mr. Smith. This briefing is classified."

"He has a secret clearance and is on my staff. It's okay for him to be here," Lodge said as he motioned Smith to sit next to him.

"No, he doesn't have clearance," McKnight said, holding up a hand. "He had clearance until a few weeks ago, but the government revoked it for cause."

Lodge spun around in his chair to look at Smith.

"Perhaps he didn't share that with you, sir?" McKnight said. "At any rate, he can't stay. He doesn't have clearance."

Smith stood and glared at McKnight, who held his gaze without emotion.

"But you let him stay for the briefing last time." Lodge said.

"Last time, Senator, we weren't sharing any information about time travel or the case that wasn't already available. We also assumed Mr. Smith had top secret clearance. Our mistake and yours. Since that first briefing, we checked his clearance and learned it's been pulled. In your office, you are free to make whatever assumptions you like about the disclosure of classified materials and who has access. But for my briefings, I take clearance seriously. He's out. If you insist he stay, the briefing is over."

Lodge looked around the room as if gauging the resolve of the team members. He turned to Smith and said, "Wait outside."

Smith glared at McKnight for a moment, then turned on his heel and left the room.

Lodge moved to speak, but Drake held up his hand, picked up his phone and speed-dialed a number. "Mr. Matthews? Would you please tell Mr. Smith that Senator Lodge suggests he go back to the Senator's local office and wait there for him there?... Yes, thank you."

He disconnected the call. "I want that person as far from here as possible," he said to no one in particular. When Lodge objected, Drake held up his hand again and said, "Please wait a moment, Senator."

Drake paused and watched the door. After a moment, Matthews came in, nodded and sat at the far end of the table.

Drake nodded back and turned to Lodge. "Sir, I know how that may have seemed to you, but I assure you I didn't send him out to piss you off. They pulled his secret clearance earlier this year because he shared classified information inappropriately. I won't share the details, but the record says he used classified information to impress and seduce impressionable young women. We believe he's responsible for the leak to the press of time travel technology and Doctor Astalos's involvement. I don't know about you, but there are things said in my office I don't want shared outside. You probably feel the same. Regardless, I suggest you review Mr. Smith's credentials and ensure he still has the level of clearance you need and want on your team."

Lodge studied Drake for a moment, then said, "I suppose I owe you my thanks. I'll investigate myself and see what's what."

"Good. Now, let's get to the readout. Doctor Wu, please invite the lady to join us."

"Yes, sir. I'll be right back." She stood and left the room.

Drake turned to George. "Mr. George, would you mind conducting the interview?"

George look surprised, but grinned from ear to ear. "Not at all, sir. Thanks for the opportunity."

Lodge's eyes fell on the ledger on the table. "Is that my father's ledger? You found it?"

"Yes, I believe it is," Drake said. "We are still reviewing the contents. I suspect you'll eventually be able to take possession. It might be awhile, though, and you'll have to negotiate with the owner to get access to it."

"What the hell are you talking about? I'm the goddamned owner!"

The door opened and a slender, elderly woman entered the room, followed by Wu. She stood very erect as women of her generation were taught at an early age, but her shoulders drooped and she was unsteady on her feet.

Lodge gasped when she entered the room. He looked stricken, but recovered and stood. "Drake, what the hell is going on here? Just what in Heaven's name are you trying to pull? I'll have you all out on the street for this! You'll regret the day you..." He stopped, looking at the woman. She was on the verge of tears. "Mom? I..."

She stood in front of him. He towered over her and she reached up to stroke his cheek. "Jimmy, please don't be upset. I asked to come here. When Mr. George came by this morning, I guessed why and I knew what he wanted. It was such a long time ago, but I remember it like yesterday. I have a story to tell."

Drake looked at Wu and George, then spoke. "Mrs. Lodge, you seem a little fatigued. Are you sure you wouldn't like to call it a day and get back together tomorrow? I can have Mr. George drive you home so you can rest."

Before she could respond, Lodge interjected, "Yes, Mom, let me call Harry. He should be here."

She looked at her son and said, "Jimmy, it isn't necessary to call Harry. Him being here wouldn't change my story in the slightest."

She turned back to Drake. "Thank you for your courtesy, Mister..."

"Drake, ma'am."

"Mr. Drake. Yes, I appreciate your concern, but I've waited way too long. I don't want to hold it inside me for another minute. Besides," she said with a shy smile and a twinkle in her eye. "You'd better get your story while you can. At my age, I might be dead tomorrow. If I could just get a cup of tea and sit down, I'll be fine."

Tyler left the room in search of tea while George pulled out a chair for her. "Would you like something to eat or to use the facilities before we begin?" Wu asked, sitting next to her. "We don't want you to be uncomfortable."

"I'll be fine, dear. Thank you." To George, she said, "Do you need to record my interrogation?"

"It's actually an interview, ma'am. But, yes, I'd like to record it if I may." Holding up a small video device, he said, "I'll place this VR on the table if that's okay with you? It'll record everyone in the room.

Otherwise, we'll go somewhere else where we can have a separate camera."

"Oh, it's not a problem," she said. "It'll be easier if I only have to tell it once."

She looked at Lodge. "Jimmy, did you ask for this investigation? I know you're involved with that time travel stuff. I was afraid you would get around to this. But, in a way, I'm glad you did."

Lodge looked uncomfortable. Drake came to his rescue. "It was my idea, Mrs. Lodge. We needed a good test of our technology. The Senator provided us with a good opportunity."

Tyler returned with a cup of hot tea and set it in front of her. She thanked him, blew across the cup and took a sip.

"Where shall I start? At the beginning, I suppose. Jim and I got married a little later in life. I was married once before and it was a disaster. Jim was considerate, at least at first, but I hesitated to make the leap again. Some of my friends thought he married me for my money, but I didn't believe it."

She stopped and smiled. "I'm not so much to look at now, but back then I cut a pretty fair swath through the young men. There were plenty that came around. I like to think he loved me in the beginning, though, but our family was well connected and he was ambitious. And he was handsome and making good money. The attention he paid me went to my head, I guess, but it seemed like a good idea to marry him. My family wasn't excited about the idea, but they knew how stubborn I can be and remained neutral—except my sister Dianne."

"What about Dianne?" George asked.

"She died last year, God rest her soul. She hated Jim. I didn't find out why until that night. A few years before I met Jim, she dated him. He told her he loved her and wanted to marry her, but he was just trying to get her into bed. Then he dumped her for someone else about two weeks later. I don't know how he convinced her to keep quiet about it. Maybe she thought I wouldn't listen. Anyway, she never mentioned it until that night. But, now, I'm getting a little ahead of myself.

"As time passed, I saw a cold side to Jim Lodge that he hid from most people. I don't think he really cared much for anyone."

She looked at Lodge. "Except for you, Jimmy. There's no question in my mind he loved you. In our last few years together, the only real warmth I saw from him was directed at you. To be honest, I was a little jealous. Oh, but don't be thinking about that, Jimmy. He provided well for me and I had my charities to work in. I had a good life."

She looked at her hands in her lap. "But I guess I'd better get to the point. I was there that night. I talked to Jim on the phone earlier in the evening and got pretty upset. He promised to come to my United Way fundraiser at the Ritz-Carlton in Buckhead and was late. So I called him from my room and he gave me a phony-baloney excuse about having to work late. I suspected he was unfaithful, and I convinced myself he was with someone else that night."

She looked up from her lap. "I know there were many. I heard the rumors about the women who came to his office after hours. And some of them worked there. Anyway, Dianne came up to check on me and, well, I was pretty much a wreck. I poured out my heart and my suspicions to her.

"She had too many drinks and told me about her history with Jim and how she really felt about him. I got mad, and we yelled at each other and then we cried together. Then I forgave her and thought of all the things I had put up with over the years. Then I got mad at him again.

"But this time I didn't get mad-upset. I got mad-cold, if you know what I mean. I was determined to catch him in the act, get some leverage, and demand a divorce." She reached inside her purse. From it, she pulled a tissue and an old weathered NewT Center ID card.

She held up the ID card. "It was Jim's. I took it from his jacket pocket one night six months before his death. I suspected infidelity, and I knew he'd get another one. My plan was to use it to catch him cheating, but he was nice for the next few days and I forgot about it. It was still in my purse.

"Somewhere along the line, I realized Jim was keeping tabs on me. Not close, mind you, but subtly. I once asked about it and he admitted he had a man that stayed close for my protection. He hinted it was because I was the wife of an executive of a major corporation and was a potential target. But I always thought it was an excuse to know where I was. He always knew when I was visiting the building. I was pretty sure the folks in security would alert him if I showed up unannounced. So, I determined that, if I wanted to catch him, I'd have to sneak in somehow. That's why I took the ID. I was sure I'd never surprise him unless I could get in without signing in at the desk."

McKnight looked away from her, to George and Matthews. They nodded at one another in silent agreement. "Mrs. Lodge, if you could wait for a second before continuing…" he said. "Mr. Matthews, I'd expect the security office to expedite a new ID for an executive. But why wouldn't they deactivate the lost ID?"

Matthews nodded. "A fair question. That's general policy and we do deactivate missing IDs for everyone else. With executives, we don't do it right away. Sometimes they find it right after reporting it missing and try to use it. If it's deactivated, it fails and they're inconvenienced. We try to avoid having inconvenienced executives. So we tag the ID in the system to be deactivated at a future date after the executive gets a new ID, which takes a couple of days. But it wouldn't be that unusual for it to remain usable for years. It's a low priority item, and people get busy and forget."

"Thanks," McKnight said. He looked back at Mrs. Lodge, who had been following the question with interest.

"Why, I never thought of that," she said. "I thought it would work forever."

"Not usually, ma'am," Matthews said. "But you were saying?"

"Oh, yes. Thank you, Mister…?"

"Matthews, ma'am. Walt Matthews."

"Mr. Matthews. Yes. Oh, and so Dianne returned to the event and told everyone I was sick and resting upstairs. I slipped out of the hotel, got in my car and drove to NewT Center."

"I don't even remember driving there. I mean, I drove there, but I was on auto-pilot, you know? All I could think of was he ditched something important to me for some little…"

She dabbed at her eyes with the tissue, then looked up at Drake. "I did love him. Despite all the good reasons I shouldn't, I still did."

Drake nodded, "Yes, ma'am, I know. I'm sorry."

Mrs. Lodge searched the faces of everyone except her son. Lodge's face was a visage of stone. He was struggling with his emotions and there was no convenient outlet.

George spoke. "And then what did you do, Mrs. Lodge?"

"I drove into the parking garage. I thought, if I used the card for entry, some sort of record would be made and someone would alert him. So I took a ticket and drove in to park."

"There is public parking in the deck at night?" asked George, leaning back and looking at Matthews.

"Yes," Matthews said. "We open the deck for events at the Fox Theatre. We control access and channel the crowds with steel curtains in the elevator lobbies. From the Fox parking lot, they can get into our parking deck and the food court area where the security counter is. From there, they can get to the train station, which is why the access is available." He looked at Mrs. Lodge and said, "But you knew that, didn't you, ma'am?"

"Doesn't everyone? If you've been to an event at the Fox and don't mind paying for parking, that's where you go. It's convenient and easy to leave when the event is over."

"I see," George said. "Please continue."

"Well, I didn't want anyone to let him know I was coming, so I went up the back way."

George, Matthews, and McKnight shared knowing glances with each other. They had guessed right. "How did you know about the back way?" George asked.

"Why, my husband took me that way once. We had to stop by the office once on the way out of town for vacation. Jim needed something from his office, but didn't want to be held up and have to work, so I went with him to give him a good excuse for not staying. We went up the back way so he wouldn't run into anyone who wanted to talk to him."

"Just for the record, ma'am, could you please tell me which way you went?"

"Certainly. I stayed out in the hall next to the parking garage elevator until a loud group came through. Then I walked behind them into the food court. While they distracted the guard, I stepped over to the door to the loading dock. I used the ID to open the door and walked down to the end of the hall. I peeked around the corner and saw the guard talking to a custodian, so I stepped over to the door at the elevator area and walked in. I got in the elevator, rode up to the bridge floor, crossed the bridge into the conference room floor, and got on the freight elevator. I rode up to the executive floor and then walked to my husband's office. Simple."

Matthews nodded and leaned back in his chair, looking up at the ceiling. Drake guessed he was already planning changes to his security procedures so no one could ever again get into NewT Center without being observed.

"So that's how you got to his office?" George asked.

"Yes, that's correct."

"Did you see anyone on your way up to the office? I mean, like a janitor or anyone?" asked George with a sidelong look at McKnight.

"It was such a long time ago. I don't… Wait a moment. When I came around a corner, but before I crossed the bridge, I thought I saw a flash of light in the little lobby area there. I thought there might be something going on and it put me off for a minute, but when I got on the other side of the bridge, there was nothing except that guard."

"What guard?" George asked.

"Why does it matter? Well, I guess it makes no difference now. I'm sure she's long gone and won't get fired for something I might say. There was a young blonde girl, sleeping in a chair. She was wearing a uniform, so I figured she was a guard taking a nap. Is that important?"

"Not at all, ma'am." George said. "Please continue."

"It's funny what you remember, isn't it? I remember that girl plain as day, but I don't remember being on the elevator. But how else could I have gotten upstairs?"

"That's right, ma'am. Our memories fade, but they're still there, waiting to be reawakened," George said. "So you took the freight elevator up to the executive floor?"

"Yes, I did." She smiled. "I was very proud of myself, you see. Normally, I wasn't very independent, but I was in the building and I slipped in without him knowing about it."

"So I went up to his office. The halls were all dark, with a few lights on here and there. There was no light coming from under the door. I remember thinking, if he has someone with him, the lights are off. I got madder, just thinking about it. So I went right up to the door and turned the doorknob. It was unlocked. So I pushed the door open and peeked inside."

"A tiny lamp was on, lighting his desk. It's a big office and the rest of the room was dark. When I stepped inside, I heard the fan in his bathroom going, so I knew he was there. I waited to see if he had someone with him. I stood by the window, and that's when I saw it."

"Saw what?" asked George.

"Why, his damned ledger, that's what!"

George hesitated. "What about the ledger? Why was it so important? What was in it?"

"Well, he had this ledger book he carried everywhere with him. He was very secretive about it. He never left it lying around, he always locked it up when he wasn't working in it. To be honest, I always wondered what was in his ledger. Until that night, I had no idea. So there it was, lying open on his desk.

"My curiosity got the better of me and I couldn't resist. I thumbed through it. I saw a lot of financial stuff in there I didn't understand. To be honest, I didn't care about that stuff. But then…"

She looked around the room as tears spilled down her cheeks. "But then I found what he wrote about that poor girl." Her words trailed off into a sob.

In a soft voice, George spoke. "What did he write, ma'am?"

"He was bragging about a girl he slept with—the one who killed herself. I guess I saw the real Jim Lodge then for the first time. He wrote about her like she was a minor loose end that got tied up most agreeably. She killed herself and his only thought was that he got rid of her and it hadn't cost him a cent!"

"I remember thinking, this is the man I married? The man who fathered my child?"

She began to cry again. Wu slid her chair over next to her and took her hand. Mrs. Lodge smiled at her through her tears and patted Wu's hand. "Thank you, dear," she said in a hoarse whisper. She took a couple of deep breaths and nodded to everyone. "And thank you all for letting me get this off my chest. There's just a little more to tell."

Lodge spoke for the first time since the interview started. "Mom, are you sure you don't want to wait for Harry? I can have him here in a half hour. He would be happy to come and help."

"No, dear," she responded. I'm fine." Her voice grew hoarse again and the tears started again. "No, I want to tell the story. It's been on my heart for too long."

"Are you sure, Mrs. Lodge?" Drake said. "We can talk more tomorrow."

"No," she said. "It's time to tell the whole story. As I was saying, I was so upset, I sat on the sofa in the dark, trying to pull myself together. I was there for only a minute when I heard a noise from the bathroom. It was water running. I was afraid to see who came out. Would it be my husband alone? Or him with some woman? I sat there, trying to decide what I would say, depending on who came out. But I couldn't get that poor woman out of my mind."

"Then the water in the bathroom stopped, and he flipped off the light in the bathroom area as he came back in alone. I was relieved, but I was still livid about what I read. He didn't notice I was there, so I sat still, hardly breathing. But then, I decided to make my presence known. I intended to confront him, to show him he couldn't control me, that I'm liable to show up anywhere and anytime. I had this feeling of power that, from now on, he would always look over his shoulder for me when he was with another woman."

"So he didn't see you right away. What did you do next?" George asked. The room was dead quiet. Lodge stared at his clasped hands before him on the table. Everyone in the room listened with rapt attention.

"Well, he sat at his desk and stared at the ledger for a second, fingering one of the pages—I forgot to turn the ledger back to the page he was reading before. So I stood up, there in the shadows of the room. He heard me because he looked up. I stood still as a statue. He squinted to see, but couldn't really see me. I was ecstatic because I saw fear on his face. I have to admit I enjoyed it. I scared him. He said, 'Who is it?' and I heard the fear in his voice. I stepped forward.

"When he recognized me, his face changed from fear to..." She faltered for a moment. "...To contempt. I saw for the first time he didn't love me or even respect me. In a nasty voice, he asked me what I was doing there. I didn't say anything—I was too furious to speak."

She stopped and stared ahead as if reliving in her mind what happened next. No one breathed a word.

After a moment, Wu spoke. "Mrs. Lodge, are you all right?"

Mrs. Lodge blinked twice, turned to Wu, and smiled through her tears. "Yes, I'm fine, dear. I just can't believe it. It happened so fast."

"What happened next, Mrs. Lodge?" George asked.

"Well, I was beside myself with anger. I called him a bastard and told him I read about the girl in his ledger. That made him really mad."

"That you knew about the girl?" George said.

"No! He was angry because I read his ledger! He called me an ugly cow and other profane names and threatened to divorce me. I told him we'd see what would happen after I told everyone about his precious ledger. Then he grabbed me by the throat and swore he'd kill me if I breathed a word about it.

"He drew back his fist. I thought he was going to hit me in the face, but he punched me in the stomach instead. He pushed me backwards, and I fell into the chair next to the coffee table. He turned around to pick up his damned book. I saw the statuette on the coffee table and I grabbed it. I hit him as he turned back around. He fell backwards and hit his head on the desk."

She stopped and looked around the table. Her eyes finally rested on her son. "Jimmy, I'm so sorry... I don't know what to say... I know you looked up to him, but... I'm so sorry."

Lodge's face was a picture of anguish.

To the group, she said, "I suppose you must all think I'm an awful person, but I couldn't stop myself. I was hurt and angry and I felt betrayed. I didn't mean to... I..."

Wu shook her head in denial and George spoke. "No, we don't think that, Mrs. Lodge. We don't. He deserved it. His own actions caused his death."

Drake turned to look at George. Sympathizing with a suspect was an effective method to keep them talking. In this case, sympathy wasn't hard—the victim was a vicious predator.

"What happened then, Mrs. Lodge?" George said.

The old woman sat motionless for a long moment.

"Mrs. Lodge?"

She blinked. "I'm sorry. What happened next is a little fuzzy. I'm trying to verbalize it. After I hit him and he fell, it was suddenly so quiet I could hear the blood rushing in my ears. I nearly fainted.

"As I recovered, I felt... triumphant. I remember I stood over him for a minute. Then, I knelt beside him and tried to feel the pulse in his neck, but I couldn't find it. I was hoping against hope I hadn't killed him and that, if I found a pulse.... well, I guess you understand. I stood up and then panic set in.

"I was sure I would go to jail and Jimmy would be all alone. I didn't want either of those, so... I decided to avoid it. I took the statuette with me. I figured it would be better if no one ever found it. I took out my handkerchief and wiped down everything I had touched. The leather sofa, the desk, the coffee table, and the ledger itself.

"Before I walked out the door, I went back to the desk and picked up the ledger. I'm not sure why, but I thought maybe I could use it in my defense if I ever had to. And I didn't want the stuff in the ledger to become public knowledge. All that stuff about his flings and finances... It would have been so humiliating. So I took it with me."

George nodded. "So you locked the door and left the building the same way you came in?" he asked.

"Yes, that's right."

"Mrs. Lodge, may I ask you another question?"

"Certainly."

"What color dress did you wear that night?"

"I beg your pardon?"

"Yes, ma'am, what color was the dress you wore when you came to your husband's office?"

"I wasn't wearing a dress. I wore a blue strapless gown earlier in the evening, but I changed into a sweat suit before coming to the office."

"And your sister Dianne? What color dress was she wearing?"

"What?"

George paused a moment to ensure he had eye contact with her before continuing. "Mrs. Lodge, what color was Dianne's dress? If I took a wild guess and said it was red, would I be right?"

"Yes," she said and looked at the floor.

"I'm sorry to ask all these questions, ma'am, but I need the whole story. I think I know most of it, but I need your help. She came to the office with you, didn't she?"

"Yes, but she didn't confront him with me. She had nothing to do with what happened."

"I know, ma'am. But things didn't happen exactly like you said, did they? I mean, you said you tidied up the room and took the statuette, but that isn't really what happened, right? Wasn't it Dianne who did that?"

Mrs. Lodge sighed and shrugged. "Well, I guess it doesn't matter now. Yes, she did. When I came out of the office, I was hysterical. She calmed me down long enough to find out what happened and went back into the office to clean up after me. Poor dear! She was so concerned about me and Jimmy and she wanted to protect us. So she went back into the office to wipe off everything. She had the presence of mind I didn't, because she brought the statuette and the ledger out with her. She wanted to make sure there was nothing in his office that might lead anyone to me. She saved me. But I guess my sins have caught up with me now."

George smiled at her. "It's okay, Mrs. Lodge. We're almost done. Could you tell me what you did with the statuette?"

"Yes. As I was driving back to the hotel, it occurred to me I shouldn't keep it. So I stopped off at Lenox Square Mall and put the statuette in a dumpster outside the food court. I wiped it off before tossing it in."

"And the ledger? I know they searched your house as part of the investigation."

"Yes, they did," she said. "Dianne suggested I give it to her for safekeeping, just in case. I don't know where she kept it because they searched her house and never found it. I wondered later if Jim had written in the book about her, too. Maybe that's why she was so eager to keep it for me. But anyway, I thought it was a good idea to send it somewhere else for a while. After a year, when she got married again, She gave it back to me. Neither of us wanted someone outside the family to see it."

"I understand," George said. "Thank you, Mrs. Lodge, for your candor and for spending the time to explain your story to us. We've taken enough of your time today. I wonder if you would come downtown to talk to me tomorrow after I have a chance to digest your story and the rest of the facts?"

Mrs. Lodge looked at him with tears in her eyes, her shoulders trembling. "Am I under arrest? I have to pay for what I did."

"No, ma'am, you aren't. But I would consider it a great favor if you would meet with me tomorrow and help me fill in the loose ends. You should bring along your lawyer and we'll talk about any items we didn't cover today."

Gratitude showed in her eyes. Her voice trembled as she said, "Yes, I'd be glad to meet with you."

With that, George said, "Kathy, would you mind taking Mrs. Lodge to the ladies lounge so she can freshen up and then arrange a ride home for her?"

"I'd be delighted to. Come along, Mrs. Lodge." She helped the elderly lady to her feet.

Mrs. Lodge looked around the room. "Thank you all for your kindness. Mr. George, I'll call in the morning to arrange an appointment." She turned to face her son. "Jimmy? Are you okay?"

Lodge responded weakly, still struggling with his emotions. "Yes, ma'am. I'm okay. I'll be by the house to see you later today."

CHAPTER 31

3:30 pm – Friday, July 13th, 2035 - NewT Center, Retail Mall

McKnight, George, and Tyler sat at a table in the food court of the retail mall, half-drained cups of coffee before them.

"Mr. George?" Tyler said. "We'd like to wrap up a few loose ends for the mission. I have a couple of questions for you."

"Lieutenant, please call me Trevor and I'll call you Winnie, if that's okay?"

"Sure. So here's my first question. Why did I change again even though Marc didn't interfere with my grandparents meeting? I'm not sure I get that."

"That's a question for Captain McKnight, I think. Something happened that might have stopped them from connecting. Captain?"

McKnight looked up and shrugged. "I'm not sure. I think a connection existed between the younger Merrie and me. Maybe I intrigued her?"

"Yes," George said. "You may have something there. Maybe she got interested in you and, when Churchie called, she blew him off because she expected to run into you again. Who knows? But that's a fair guess."

"Okay," Tyler said. "Question number two. When I changed the second time, we assumed the recall light flash delayed Mrs. Lodge… or rather, both women, right?

"Yes, in hindsight, I think that's a good assumption. They were likely delayed in getting to Lodge's office for approximately five minutes."

"So they trashed Lodge's office?"

George shrugged. "Maybe Mrs. Lodge did that by herself. Here's what I believe happened. The light flash delayed her, so she arrived at the office after Lodge came out of the bathroom. She didn't look at the ledger, didn't find out about the dead girl, and didn't get angry enough to hit him with the figurine. She expected to find another woman and got pissed because he didn't even have that excuse for blowing off her event. It wouldn't surprise me if there's a big temper hiding in that sweet refined lady."

"So she trashed his office, and he covered for her by reporting it as vandalism?"

George nodded. "That's what I believe. So when we put them back on track... Well, you know the rest of the story. Anyway, no way to confirm. At least, not without going back and re-creating the situation again."

"No, thanks," McKnight and Tyler said in unison.

"Aw, c'mon. Where's your sense of adventure?" George whined, then grinned.

"I've had enough fun for one weekend, thank you very much," McKnight said. "Slender threads."

"What?" George said.

"Just imagine." McKnight said. "What if they caught another red light on the way over here? Or the elevator took longer to carry them upstairs?"

"Right," George said. "Or, if she decided to wait and confront him when he got home and never made the trip downtown. You know, all of a sudden, I'm exhausted. I think I'll go home and sleep for a couple of weeks."

"Or at least until your appointment with Mrs. Lodge?" Tyler said.

George grinned. "Or at least 'til then. Right. You have a great evening, gentlemen."

He shook their hands and walked to the NewT Center garage. Tyler and McKnight watched him until he was out of sight.

McKnight looked at the security counter across the food court. It was where Churchie Tyler first met Merrie McAllister and said enough of the right things that she shared her telephone number. It was the site of a significant event that shaped Winnie Tyler's life, fifty years ago.

Tyler turned to face his friend. "Well, what do you think, Marc? Will we have to put up with the Senator interfering with the program anymore?" Tyler gripped his cup in both hands and stared at it.

"Well," McKnight said. "Maybe not for a while. I don't suppose he'd want the contents of that ledger to become public knowledge."

"What's in it?"

"Note it's still classified, Lieutenant, for future reference," he said. "The Senator's father wasn't an honest businessman. He embezzled money from his company and he had a few shady deals on the side. That book was his record book. No wonder the Senator wanted us to find it for him."

McKnight stopped talking.

"What else?" Tyler said.

"Something else occurred to me. I suspect there's money accumulating somewhere that no one but Lodge Senior knew about. That might explain the Senator's obsession for getting the book back, and maybe even his motivation for investigating the murder. Considering that, this whole thing didn't turn out like he wanted."

"I feel so sorry for him," Tyler said. The tone of his voice was not one of sympathy.

"Me, too," McKnight said. "To your question, I didn't have a chance to review it as closely as the General did, but I saw enough to know it would not be good for the Senator's career to have that ledger get out. He's spent time and money over the last twenty years, trying to clean up that image and this would be a major setback. But you never know. If something comes along that's more important to him, I wouldn't put it past him to get back in our face."

"What do you think will happen to Mrs. Lodge?"

"Not much. She's nearly eighty, and anything we bring back from the past is, by law, not admissible in court as evidence. We're required to keep the film disk in the mission records and it might one day be open to legal proceedings, but not in her lifetime. The Senator could make a big deal out of it, but I can't see that happening."

"Will George tell her what really happened?" asked Tyler.

"Yes, Her sister is dead and he'll want to take away the guilt. No need for her to carry it any longer."

"What else?"

"George, you mean? I think he wants to learn all the details about the case since he studied it for so long."

"Is that why he asked her to come downtown?"

"That and he wants to tell her the truth. She was upset last night and I suspect he wanted to give her a chance to rest before learning that her sister killed her husband and she didn't. He'll give her a chance to say anything else she wants to share. You know, lay the matter to rest. It'll work out fine for Mrs. Lodge. I believe she's relieved that the truth is out."

"So you think they'll go downtown to talk and then he'll let her go?"

"He has no grounds to hold her. I suspect he will make her as comfortable as possible, explain her rights and that she is free to go, remind her to listen to her lawyer, but ask her for a favor – Could she please help him fill in the blanks in the case? Everything she says would be off the record. I think she'll have no problem with doing that. And I doubt George will record much of it, except where the details help answer questions about the case. He just wants to know how everything happened. He's been studying this case for a while and he wants to close out his questions and related theories."

"He's a sharp guy. Was the General serious about offering him a job?"

"I believe so. He's sharp as hell, very curious, and has other skills we don't have."

"Years of experience as a criminal investigator, for example?"

"Yes, and as an interviewer. He and Kathy will make a great team. There won't be much that gets past those two."

"I heard," Tyler said. "And they seem to be hitting it off, too."

"You think?" McKnight said with a laugh.

He held up his cup to his friend. "Salud. I'm glad you're back."

Tyler returned the salute with his cup. "Me, too. I'm glad the mission is over."

McKnight caught Tyler's eye and said what was on his mind. "Winnie, I'm sorry you had to go through what you went through because of my mistakes."

"Shit, Marc. Are you still worried about that?"

"Yeah, I am. I can't help it. I could have wrecked your life forever. It would be bad enough that I changed history, but if I had screwed up the life of someone under my command–"

"Or a friend?" finished Tyler.

"Or a friend," McKnight acknowledged with a smile. "Now that you mention it."

"Look, from what I understand—now that my mind is clear and I've read the transcripts—I don't see how any of it was your fault. Somehow, Gramma got in your way. It might have been inevitable." He held up his hand as McKnight started to speak. "I know, I know… But consider this. What if there are forces at work during time travel that we don't know about? What if they come into play and affect time and space in ways we don't yet realize?"

"I don't think I understand," McKnight said.

"I can't explain it, but there's a special connection between you and Gramma."

McKnight shifted in his chair and opened his mouth to speak.

Tyler waved him off. "Now, don't go defensive on me, I wasn't implying anything there. I'm saying I can sense something there. Laugh it off if you want to, but I'm serious."

McKnight considered this new idea.

"But, do you understand what I mean?" Tyler said. "You met her and enjoyed being around her here in the present, and in the past you couldn't avoid her. She couldn't have known about you and you weren't trying to contact her. Yet, you still ran into each other again and again. And don't forget what you experienced when she was in the attic."

McKnight held up his hand. "Okay, I respect your opinion, but I don't get it." He shrugged. "On the other hand, I don't guess I have to. Okay, so document it. Spend enough time to make sure you capture the idea as clearly and succinctly as possible, including all your impressions, theories, and ideas. Pour them out on paper. We'll let Kathy and the General chew on it for a while and involve Doctor Astalos. If you're right, then this attraction or magnetism—or whatever it is—is something we need to study. If it's a real thing, it'll happen again on another mission and we'll need to factor it into our planning checklist. Make sense?"

"Yes, sir. Will do."

"Thanks, Winnie," McKnight said, switching gears. "So, what's the plan for tonight?"

"Well, I talked to Gramma a few minutes ago. She's invited us back to the house for drinks, dinner and an overnight stay. We can head back to DC tomorrow. Remember, the invitation is still open for you to stay here a few days for vacation. That is unless you're just dying to get back to DC?"

McKnight considered it. "Well, no matter what, I could use a beer and a good night's sleep. Your grandfather's place sounds good. Why don't you go ahead and I'll cab to the house when I'm done here? I need to debrief with Kathy and the General first. I'll be out there in two hours. Will that work?"

"N-P, Marc," Tyler said, rising to leave. "I'll see you then. Don't get lost."

Tyler picked up McKnight's overnight bag and grinned at him. "I'll carry this on home for you. That way, you won't get lost. See you later." With that, he came to attention and saluted his friend, turned, and strode across the retail mall to the Marta train station.

McKnight sat still for a moment, fingering his coffee cup. He needed to debrief with Wu and the General, but first he needed to be alone for a few minutes. He was beyond tired, but his brain was still in overdrive. He re-traced his steps in the mission, noting what he might have done differently.

I wonder if there's anything to Tyler's connection theory? Bah! That's too much to think about right now.

His internal critique of the mission completed, he walked to the trash bin and threw away the paper cup.

Guess I'd better go talk to Kathy and the General and get this closed out.

CHAPTER 32

3:50 pm – Friday, July 13th, 2035 - NewT Center

He headed for the private conference room Matthews reserved for their debrief.

The General didn't have much to say. He asked McKnight for his final report on the mission and his comments. He praised him for the results, but tore him a new one for the unplanned people contact.

McKnight kept his mouth shut and replied 'Yes, sir' at the right places in the debriefing. He asked Drake if he had more thoughts about the second female security guard. Drake responded by asking him if he remembered anything new. When he admitted that he didn't, Drake put it off and commented that Doctor Astalos might have ideas.

Drake listened with interest to McKnight's outline of Tyler's theory about the coincidental meetings. He asked to see Tyler's report as soon as he provided it. McKnight made a mental note to let Tyler know the General was waiting for it.

Kathy Wu was kinder to him. She went back over the events to make sure she captured everything in her report. As he expected, there was little he could add. After a few minutes, she thanked and released him.

McKnight called Wheeler to touch base. The lieutenant was packing up the Engine and getting it shipped back to DC. McKnight thanked him for his work.

McKnight couldn't think of anything else to do, so he went back downstairs and headed out through the retail mall to hail a cab.

He wasn't ready to deal with social chitchat, so when he walked by a small bar and grill near the street exit, he stepped inside.

He picked up a Blue Moon at the bar and sat in a corner booth. He savored the wheat aroma, the orange slice and the condensation off the cold glass. After a long drag on the beer, he checked his email.

But his heart wasn't in it. After staring at an email for too long, he pocketed his phone, took another sip of beer and looked around the bar.

Like many sports bars in the South, they covered the place with memorabilia from the region's college teams. High on the wall was an assortment of college football banners for Georgia Tech, the University of Georgia and other regional schools.

He thought of Merrie. In his mind, he divided her into Merrie the Younger and Merrie the Older. He admitted he had a thing for Merrie the Younger and she connected with him, at least back in the past. She moved on after he didn't come back. After all, they only talked for a few minutes on the one occasion she would remember.

He smiled.

There was definitely a spark there.

For a moment or two, he toyed with the possible options, including disappearing into the past. If he chose to, he could create an identity, set up a life. It'd be easy. He could work the stock market. Hell, he knew what would be big in the future. It'd be simple.

But it was just fantasy and nothing more. No matter how he looked at it, love for his friend, loyalty and honor trumped all those ideas. It was only a brief flirtation with a romance that could never be.

There was only one real choice. He would enjoy the friendship and company of Merrie the Older and forget Merrie the Younger. He took a deep breath, exhaled and, in doing so, signed a mental contract with himself.

Out of the corner of his eye, he saw honey-blonde hair walk by the bar window. His eyes leaped to the next window in anticipation. The woman passed in front of the second window and he had no doubt.

Impossible. How could Merrie the Younger be here in this time and place?

He jumped to his feet and ran to the bartender. "What do I owe you?"

"Eight bucks, even," the bartender said. He pulled several bills out of his pocket, threw them on the bar, and dashed to the door.

Once outside, he looked in the direction the woman had been walking. She was nowhere in sight, but there was a corner a few dozen feet further. He ran to the corner and looked both ways, up and down Third Street. There was no sign of her. Fifty feet away, a cab pulled away from the curb, but he didn't get a look at the passenger.

McKnight closed his eyes and allowed himself to fall backward to lean against the building.

Get a grip!

He rubbed his eyes with the heels of his hands and looked both ways again.

Did I imagine that whole thing? Am I losing it completely?

He closed his eyes again and slowly banged the back of his head against the building several times. He forced himself to relax and slow his breathing.

Okay. I need sleep. Let's do that before we do anything else.

He flagged down a taxi and gave the address.

McKnight stared out the window of the cab, thinking about everything and nothing. He nodded off more than once. It seemed only a moment passed before he arrived at the Tyler mansion. After he paid the driver, he walked to the door and knocked.

The door opened and an attractive woman with shoulder length red hair, plenty of freckles and a big smile greeted him. It was Sarah Davis, Tyler's fiancée. "Well, good evening, Marc. Winnie said you'd be joining us. Please come in."

"Hi, Sarah," he said and kissed her cheek. "How are you?"

"A little tired from the trip, but great now that you two are finally off work. Everybody's waiting for you out on the terrace. Shall we go on out?"

"Actually, Sarah, I'd like to grab a quick shower first. Maybe I can–"

"Oh, Winnie said you might want that. They kept a room for you, the one you used the other day. He put your bag in that room and there's an adjoining shower. He said you should make yourself at home. Can I get you anything? A drink, perhaps?"

"Sarah, I'd love to have one after I get a shower. I'll be right back down. Would you tell them I'll be a few minutes?"

"Sure. Don't be long now."

"Thanks, Sarah," he said as he turned and climbed the stairs. He found the room and stripped off his clothes. Once in the shower, he pushed the heat in the shower up as hot as he could bear and stood there, allowing the water to beat on his neck and upper shoulders. He took deep, slow breaths, willing the stress and fatigue to drain off his body with the water. He brought the heat down and washed, then switched to cool water to bring his body temperature back down.

When he stepped out, he was still tired but felt like a man who had cast off a burden. He dressed in a polo shirt, slacks and a pair of flip-flops.

Sarah met him at the bottom of the stairs with a Blue Moon in her hand.

"First order of business," she said, holding up the beer. "Winnie had to run an errand, so he asked me to take care of you."

She slipped her arm inside his and walked him toward the back porch.

"I've been hanging out here for two days, waiting for you two. So you two gentlemen will have some days off now, I hope?"

"Yes, ma'am. So you're still hanging out with this weirdo, then?"

She smacked him on the arm. "Oh, stop! You guys think you're so funny. You bet I am. My parents even like him, which is usually the kiss of death for a boyfriend. So, anyway, Winnie will be back soon. Let's go see what everybody's up to."

They walked through the back door and onto the porch. A gentle breeze was blowing and the scent of pine trees wafted across the yard. There, in the shadow-streaked lawn, were Tyler's parents and another couple. He recognized the woman as Tyler's aunt Janet, who introduced him to her husband Steve.

Tyler's voice came from behind him. "Hey, Marc. I see you found your way back."

McKnight turned to greet him, but the words stuck in his throat. There, with Tyler, was Merrie the Younger. All McKnight could do was stand there and stare.

"See? I told you she was hot."

The young woman punched Tyler in the arm. "Stop it, you ass!"

"You're..." McKnight stammered.

She thrust out her hand. "Hi, I'm Megan. I'm Winnie's cousin. I guess you've already met my Mom and Dad here."

McKnight shook her hand and stared at her. With an effort, he managed to put two more words together. "Winnie's cousin...?"

Tyler stepped to McKnight's side, laid his hand on his shoulder and spoke to Megan. "Yeah, he doesn't know how to talk, but he's decent company once he learns how again."

He clapped McKnight on the back. "Stop embarrassing me. I told her you were smart. Look, please excuse us, but I have friends to introduce Sarah to. Come on, Sarah, let's go."

"See y'all later, Marc. Nice to meet you, Megan," she said and walked away with Tyler.

McKnight found his voice. "Sorry, can we try again? I'm Marc." He offered his hand to Megan.

She laughed. "Yes, we can. I'm Megan," she said and shook his hand again.

He looked over towards the gazebo and saw Merrie and an older gentleman sitting there. To Megan, he said, "Did anyone ever tell you–"

"That I look like Gramma? This is the first time... today. Yes, it happens quite a lot." She laughed, and the sound of it was a balm for his battered soul.

"I think your eyes may be a little bluer," he said with a smile.

She smiled back. "Thanks. Tyler wanted me to meet you the other day, but I had to work."

"It was a crazy day," he said. "May I get you a drink or something?"

"You're drinking my favorite beer. I'll go get one out of the fridge. Would you pardon me for a few minutes?"

McKnight didn't want to let her out of his sight. "How about I tag along?"

"Whatever suits you just tickles me plumb to death," she said, and turned to go into the house. He jogged to catch up and fall in step with her.

"Excuse me?" he asked. "What did you say?"

"Oh, nothing. Just something Gramma says. It always makes me laugh."

"From an old movie, right?"

"Hmm. I think so. Why?"

"Oh, it seemed familiar, that's all. Where's the fridge?"

"Right here in the pantry. Hold on." She stepped into a large walk-in pantry, opened the refrigerator, and brought out a beer. She handed it to him and said, "Do you mind?"

"Not at all," he said, twisting the cap off the beer and handing it back to her. "There you go."

They walked back outside again. "Want to sit down and talk awhile?" she asked.

"I'd like that," he replied. They walked to a dogwood tree and sat underneath it in two wooden lawn chairs.

"This is my favorite time of day," she said.

"Mine, too."

A memory surfaced. What was it Merrie said to him the day they met? *You know, you should meet my granddaughter. She feels that way, too.* He chuckled to himself.

"What?" she asked.

"Oh, nothing. I understand your grandmother likes it, too. You said you were at work the other day. What do you do?"

"I'm in the security business."

The hair on the back of McKnight's neck stood up. "Where do you work?"

"I work at NewT Center in the security department. I help the Chief run the office."

"What's his name?" asked McKnight, certain he already knew the answer.

"Walt Matthews. He's a good guy. I've been there almost two years."

"I've met him. Winnie and I were there the last couple of days, working on a project. How come I didn't meet you?"

"I was off this weekend."

"Are you aware that your grandmother used to work there?"

"Yes. I asked her for advice on working there, and I followed it."

"Really? And what was that advice?"

"She said I shouldn't use my first name while working there. She said there were a lot of jerks out there and using my middle name would make it harder for them to find me outside work."

McKnight searched his memory again. "Good advice. And let me guess at the name you used. Would it be April?"

Her mouth dropped open in surprise. "How did you know? Did Winnie tell you that?"

"Mr. Matthews mentioned his assistant named April and wished she were there to help us with our project. He was very complimentary. And that was the last question. Well, actually, if you don't mind, there is one more question I'd like to ask you, if I may?"

"All right," she said. "One more question."

He sat up in the chair and leaned forward. He noticed a few freckles on her nose that Merrie the Younger didn't have. She was as beautiful as her grandmother was fifty years—or forty-eight hours—ago.

"Thanks, I appreciate it. And the question is, were you there today, about an hour ago?"

Her eyes widened a little. "Why, yes, I was. I took a cab over, ran in to get my paycheck, and ran back out. I was only there for five minutes. Why?"

McKnight grinned at her and said, "Thanks. You just proved that I'm not crazy."

He laughed out loud. "I had this vision of a devastatingly beautiful woman. I ran after her, but she disappeared. And now, here she is." He pointed his beer bottle at her. "I thought I was going crazy, but now I know she is real. And all is right with the world." He leaned back in the chair and took a long swallow of his beer.

She blushed and cast her eyes downward. When she looked at him again, her eyes carried the same twinkle Merrie's did.

"For a guy who can't talk, you do pretty well," she said. "Will you be around for a few days, I hope?"

"I am, now," he said. "I am, now. Shall we join your grandparents in the gazebo to enjoy the sunset?"

She laughed. "Good idea! It'll give me a little more time to figure you out." She winked at him and they clicked their beer bottles together in the hopes of the start of a beautiful friendship.

CHAPTER 33

<u>7:30 pm – Saturday, July 21st, 2035 - Buckhead Neighborhood, Atlanta, GA</u>

McKnight and Tyler strode across the expansive lawn, headed toward the gazebo. McKnight smelled pines and a hint of magnolia in the air. Looking over his shoulder at the porch, he saw Sarah and Megan in rocking chairs, talking away, just where he and Tyler had left them.

He looked ahead.

Has it only been a week since our first time here? It seems like much longer.

He glanced at Tyler, who was focused on the gazebo. He had a vacant smile on his face and was staring ahead. As he watched, a big grin broke out on Tyler's face. McKnight followed his gaze and saw the reason.

Merrie sat in the gazebo. She wore the same color of blue she wore before. And she was as radiant as McKnight remembered.

They stepped up into the gazebo.

"Well, here he is, Gramma, as promised. Now, if you two will excuse me, I'll leave you to it." Tyler turned on his heel and walked back down the lawn toward the house.

Merrie stretched out her hand and said, "It's good to see you again, Marc."

McKnight took her hand in both of his and squeezed it. "It's my great pleasure again, Merrie. Thanks for inviting me back."

"Sit with me, please," she said, patting the seat beside her. "Was your mission successful?"

He looked up at her. She smiled, but there was something else in her eyes.

"Yes, ma'am, it was."

"Good." She said. She reached down beside her chair and produced two Blue Moons and handed one to McKnight.

"I hear you accepted our invitation to take some leave and stay here a few days. I'm glad you did."

McKnight's eyes strayed back to the mansion, and to Megan, who so resembled her grandmother he thought she followed him back through time.

"I also hear you've taken a shine to Megan. That pleases me. I think you two will get along well."

"Why do you say that?"

"Because she likes to come out here and sit with me at the end of the day, like now. I remember you said this is your favorite time of the day."

"And it's your favorite time, too, if I remember correctly," McKnight said. "It's nice out here." He looked toward the west, seeing that the sun had dropped behind the trees. It would be sunset soon and the air was cooling. Red, rose, and pink colors were already showing in the clouds near the horizon.

McKnight turned back to face her. Her blue eyes narrowed, and she studied him. "It was you, wasn't it?" she said.

"I beg your pardon?" he said.

"All those years ago. In the meditation room at the NewT Center? It was you."

"Ma'am? I'm sure I don't know what you mean." He looked into her eyes and did not blink.

She searched his face, then said, "Well." She paused. "Can I tell you a story?"

Relieved to move to a different subject, he responded. "Sure, Merrie. I'd like to hear it."

"Okay. Have you ever wanted to do something crazy? I mean, something that is so out of your character you don't even recognize yourself. Like someone else was doing it? Do you understand what I'm talking about?"

"I do," he said. "Sometimes you have to act a little crazy to let out the stress."

"Yes, that's exactly what I mean. I wanted to do something crazy." She searched his face again. "Megan told me you and Winnie were working on a project at NewT Center. I was on the security staff at NewT Center many years ago—back when that terrible murder happened."

McKnight shifted in his chair. The conversation was moving toward the mission. *Not good.*

"But that's not what my story is about," she continued. "It was the day before the murder. It was so many years ago. But it was my birthday, so right before I got off work, I did something crazy. I'm not sure why, but I guess my soul was crying out for excitement. Do you know what I mean? Anyway, back then, at the end of my shift, I'd usually go to the bathroom in the office and change clothes before leaving. But this time..." She blushed. "But this time, I went up to the attic and changed my clothes right out in the open."

Involuntarily, the memory of her standing there at the edge of the platform filled his mind. That vision of her still moved him and touched his emotions.

"Merrie, I–"

"I've never told anyone about this before, not even my husband. Do you think I'm crazy or a loose woman?"

"No, I don't," McKnight said, the scene etched in his memory. "We all feel that way at times. Sometimes, you have to do something risqué, something off the beaten path, right?"

He paused. "How did it feel?"

She visibly relaxed at his response.

"Well, at first I felt stupid. Then, I had a flash of insight. I spent my life up to that point, not lived it. I decided that, from that moment on, no matter what, I would change my life. From now on, I would grab life with both hands and hang on." She looked him in the eye. "It was one of the defining moments in my life. And it happened that night."

"What happened, Merrie?"

"I raised my hands to… I don't know… Heaven, maybe? Or maybe to the world. But I swore on my soul that, from that moment on, I would stop being so logical and I'd follow my heart. I was filled up with emotion, I felt so powerful, and… you know what else?"

"What?"

"I wasn't alone."

"What do you mean? Like God or something?"

"I mean like someone else was there. I don't know. What do you think?"

He smiled.

"Well, I don't know about that, but it sounds like you had enough emotion inside you for two or three people. Maybe that's what you sensed."

"Maybe," she laughed. "Yes, that was probably it." She looked McKnight in the eye. "But you wouldn't know anything about that, would you?"

"No, ma'am. I don't see how I could."

Merrie didn't appear convinced. After a moment, she shrugged and smiled at him. "Well, I don't want to keep you. Would you and Megan like to join me here and watch the sunset? If you do, why don't you find her and come back out?"

"I'm sure we'd both love that, Merrie. I'll go get her. Should I bring out more Blue Moons?"

With that twinkle in her eye that so captivated him, she said, "Whatever suits you just tickles me plumb to death. I'm blessed."

He smiled back and marveled at his good fortune.

Me, too.

Then he winked at her and started for the house.

THE END

A Note From The Author

Thanks for reading this book.

Scan the QR code below for a short note from me.

Cheers and Regards,
Kim

The Marc McKnight Time Travel Adventures

Book 1 – TIME LIMITS

Book 2 – THE TIME TWISTERS

Book 3 – TIME REVOLUTION

Book 4 – TIME PLAGUE

Coming Soon

A new series for Marc McKnight and the HERO Team:

THE TIME PATRIOT

ABOUT THE AUTHOR

Kim Megahee is a writer, musician, and retired computer consultant. He has a degree from the University of Georgia in Mathematics Education. His background includes playing in rock bands, teaching high school, and much experience in computer programming, security and consulting.

In addition to writing, he enjoys hanging out with his wife, reading, boating on Lake Lanier, playing live music, and socializing with friends. Kim lives in Gainesville, Georgia with his soulmate wife Martha and Leo, the brilliant and stubborn red-headed toy poodle.

www.AuthorKimMegahee.com
Facebook: author.kmega